Death on the
PATAGONIAN
EXPRESS

Also by Hy Conrad

Dearly Departed

Toured to Death

Published by Kensington Publishing Corporation

Death on the
PATAGONIAN
EXPRESS

HY CONRAD

KENSINGTON BOOKS
http://www.kensingtonbooks.com

KENSINGTON BOOKS are published by

Kensington Publishing Corp.
119 West 40th Street
New York, NY 10018

All Kensington titles, imprints, and distributed lines are available at special quantity discounts for bulk purchases for sales promotion, premiums, fund-raising, educational, or institutional use. Special book excerpts or customized printings can also be created to fit specific needs. For details, write or phone the office of the Kensington Special Sales Manager: Attn. Special Sales Department. Kensington Publishing Corp, 119 West 40th Street, New York, NY 10018. Phone: 1-800-221-2647.

Kensington and the K logo Reg. U.S. Pat. & TM Off.

ISBN-13: 978-1-61773-688-9
ISBN-10: 1-61773-688-0
First Kensington Hardcover Edition: January 2017
First Kensington Mass Market Edition: July 2018

eISBN-13: 978-1-61773-689-6
eISBN-10: 1-61773-689-9
Kensington Electronic Edition: January 2017

10 9 8 7 6 5 4 3 2 1

Printed in the United States of America

AUTHOR'S NOTES

Alas, there is no actual railway connecting Argentina and Chile, although there should be. There is also no Carmelite monastery in the shadows of Torres del Paine. My goal in setting a mystery in Patagonia was not to replicate every detail of this wild, fascinating corner of the world, but to try to give a true sense of the place—and to tell a good story.

In all other ways, I've tried my best to get things right—the food, the people, the wind, and the solitude. The credit for whatever accuracy I've achieved should go to my guides, Pablo and Nicolas, who spent a total of three weeks with me, showing off their own private Patagonia. Both were incredibly generous and patient, especially when my questions included ones like, "What animals around here would eat a human corpse?"

As long as I'm veering into the realm of acknowledgments, I feel that I have to acknowledge Jeffrey Johnson, my husband and traveling companion for the past thirty-seven years. He has put up with much more than Pablo and Nicolas ever did, and he never even got a character named after him.

PROLOGUE

TrippyGirl was not prepared to die in Patagonia.
The first fall had broken my left leg. The second fall
wasn't technically a fall. It was a deliberate, painful leap
from the cliff onto my saddle, which Milly, the horse under-
neath the saddle, didn't seem to appreciate. As I lay on the
hard, dusty ground and touched my side, I could feel the
freshly broken ribs from where Milly had landed a kick right
before abandoning me here on the windy, arid plain. Enough
adrenaline was coursing through my system, to keep most of
the agony at bay. But it would come. The worst pain I felt at
the moment, more than from the ribs and the broken leg, was
from looking at my black Lafonts, my favorite frames,
which had been all but destroyed in my attempt to escape
this cold-blooded killer.

Fanny pushed herself back from the keyboard,
picked up the earthenware gourd, and sipped through
the metallic straw. She refused to acknowledge the
presence of the woman right behind her, who was
reading over her shoulder.

"Mom, that's not how it happened."

Fanny mashed the herbal mixture, took one more sip, then turned to face her. "Your leg is in a cast," she said, pointing to the cast. "You have two broken ribs. Your left eye is all black. You have more cuts and scrapes than a creature in a horror film. . . ."

Amy's hand went to her face. "Is it that bad?"

"Not quite. The sunburn gives you a nice healthy glow. But . . ." She pointed to a pair of black Lafont frames on the kitchen counter, the two sides loosely held together with electrical tape. "Those *were* your favorite glasses, if I'm not mistaken."

"Yes, but I can get them repaired."

"Okay, I'll change it. Not destroyed."

"That's not what I meant. Everything you write is an exaggeration."

"Excuse me for trying to liven up the truth."

"It doesn't need livening up."

An impartial observer, someone just walking into the living room of the Greenwich Village town house, would probably have sided with the younger Ms. Abel. Amy was in her early thirties; relatively tall at five-ten; with brown, shoulder-length hair; brown eyes; and pleasant, unremarkable features. She was indeed decked out in a leg cast, with bandages holding her ribs in place, and various bruises decorating the rest of her body, including a sunburned face. The truth, whatever it was, probably didn't need livening up.

Her mother's appearance was tamer by comparison. Fanny was a good eight inches shorter than Amy, shaped like a curvy fireplug crowned in a henna-dyed pageboy. At the moment, the pageboy was covered by a Peruvian wool cap with a red pompom on top and a silver Batman insignia, like a mirror, adorning the front.

"Everything needs livening up," said Fanny. And she punctuated this statement with a long slurp from the earthenware gourd.

CHAPTER 1

Two months earlier . . .

Amy gazed out at the lazy, uncommitted snowflakes, then reluctantly returned her focus to the over-heated confines of the Village Gastropub.

For as long as she could remember, since her kindergarten days, when she'd first learned to order from a menu, this space had belonged to Tony & Bill's, a dusty Italian eatery revered for its unchallenging menu and unchanging prices. Now it had been turned into a trendy, faux-casual café, with burnished redbrick walls and a polished bar and featuring Kobe beef burgers and white truffle mac and cheese.

She was sitting alone at a window table for three—not physically alone, since her mother was seated just opposite her. But for all practical purposes. "You're like a teenager," she complained and got no reaction. "Hello?"

Fanny readjusted her reading glasses but did not

look up from her phone. "Just doing some tweeting. My public expects it of me."

"Since when do you have a public?"

"Aren't you being a tad jealous of Trippy? You shouldn't. I love both my girls equally."

It was a joke. But Amy couldn't help seeing the truth underneath.

She had never been impetuous, unlike Trippy. She had always thought too much about what could go wrong. She had just begun to overcome this trait, one that she'd inherited from her calm and passive father, when the violent death of her fiancé, Eddie, plunged her back into her quiet, unadventurous existence.

This had been three years ago, and Fanny had tried everything to bring her daughter back into the world of the living. The eventual solution was to start a business together, a travel agency focusing on exotic, action-filled vacations. Amy would be forced to face people and problems again and would be rewarded by going around the world. Travel had been her and Eddie's mutual passion. And Amy's Travel, a cute little storefront on Hudson Street, was founded as a living tribute to their life together, the life they'd almost had together.

In retrospect, it wasn't the best business plan. The Internet had nearly destroyed the brick-and-mortar agencies. And the fact that Amy's Travel periodically showed up in the news in conjunction with murders and arrests worldwide didn't make things any easier.

The saving grace had turned out to be *TrippyGirl*, a modest blog that Fanny had come up with on her own, featuring the fun-loving, carefree girl that Amy wasn't. Almost without knowing it, the Abels had a viral smash, allowing them to sell ad space and drive traffic to a myriad of other travel sites. In some ways, Trippy had become an alter ego, the fearless daughter that Fanny could approve of without hesitation. Without the daily fights over everything that actual mothers and daughters fought about.

Fanny returned to her tweets, thumbs flying. Amy retaliated by taking out her own phone and pressing the Facebook icon. She scrolled down through the array of cat videos and political calls to action and selfies featuring people she barely knew. "Oh, my!" she exclaimed a few seconds later. Her tone was shocked and sad and genuine enough to make Fanny look up.

"Oh, your what?"

"You remember Danny D'Angelo from high school?"

"Of course. Danny Angel. You had a crush on him."

"No, Mother, you had a crush on him."

"Well, the boy was adorable, and he knew it. A very high opinion of himself. What's he doing? Starring in a movie?"

"Danny D'Angelo died," Amy said, scrolling farther, trying to piece together more information from the Facebook comment section.

"Oh, that's horrible," said Fanny, hand to her heart. "The poor family."

"He was on a vacation somewhere." Amy read the next part twice and even then paused before saying it. "Apparently, Danny was killed by a mirror."

"By a mirror? That's ironic. Mirrors were always his friends."

"Must be an AutoCorrect error."

"Did he like younger women? Maybe he was killed by a minor."

Amy was still scrolling when the last person in their party arrived. "Sorry I'm late," she said. "So great to finally meet you." What looked like a sixteen-year-old girl stood there, smiling anxiously as she whipped off her plaid Eskimo parka and her knit winter cap. She was dark and short, rather waiflike, with curly hair and shining teeth that seemed a size too big.

"Great to finally meet you," echoed Amy. Both Abels rose for the obligatory hugs and air kisses and general assurances that everyone looked wonderful. During all of this, Amy slipped her phone off the table and glared until Fanny did the same with hers.

It was odd that they'd never met Sabrina before. But that was the way it was. You could communicate a dozen times a day, gush over their children or fiancés, and donate money to their next 5K run without ever physically meeting. You could find out how they reacted to a midnight e-mail sent after you'd had one too many glasses of chardonnay. As far as Amy had been able to tell, Sabrina Marx was quite a nice person—energetic, personable, willing to share, even by Fanny's intrusive standards. But, surprisingly, just a kid.

Book editors were getting younger, Amy knew, a result of low pay and the changing dynamics of publishing. But still. It was hard to look at this youngster and not ask what subject she was majoring in.

"Banyan Press is so excited about *TrippyGirl's World*," Sabrina assured them. "We've got contracts lined up with Audible and the Literary Guild. We even have some top-notch travel writers wanting to review it. The crossover potential is going to be super."

"Real travel writers?" Amy asked, trying to sound more excited than frightened at the prospect.

"For real. Todd Drucker from *TD Travel*."

"You mean the magazine's owner and editor? That Todd Drucker?" Amy knew of him, of course. This was the man who had, in the past decade, taken the world of travel writing up a good five notches, the single biggest force in making exotic travel part of the mainstream. And, according to all reports, not a very nice or forgiving guy.

Sabrina grinned at her coup. "Uh-huh. As soon as we did our first press release, he was all over us about a review copy." She dumped her coat into a nearby chair, settled in, and raised a hand to catch the waiter's eye.

"Imagine that," Fanny gushed. "A big-time writer reviewing a book made of my little blogs."

The personal pronoun (singular) hung in the air as their waiter stepped up, introduced himself (Bradley), and took their orders for three iced teas, passion fruit and mango. Amy tried to secure a plain iced tea, but passion fruit and mango was as close as the Village Gastropub was willing to go.

Last year, when the publishers first started calling, Amy had emphasized that the *TrippyGirl* blogs were a collaboration, with her mother taking Amy's real-life escapades and embellishing them. They had labeled the work faction, like a nonfiction novel, which in hindsight was probably being generous. For example, the blogs about the Taj Majal murder were largely true, while the ones sent from the Trans-Siberian Express were entirely made up. The editors had to understand that TrippyGirl was not Amy Abel, and this was not a memoir. After hearing this disclaimer, several publishers had lost interest, but not Banyan. Or maybe Banyan just hadn't wanted to hear. All they'd heard was that Amy and Fanny had a blog with an avid readership of over a million and growing.

Sabrina waited until the waiter had recited the lunch specials and retreated. "You write the blogs together?" she said, phrasing it as a question.

"Of course," said Fanny.

"Actually, no," Amy said, clarifying. "I read the drafts and make suggestions, but Mom does the writing. It's her style that everybody loves."

"I understand," said Sabrina in a tone that said she didn't. "But photos of you are on the site, Amy. That leads people to believe you're at least a coauthor."

"But I'm not TrippyGirl. No one is."

"I understand," Sabrina repeated. "But when you post a photo of yourself on a train in the snow . . ."

"That was a PATH train in New Jersey during that December blizzard."

"That was some blizzard," Fanny recalled. "I couldn't get out of the house."

"But you used it to illustrate a blog set in Siberia, if I'm not mistaken." Sabrina stopped a moment to think. "Why didn't you use a photo from your trip to Siberia?"

"Her camera was stolen," said Fanny.

"I was never in Siberia," Amy said, clarifying some more. "That part of the book is more fiction than the rest. Again, we don't claim that the blog is real, and everyone seems fine with it."

"I understand, too. But when you show yourself in these settings, that's what people imagine. What I imagine. No one wants to find out that Trippy is—no offense—some older, stay-at-home mom who's making it all up. That's not your image."

"Ooh, boy," muttered Amy.

Sabrina must have heard. "No offense," she repeated with an anxious smile. "I mean, if it was Amy exaggerating the facts . . . well, that's one thing. Kind of an irreverent, young thing."

"Upper end of young," Fanny pointed out.

"And," continued Sabrina, "Amy is this world traveler who's known for getting into weird scrapes."

"Right. So what am I?" demanded Fanny. She kept her gaze steady, straight in the eyes, and her voice low. "Some troll under a bridge? Some deformed, old Rumplestiltskin who sits in a dark corner and spins the worthless straw into gold?"

"No, no, no." The young editor almost physically backtracked, holding out her hands as if to brake Fanny's momentum. "I'm so sorry. Please. Fanny, you're wonderful. I love your style. And you're not a rumple . . . whatever." She made a helpless, childlike face. "What is that, exactly?"

"Rumplestiltskin?" Amy couldn't believe it. "A fairy-tale character. You never heard of Rumplestiltskin?"

"I don't see many Disney movies," Sabrina admitted.

"Not all fairy tales are made into Disney movies," Amy said. "Didn't your parents ever read to you?"

"Not about Rumplestiltskins."

"It's a classic. How could you not know . . ."

"I think you're missing the bigger picture," snarled Fanny through clenched teeth. "The bigger picture is that you're embarrassed by me, aren't you? You are. I'm the real TrippyGirl, and my own editor is embarrassed."

"Amy and I are not embarrassed," pleaded Sabrina. "But public perception is everything."

"I'm not embarrassed at all," said Amy. Sabrina didn't have to go home and live with this. "Let's change the subject, okay?"

Somehow, they made their way through their hour plus at the gastropub intact. Amy, Fanny, and Sabrina all managed to call a truce and order their salads from Bradley. Like a mother at a bedside, Fanny informed their child editor of the whole *Rumplestiltskin* fable, and they all could agree that (a) the king was a jerk for wanting a wife who could spin straw into gold, (b) the peasant girl was irresponsible for agreeing to give up her firstborn child to some trollish dwarf named Rumplestiltskin, and (c) being saddled with that last name alone would wreak havoc on any child's self-esteem, not to mention being given up by your mother and raised by a dwarf in a cave, which luckily never happened. And if the peasant girl hadn't lucked out and guessed the dwarf's name, how the hell was she planning to explain the whole thing to the baby's father, the king? All in all, a very unsatisfying, un-Disney tale.

The lazy snowflakes had stopped by the time mother and daughter stepped out onto Bank Street and headed toward the Barrow Street house. Neither said anything during the six-block walk, and Fanny did not do any *TrippyGirl* tweeting along the way, which was probably a good idea, Amy thought, given her almost combustible state of mind.

Their silence lasted until they got into their separate apartments, Fanny on the lower two floors of the Abel brownstone and Amy on the upper two. Amy went immediately to her greenhouse office on the top floor rear and brought her computer out of its sleep mode. A few minutes later she came down the three flights and found her mother in the rear garden, in a corner next to the wall, out of sight of the upper-floor windows.

"I'm not even going to mention the fact that you're smoking."

"Too late," said Fanny. She took one long, last inhalation, then dropped her stub onto the gray slate tile and ground it under her heel. "The dwarf in the dark corner smokes. What can I say?"

Amy took a deep, sighing breath. The smoking argument could be left for another day. "Mom, you know I'm on your side. You created Trippy. She's you."

Fanny blew out the smoke in an even stream. "The me I wanted to be forty years ago maybe, before I settled into being this old stay-at-home mom. Not that I'm blaming you for putting me in that position."

Amy lowered herself onto one of the metal garden chairs. It was still wet from the melted snow, but she hardly noticed. "First of all, what does Sabrina know? She's a teenager. And second, that's still you. I don't joyfully run into the face of danger, not on purpose. But Sabrina was right. We do have to start being careful about Trippy. That's what she meant."

"I know what she meant," said Fanny. "Your adventures are exaggerated and fun. Mine are made up and desperate and sad."

"Now you're being maudlin."

"Desperate and sad and maudlin, right." She tapped her skull. "Duh. How could I have left out maudlin?"

"Okay. Changing the subject now." Amy stood, the wet chair finally beginning to annoy her.

"That's right. Change the subject."

"I'll do my best." She paused dramatically. "I found out how Danny D'Angelo died."

"Oh?" Despite herself, Fanny was curious. "Was it a full-length mirror? They can be dangerous."

"Apparently, he was on a motor scooter in Old San Juan, in Puerto Rico."

"Was he checking his hair in the rearview mirror? Because you have a tendency to do that, too."

"No. He was riding down a very narrow street, trying to pass a bus. He got clipped by the bus's rearview mirror and landed on his head on the cobblestones."

"Poor Danny." Fanny stared off into the distance as the news of the tragic, random accident slowly sank in. Then she brightened. "You know, I think I can use this. Change Danny's name and make him Trippy's old high school flame." Her excitement grew as she spoke. "He's riding down an old narrow street, on his way to see her for the first time since graduation. Meanwhile, Trippy's in that same fateful bus, looking casually in the rearview mirror, when she sees Danny in the mirror. Her heart leaps. Danny! He comes closer and closer to the mirror. And then *bam* . . . What a scene! Is that near enough to the truth for you?"

Amy didn't know what to say. "Fine."

CHAPTER 2

Over the next few days, Amy spent more time than usual at Marcus's, dropping by every evening after her workday and hanging out until one of them got hungry enough to pull the take-out menus from the wicker basket under the TV. It was a small two-bedroom, a third-floor walk-up in a brownstone just off of Sixth Avenue. The whole place was a little cramped and shabby. But for Amy it had the distinct advantage of not being home.

"I like this," Marcus said on the third evening in a row, as they lounged, cradled in each other's arms, with just enough of his right arm free to work the remote. He was flipping through the Time Warner channels, not really paying attention. He gave up and pressed the *OFF* button.

"It's so nice when Terry's not here," Amy said and snuggled a little deeper. Terry was Marcus's roommate and had been surprisingly absent during these blissful, long evenings.

"I think Terry and Fiona are getting serious," Marcus whispered in her ear.

"That's good." Amy was grateful that Terry was otherwise occupied, but she always felt a twinge of jealousy when other people were getting serious in their relationships and she wasn't.

"Not so good, maybe," said Marcus. "Or maybe very good."

Amy lifted her head half an inch from the warmth of his chest. "What do you mean?"

"I mean Fiona has two roommates. And this apartment is legally in Terry's name."

"Yes, of course." She had known this fact and what it meant. It was an essential part of a larger discussion that they'd been having for almost a year now.

Amy and Marcus's relationship seemed to have two settings, high and low. High was full of adrenaline and passion and arguing about how to get out of one scrape after another, usually involving a murder. Low was most of the time in between, the months in which Marcus retreated into his unknowable self, and Amy had the time to look closer at the infuriating man who could lie even better than her mother and feel even less remorse. True, they were never big lies—details about his past or what he'd done yesterday. But they always wound up putting some emotional distance between them.

"This could be our chance to move in together," said Marcus. The words hummed up through his chest.

Amy had to remind him. "The last time we looked for a place, you'd just lost your job and didn't tell me. Oh, and my company was on the verge of bankruptcy, and you didn't tell me that, either."

"But now we have more money," said Marcus.

"Do you still have your job as a concierge?"

"I do. I even got a raise when they moved me to the Ritz-Carlton in Battery Park."

"You switched hotels?" She lifted her head again. "When did that happen?"

Marcus had to think. "A month? My old boss never liked me, so Fanny and I arranged to get him fired."

"You got him fired?"

"It was Fanny's plan. Anyway, things got awkward after that, so . . ."

"And you never thought to tell me?"

"You would have wanted the ugly details, and Fanny made me promise." He eased her head off his lap, and they both pushed themselves to a sitting position on the sofa. "The point is we can piece together a first and last month and a security deposit and an agent's fee. Or . . ." And here he practiced his smile. It was hard to resist his smile. "Or we could save money. I happen to know of a fabulous two-floor walk-up on Barrow Street."

"No, you are not moving in with me."

"Why not?"

He knew the answer, so she didn't have to repeat it. Her move back home had been a temporary necessity after Eddie's death. The house signified a childhood she would never be able to leave behind, not as long as she continued to live there. Plus, cementing their relationship would be impossible with her lovingly intrusive mother living mere feet away. And, most crucially, Fanny and Marcus were besties, cohorts in crime who shared a common sensibility and could outvote Amy at every turn. She had to at least try to keep them separated.

"Okay," said Marcus. His nod was reluctant and barely visible. "But we have to start thinking about an apartment. At least I do."

"Then let's do it," said Amy, pleased by her deci- siveness. "Let's pull the trigger. We can call an agent in the morning."

This practical discussion had sucked all the ro- mance out of the moment, even though they were once again considering a commitment. The TV went back on. And when Terry finally walked through the door, looking tired and smugly happy, Amy took her cue and left.

The night air was bone-chillingly damp as she wan- dered along the side streets off of Sixth Avenue. She could have cabbed it. It was just far enough, given the weather. Several taxis were cruising by, their roof lights aglow with welcome. But Amy needed to clear her head.

By the time she got out of the shower the next morning, everything looked brighter. This was al- most always the case. If Amy had a talent, it was for ig- noring her doubts and starting fresh. And nothing symbolized that better than a hot shower on a new day. She and Marcus would work things out.

As for life with Fanny, there the prospects didn't look so bright. The past few days had been unevent- ful, the predictable aftermath of an Abel family fight. The tradition dated back to when Stan Abel had been alive and, despite his best efforts, had managed to annoy his wife. Fanny would behave as though noth- ing was wrong. She would smile and wave away any mention of the presumed slight. But this was the calm in the eye of a hurricane, and soon enough she would find a way to make Stan pay. That was the main rea- son why Amy had been spending so much time over at Marcus's. This hurricane calm could make you crazy.

Amy's phone dinged just as she was finishing with the blow-dryer. A text from Fanny. Was Amy up and in the mood for fresh coffee and bagels? Her heart clenched as she quickly messaged back. **Love it!** Just for safety's sake, she made sure to get fully dressed and make herself presentable to the world, grabbing a pair of black matte Lafonts from the dresser so she could see her way down the stairs.

CHAPTER 3

When she walked in, Amy found a middle-aged gentleman sitting opposite her mother at the old oak table. She hadn't anticipated this precise turn of events, but she wasn't surprised. The man rose to his feet, as if royalty had entered the brown, cluttered, middle-class kitchen. "TrippyGirl," he shouted almost joyously, the same way other people might shout "Happy birthday."

Even with that one word, Amy could sense an accent. Spanish? He looked Spanish. A man of medium height, dark complected, with a perfectly fitted black suit over a thin frame just beginning to show a middle-aged gut. His hair was long, thick, and wavy, black but streaked with silver, the way she thought Marcus might keep his in twenty years, if he managed to keep it.

"Amy," she said, correcting him, reaching out to shake hands. The man ignored the hand, reached for her shoulders, and drew her into an embrace, kissing her on both cheeks before letting go.

"Yes, please forgive me. I am just such a fan of your

Trippy. Jorge O'Bannion," he announced, releasing her and bending at the waist in a courtly bow.

She smiled back but didn't ask questions. This was her mother's game. She would find out the details soon enough.

"I didn't tell you Mr. O'Bannion was visiting?" asked Fanny. "I thought for sure I did."

"You didn't."

"Well, I meant to, but you were always over at Marcus's." Fanny was on her feet now, too, scurrying around the kitchen in imitation of a caring hostess. "Coffee with cream and an everything bagel, toasted." She ducked around the refrigerator. "I'll put on a second pot. Don't let me get in the way. Jorge contacted us two days ago with a very interesting proposition."

"Two days ago?" Amy said. This couldn't be good.

"I'll let Jorge speak for himself. Can I call you Jorge? Americans are so much less formal than Chileans, I imagine. That old-world charm, except that it's in the New World, isn't it?"

"Your mother is extraordinary," said Jorge O'Bannion with obvious amusement. He settled into a straight-backed chair, folded his hands gracefully across his waist, and began to explain himself. His voice rumbled with soothing authority.

The saga, whatever had brought him here, had begun with his grandfather, Timothy O'Bannion, who emigrated as a boy from Ireland to Chile. Timothy was still a young man when he saw the potential for sheep ranching in the wide-open spaces of Patagonia, the rugged southern section of the continent. With a small inheritance and a lot of ambition, the Irish lad bought up land and political connections

and transformed himself into a South American gentleman, marrying into one of the best families of old
Chile.

Generations of generous sheep had been good to
the O'Bannion clan. The animals thrived in the grassy
foothills. And when they produced too much wool
and meat for domestic consumption, Timothy and a
few other landowners persuaded the governments of
Chile and Argentina to build railroads connecting the
wilds of Patagonia to Buenos Aires on the Argentinean
East Coast and to the town of Puerto Natales, far down
on the Chilean West Coast. From there, O'Bannion
wool went worldwide.

"It was a good life," said Jorge, warming his hands
on his newly delivered second cup of coffee. His English was fluent, and his delivery self-deprecating and
charming. "Or so the photographs show and my parents said, too. Those days were gone by the time I was
born."

The two family ranches—estancias, as they were
called—did well, he explained, even during the Second World War, supplying wool for uniforms and
meat for a ravaged and hungry population. But with
peacetime came hard times for the O'Bannions. The
rest of the world started raising sheep again. And the
wartime innovation of synthetic fibers made their
old-fashioned wool seem suddenly itchy and uncomfortable and unpopular.

"When my papa inherited the estancias, we were
reduced in circumstances." A wistfulness tinged his
words. "Much of the family's grazing land he turned
over to tenant ranchers, who managed to eke out
their lives. The big houses, with golden teak and mahogany floors from the Amazon forests, they were half
empty and sad all throughout my boyhood. Ranching

would never again be what it was. But my papa, he did not give up. He had a plan."

Fanny sat riveted. So did Amy, despite herself, despite the fact that she knew she was being manipulated. Manipulated into what, she didn't yet know.

"After the war, the outside world discovered the romance of South America," Jorge O'Bannion said, perhaps even enhancing his romantic accent. "The gauchos of the pampas. Carmen Miranda. Fernando Lamas."

"Ricardo Montalban," suggested Fanny.

"Montalban was Mexican. But he played South Americans in the movies," Jorge noted graciously. "In the nineteen fifties, North American tourists began coming. That gave Papa his plan." He leaned across the table to both of them, as if sharing a secret or a million-dollar recipe. "He envisioned the tourists flying into Buenos Aires, taking luxury sleeper trains across the plains and getting off at South American ranches, what you call here dude ranches. They would stay in our estancias, ride horses into the mountains, camp out under the stars of the Southern Cross. All in first-class luxury."

"Sounds heavenly," cooed Fanny, who had, to her daughter's knowledge, never camped out or ridden a horse. At some point, she might have gazed up at a star.

"But this plan never happened," Amy guessed.

"No," Jorge said flatly. "Papa borrowed against our income, sold a few hundred acres, which became part of a national park. He bought fancy sleeper cars and began to restore the estancias for the visitors to come. But then governments changed. They were not so interested in supporting the sheep industry. Chile stopped running the railroads and abandoned the tracks. Papa died twenty years ago, a gentleman gaucho to the end, barely keeping the roofs from falling in, sending off the wool in trucks patched together with tape and spit."

"But times have changed again," prompted Amy. "Patagonia tourism is more popular than ever. That's why you're here, isn't it, Mr. O'Bannion?" In her mind, there were only two directions in which this could go—sheep or travel. And last time she checked, no one was tracking down the Abels for their expertise in sheep.

Jorge smiled. "Not long ago, our world was a destination for backpackers. But then the travel press discovered us. We are the Eighth Wonder of the World, they say. Now the majestic glaciers and mountains attract very high-end resorts. But we are still a five-hour car ride or a private helicopter ride from anywhere."

"It sounds like your father had a good idea with the train," said Fanny, pretending as if she'd never heard any of this before. "Ahead of his time."

"He did," said Jorge. "And so do I. And so does, I am happy to say, a wealthy and well-connected businesswoman and dear friend. It is our fervent wish to fulfill my father's dream."

"I see." Amy nodded. "So Argentina and Chile are reopening the railroads?"

"The Argentine side never closed. But yes, the Chilean government has finally seen the wisdom of promoting tourism. As I said, my investor is well connected. We are restoring the Pullman carriages my father bought from the Orient Express company. And we're redoing the estancias, more luxurious than my grandfather could have imagined. We have a name now, too. The New Patagonian Express. Like the old book."

"I know the book," said Amy. *The Old Patagonian Express* was one of the first travel memoirs she'd ever read, recounting Paul Theroux's epic journey from Boston to the tip of South America by rail. But the book wasn't about luxury travel. It was a caustic travelogue about barely surviving on some of the worst railway systems in the world.

"It's a perfect name," claimed Fanny.

"Thank you. In return for our financial gamble, Chile is giving us seven years exclusive use of the tracks." Jorge lifted his hands from his stomach, fingers still laced, reached forward, and cracked his knuckles. "As you might appreciate, Miss Abel, we have no time to waste. Now is the moment."

"Congratulations," said Amy. "When is the inaugural trip?"

"February. Next month. What they call a soft opening, to work out the flaws and generate publicity. Once we are operational, it will be a luxury assembly line. One group will be on the first train while another is at the first estancia and another on the second train—we will have two trains eventually—and another group at the second estancia. All carefully planned. My partner, Lola Pisano, hired a New York publicist, and he brought our attention to you, Miss TrippyGirl." He extended a welcoming hand. "You have already done a train trip in Siberia, yes? I promise this one will be much more comfortable."

"Are you inviting me?"

"I am, if you would be so kind. We are starting with a small group—travel writers, big tour operators. All we ask is your honest opinion in your blog. Make your trip part of an adventure, if you like. Eight days of wonder in the Eighth Wonder of the World. Do you like the phrase? I made it up myself."

The man had the charm thing down. And she sympathized with his story. More than sympathized. Her own travel business was a tribute to Eddie's dream, just as Jorge's business was a tribute to his father's. "I'm very tempted," Amy said haltingly. She hated disappointing people. "But I'm not TrippyGirl. I know photos of me show up on the site, but . . ."

"It's you and your mother combined," said Jorge with a wink. "Mrs. Abel told me."

"Jorge took me to dinner last night—at the Gastropub. Their evening menu is much more extensive. Good martinis. You should give it another shot."

"Mrs. Abel came up with our solution." Jorge beamed. "Both of you will be my guests. TrippyGirl and her mother. No one need know your secret."

Amy turned to Fanny. "You already said yes? You and me? No, no. We are not traveling together."

"Why not? We're both TrippyGirl. This is the perfect opportunity."

"To do what? Get killed together?"

"Killed? No, Patagonia is perfectly safe," Jorge said, palms raised in assurance. "Why do you say killed?"

Have you actually read the blog? Amy wanted to ask him. *Taking a Siberian train isn't the hallmark of* TrippyGirl. *It's murders happening all around. It's almost getting killed.* She didn't know why, but it was undeniably true. The only reason she'd survived the previous two trips, in her mind, was that Fanny had not been there, egging her on to even more reckless behavior.

"Amy, dear, this is our opportunity to quash those nasty rumors," Fanny said.

"What rumors?" asked Amy.

"That Trippy is a fake and I'm a troll under a bridge."

Jorge O'Bannion had probably expected a different reaction. After all, here was a young traveler, a travel agent. He was offering her a free, unique tour, two of them, in return for what she would be doing, anyway, writing about her exploits. "I thought you might enjoy a vacation."

"So did I," said Fanny. "Apparently, old Mrs. Troll was wrong."

Jorge O'Bannion had brought along a binder of promotional material, complete with glossy photos and maps and flashy hyperbole. It looked extraordinary, Amy admitted as he handed it over and she leafed through the pages. She and Fanny would certainly consider his generous offer and get back to him. Later today. Tomorrow, at the latest. It was her way of getting rid of him, and they all knew it.

"It would be such an honor to show you my corner of the world," said the courtly gentleman. "Please."

Amy stood up, checked the clock on the wall, and made some noises about having an early appointment at the store. Jorge, looking embarrassed, his charm no longer oozing, thanked them for their time.

Fanny walked him out the door and returned to the kitchen a minute later. "That was rude," she said and started busying herself at the sink. Dishes clanged against the porcelain bowl. "I can't believe you said no."

"It took me by surprise. I didn't mean to be rude to him."

"Rude to me. Implying I would get you killed! Have I ever gotten you killed, young lady? You used to love traveling with me. Our summers at the Jersey Shore? I wouldn't let you go into the ocean for a full hour after lunch. Plus, the water wings . . . That's how careful I was. But I understand if you're afraid of life. That's just who you are."

"I know. I know it's irrational," Amy muttered into her empty cup of coffee. "It would probably be an extraordinary trip, with no one getting killed for miles. And I've always wanted to see Patagonia. Unfortunately . . ."

"Don't say 'unfortunately' and whatever comes after that word. If you're not going, fine. I'll go without you. I'll buy one of those little head cameras and show you who the real TrippyGirl is."

"You are not going without me. Talk about a death wish!"

"Good. Then you're coming. I made the plane reservations last night—after the martinis. Now call Mr. O'Bannion, right now, before the man can catch a cab. Here's his number."

CHAPTER 4

Seen from a distance, perhaps from a rooftop half a mile away, the barrio most resembled a collection of paint chips—paint chips remembered from a fever dream of bad decorating. A balcony of bright orange stood next to a wall of aquamarine, with its windows etched in canary yellow, next to another balcony of bright red with flamingo-pink railings. This visual chaos went on and on, around every corner of every block of the two- and three-story buildings. It was surprising what fun a little disorganized color could add to what was essentially a working-class neighborhood.

The Buenos Aires barrio of La Boca had begun as a dockworkers' town by the river's mouth—*boca* in Spanish. Interspersed among the dry docks and warehouses were modest homes built from ship wood and corrugated iron and sheet metal and whatever else had been lying around a hundred-plus years ago. To some extent, it was still a lower-class district. But during the past few decades, the most colorful few blocks have been transformed into a place everyone had to see. Tapas restaurants and curio shops poured out onto the sidewalks. Tango dancers in full romantic regalia performed on the corners in front of the cafés, sweating in the February heat, hoping to lure customers inside. In short, La Boca was a tourist trap.

"It was almost abandoned," said Pablo as he ushered them across a cobblestone street. "Then, in nineteen-sixty, an artist, Benito Quinquela Martín, painted the walls of a few houses and built a stage for outdoor performances. More and more artists began coming to the neighborhood. . . ."

Amy didn't enjoy tours. Her feeling was that travel involved discovering a new world on your own. Sure, time would be wasted and there would always be part of a city that you didn't get to experience. You wouldn't get to hear all the facts, either, not unless you walked around with your nose in a book. But if you were lucky, you'd get lost and end up with a one-of-a-kind experience, good or bad, instead of a preprogrammed spiel from a guide just trying to make a living. Pablo, she thought, was better than most. He was young and thin, slight and energetic, with the stubble of a goat patch that either couldn't or wouldn't develop beyond a thick shadow in the middle of his chin.

They had arrived on an overnight flight, nonstop from JFK—eleven hours in business class, where the seats did lie flat but, in order to accomplish this, mechanically sank you into a narrow coffin-like bed. Fanny, who was both shorter and broader than her daughter, had wound up flat on her back, unable to turn, hands folded across her chest, looking like a body at a viewing. Although she protested that she'd barely got a wink of sleep, Amy knew better, since her mother had a habit of snoring loudly when lying on her back. It was the rest of business class who barely got a wink.

The time difference was a mere two hours, ahead, not behind, since the South American continent jutted a good deal farther out into the Atlantic Ocean. By the time they had got settled into their five-star hotel, a converted mansion more European than anything in Europe, it was time for lunch by the pool, then this half-day tour of Buenos Aires.

Pablo was to be their guide throughout the eight days. Only two of Jorge O'Bannion's guests had expressed interest in the city tour—Fanny and Alicia Lindborn, the stylish silver-blond matriarch of Lindborn Travel. Amy had been dragged along once it became clear to her that (a) Fanny was going with or without her and (b) despite her professed lack of sleep, Fanny was determined to hit the ground running. That included the use of a small sports camera, high tech and sturdy looking, mounted to the front band of her straw sun hat on a glittery red strap, ready to record whatever adventure might come along.

"Follow me," said Pablo, escorting his three charges around another multicolored corner. "This is my favorite. Not many tourists see this." He picked up speed as he walked, then led them around another corner to a short alley and around another corner to a one-story warehouse that ran the entire length of the block. The street was nearly deserted. "Here. Not pretty in the normal way. But my favorite."

The women stopped to take it in. Fanny had been toying with the buttons on her hat-mounted camera. She adjusted the hat and camera squarely back on her head, then turned slowly to record the entirety of the sight before them.

Amy had seen dozens of murals during her few hours here. They were unavoidable. More than any other city, Buenos Aires seemed to treasure its inventive, whimsical, sometimes ugly public art. They were on the sides of factories and garden walls, on office towers and government buildings, even on the blank walls of private homes. Some were true works of art, surrealist and masterful, like Salvador Dali paintings of imaginary landscapes and mythical beasts. Others depicted soccer stars, singing stars, tango couples, Eva Perón, Daffy Duck, cute kids and puppies. Even the lowliest graffiti tags seemed elevated by the city's inspiration.

This one, taking up the one long wall of stucco, was nothing more or less than angry. Angry and chaotic. The colors were bright, almost cartoonish, with bold outlines and hard angles, reminiscent of one of the paint-by-numbers projects Amy had worked on as a kid. "What is it about?" she asked. It had to be about something.

Dozens of characters stared out from the wall, peasants and laborers, some of them struggling with hard, blue-faced, rifle-toting soldiers, others seeming to struggle with the wall itself, as if trying to emerge from a dungeon. All arms and legs and desperate faces. To the far left was the oversize orange visage of an army general in his uniform. It was a nightmarish face. He was shouting orders or deadly threats, his mouth turned down at the edges, his tongue a wet blob in the back of his throat. A fat red fist held a gun, and one of the fingers of the fist was adorned with a ring, gold with red eyes—the roaring head of a lion.

"Have you heard of the *desaparecidos*?" Pablo asked, lowering his voice to a hush.

All three women nodded, including Fanny and her bobbing camera. "The disappeared ones," she said. "Did that happen here?"

Amy would have to look up the details. But in the late 1970s and early 1980s, she recalled, tens of thousands of Argentineans simply disappeared. They would be living their normal lives one moment, on the street, in cafés, answering an unexpected knock at the front door. The next moment they would be pulled in for questioning by the army, never to be seen again.

"The military dictatorship," Amy said.

She could see it now in the painting—ordinary citizens dragged from their routines, mouths gaping with fear. The soldiers, a monolithic blue wall of force, ripped at them with clawlike hands. At the edges of the mural, top and bottom, shadows of human body parts melted into a fiery background. And dominating the horror show was the orange, diseased face of the man giving the orders.

"Who is that?" Alicia Lindborn asked.

"I don't know," said Pablo. "There were many generals. Maybe this one was worse. Or maybe he's a symbol. The government said it was fighting the communists. But all kinds of people got disappeared. Artists, doctors, professors, even people who never spoke out about the dictatorship but who might have some influence if they did. Many bodies—most of them, I think—were never found. Babies were taken away with their mothers. When the mothers died, the babies were adopted by strangers and given new names. Our country is still trying to make peace with this."

"Babies?" Alicia splayed one hand of her perfect manicure over her heart. "They'd be grown-ups now.

Do they even know who their real parents were? Or that they'd been killed?"

"Some do. Some don't. If you were five years old, of course you'd remember your parents."

Fanny shuddered, then gave their tour guide the eye. "And this is your favorite?"

Pablo shrugged. "We *porteños*, the people from Buenos Aires, we love dramatizing the past and mulling over it."

"In this case, I can't blame you," said Amy. "How do you get over something like that?"

"Lucky for us, we love to get mentally analyzed." The guide chuckled at his own mistake. "I mean psychoanalyzed. There are more psychoanalysts in Buenos Aires than taxi drivers. Honestly. It's become a big part of our culture."

"Do you use a psychoanalyst?" Fanny asked.

"I use two," Pablo said, seemingly proud of his sanity.

Meanwhile, Alicia kept focused on the mural. "It's got such power," she said in a quiet voice. "More than any realistic depiction. Thank you for showing it to us." Alicia Lindborn behaved like a perfect guest, curious and considerate and open-minded, befitting her rank as a travel business legend. "Who is the artist?"

"No one knows," said Pablo. "It was painted over a period of a month, always in the dead of night. If anyone saw the painter or helped him, they never said. And no one would ever paint over this. They wouldn't dare."

For Amy, the mural would become the highlight of their afternoon. Sure, they'd been to the Eva Perón balcony and the ornate opera house and the widest avenue in the world, with sixteen lanes of traffic and a much-needed median strip in the middle to avoid getting run over. But the angry mural was what Amy would remember best.

Pablo and the driver dropped them off in front of the ex-mansion in the Recoleta district. The hotel had probably once been the city house for a family not unlike Jorge O'Bannion's, barons of the pampas, making their fortunes from sheep and cattle and wheat and cheap labor.

Amy was halfway to the doorman, envisioning a nice dinner of Argentine beef and an early bedtime, when she looked back to see Fanny, the camera still in place on her straw hat, talking to Pablo. He wrote down something on a notepad and tore off the page. Fanny was all giddy smiles as she walked up the stone path, waving the page.

"No," Amy said, guessing pretty much where their conversation was going to go. "I'm tired."

"It's two hours earlier in New York," Fanny countered. "And after all the sleep you got on the plane . . ."

"You're the one who slept."

"Really? You're quibbling about sleep on our one night in Buenos Aires? Pablo told me about this tango joint where just the locals go." She checked the slip of paper. "A *milonga*, whatever that is. And don't worry about your dinner. He says the place doesn't even open until eleven." Fanny raised the other hand to swat away her daughter's next concern. "That's nine p.m. You can't possibly want to go to bed at nine. Not in the city that invented tango."

"Do I have a choice?"

"No, dear, you don't."

CHAPTER 5

La Iglesia del Tango, the Church of the Tango, occupied a small, deconsecrated chapel on the edge of the city's business district. It seemed like an unusual concept for a "locals only" club, but it had been in this venue since the 1940s, and the inescapable parallel between dance and religion had proved to be no deterrent to its popularity. The fact that it had an old wooden dance floor with a lot of spring didn't hurt, either. When Amy and Fanny arrived, after their steak dinner and after eleven thirty, the *milonga* was already half full. A four-piece band was tuning up on the stage, where the altar had once stood: accordion, violin, guitar, and standing bass.

Amy always traveled prepared for an elegant evening, one elegant evening, with a slim, black, sleeveless Liz Claiborne and a pair of low black heels. Fanny's preparation for the evening had been more time consuming, since it had involved hiding her *TrippyGirl* sports camera in a huge artificial rose and then figuring out how to hold the rose in place in the folds of her henna-dyed pageboy. They had settled on using the band from her straw hat. The resulting look was eccentric but passable, and Amy was glad to find the club mercifully dim.

There was a free table for two, one row back from the action, and they settled in. The accordion player, a man in his eighties, struck the first chord of the evening, a breathy, elaborate glissando. A handful of couples headed for the floor almost immediately, and Fanny pointed her rose in the direction of the crowd. Meanwhile, Amy went to get them drinks, something seriously alcoholic, at a bar that might have once been part of a confessional.

Amy was good at languages. She was nearly fluent in French, thanks to high school and a cute foreign exchange student named Jules. Her Italian was also decent, thanks to her college minor in Renaissance art and a semester in Sicily. But she'd always had a deaf ear for Spanish. Despite its similarity to Italian, or perhaps because of it, Amy found herself incapable of understanding more than a few sentences in a row and unable to utter more than a few words. When she found that the busy, disinterested bartender didn't speak English, she pointed to what someone else was ordering and managed to say, "Dos, por favor." What he started making for her was a combination of rum and Fernet-Branca, which, she seemed to recall, was some sort of aromatic bitters.

The dance hall was a dusty, charming combination of the sacred and the profane, of the homey (bad paintings by local artists hanging crooked on the walls), the old-fashioned (a dangling mirror ball where a religious chandelier must have once hung), and the extremely old-fashioned (tattered red velvet banquettes inhabited by dancers whose grandparents might have sat on them in days gone by).

Amy paid for her drinks in U.S. dollars, the pre-
ferred currency in Argentina these days, and weaved
through the tightly knit dancers back to their table
for two, only to find that her chair had been taken. A
silver-haired gentleman had scooted it around to
Fanny's side of the little round table, had sat down,
and was holding out his hand in invitation. They
moved fast, these old porteños.

"Don't mind if I do," said Fanny in a tone that
needed no translation, especially when combined
with a girlish giggle. When she took his hand and
they both stood, it became apparent that the gentleman was nearly a foot taller. Many men were, including Fanny's late husband. Fanny reacted by reaching
up to adjust the artificial rose strapped to her head.
"Help me," she ordered Amy. If the gentleman
found anything unusual in seeing a woman and her
daughter rearrange the lens of an artificial rose, he
didn't let on.

Watching the mismatched pair tango away, Amy
prayed that if this wound up on the blog, she could
at least persuade Fanny to let her dub in the audio.
The last thing they needed was for their unseen
Trippy to sound like a giggling New York matron.
Amy sipped her brown concoction and winced at the
strongly bitter taste. Licorice? It certainly wasn't
Campari. She reminded herself that the Spanish for
"Campari and soda" would be *Campari y soda*. How
hard could that be? *Next time*.

The old church floor was being polished nicely by
dozens of pairs of shuffling feet traveling in straight
lines, then twirling at seemingly random moments.
All ages and types participated in the polishing, young
and old, fathers and daughters, well-dressed couples
in suits and gowns, and workmen who looked like

they'd just gotten off their shifts. As with most bands that utilized an accordion, this one instrument dominated the sound, but it wasn't unpleasant, Amy found. Quite hypnotic. Plumes of cigarette smoke wafted up from the tables toward the mirror ball, and starry beams of diffused light spun slowly through the cavernous room.

Visually she followed the beams, basking in the expanding warmth of the licorice and the friendly but foreign surroundings. Every now and then a beam would linger on a short woman with reddish hair decorated with a large rose. For someone who hadn't danced in years and probably hadn't ever tangoed, Fanny was doing well. Perhaps the tall gentleman, unlike her father, was used to taking a firm lead.

Amy traced several more lingering beams into an alcove, a space that had once been an apse, one of the short arms of the chapel. A flash of mirrored light illuminated a face just for a moment. But it was the man's hair that caught her eye, black and wavy and streaked with silver. She had met him only that once, during the breakfast ambush in her mother's kitchen. But his photos were all over the promotional materials, plus the Web site, plus the puff piece last week in *Online Traveler*, highlighting his family's story of resilience and hope for financial redemption.

Without thinking too much, Amy lifted her glass of licorice-tainted rum, took one more swig, and began to weave her way around the edges of the floor toward the alcove. She felt badly about having been so hesitant to accept his generous offer and not having taken the time to see him again during his stay in New York. This would be a chance to remedy that, she thought.

"Senor O'Bannion. Hi. I can't tell you how much we're looking forward to . . . ."

Jorge O'Bannion sprang to his feet and greeted her with a warm, toothy smile and his usual courtly bow. "TrippyGirl. Just this moment, I saw your mother dancing. *I must be hallucinating,* I told myself. Why would two sophisticated New Yorkers be in a humble dance hall? I hope Pablo didn't send you. I'm going to have to have a talk with that boy."

Amy was familiar with this kind of faux modesty. What it usually meant was, "There are private places we like to keep off-limits from gawking tourists. But, oh well, what can you do?" "No, we found it on our own," she lied. "Happy accident. What a wonderful place."

"Yoo-hoo," came a voice from behind them. Amy moved out of the way just in time. In some unfathomable way, Fanny and her partner had tangoed themselves through the tables of the alcove. "Jorge, hello." The face under the oversize rose smiled broadly. "Smile. Smile and wave." But before Jorge could react, Fanny's tall, accomplished partner was sweeping her into an abrupt turn. "Gotta go." And just like that, they were weaving back through the tables to the dance floor.

Jorge looked puzzled. "What was on your mother's head?"

"Just a rose," said Amy. "We're so looking forward to tomorrow."

"I am, also."

Jorge turned to the other person at his table, a figure half hidden in the shadows. The woman rose regally and extended her hand. Amy didn't know whether to shake it or kiss the woman's large, square-cut emerald ring. She settled on a light shake. The woman said something softly in Spanish. Jorge did both sides of the translation.

"Lola Pisano, Miss Amy Abel. Senora Pisano is my partner in the New Patagonian Express. Her late husband was a school chum who many years ago traded his land holdings for more profitable things. But Lola shares my passion. It is her dream, too." And here Jorge switched into Spanish, reiterating, in Amy's best guess, what he'd just said, plus giving some indication that Amy was important and Lola should make an effort to be pleasant.

Lola Pisano was a hard-looking woman. Thin, with a face that seemed all angles, like a Picasso portrait. She attempted to soften her look with a helmet of ash-blond curls. Although probably no older than Jorge, she utilized several ounces of make-up, evident even in this light, which, Amy thought, served only to age her more. One side of her head she kept subtly averted from Amy's gaze. When Senora Pisano half stood and leaned up to speak again, Amy could make out the contours of a dark mole just below the woman's left cheekbone. It was just large and protruding enough and in the right/wrong place to be considered disfiguring. This sight—and her own curiosity—embarrassed Amy enough to make her look down and take one more sip of her bitter rum.

Whatever Lola said, it was accompanied by a scowl and a beady stare. Instantly, Jorge was back in his English mode, moving a step in Amy's direction, upping the charm as if to compensate for whatever she had not understood. The Abels were such adventurous travelers! He had been so right to invite them on the tour! And the tango? He had no idea Fanny was such a good dancer. Just look at her out there!

"Jorge, *mi corazón*." Senora Pisano was on her feet,

arranging a green patterned shawl across her bony
shoulders. Again, the black mole was visible, and
Amy took another bitter sip in an almost Pavlovian
response. Lola's next few phrases were quick and un-
intelligible, but the annoyance in her tone was clear.

"Excuse me, dear Amy," said Jorge, looking well
chastened. "I look forward to tomorrow. The start of
our adventure, yes?" He kissed her hand, and they
both heard a jealous intake of breath coming from
somewhere near the mole. Before Amy could say a
proper good-bye, Lola had dragged her escort out of
the shadowy apse and onto the dance floor.

It was after 2:00 a.m. when the Abels returned to
the hotel, barely past midnight in New York. Amy
had a policy of not video chatting while buzzed. But
it was only a light buzz, she thought, and Marcus
rarely got to bed before midnight, and she knew he
would want to say good night. And, most important,
she needed to hear his soothing voice and see his
face.

She turned on her phone, ran a brush through
her hair, and straightened the neckline of her liquor-
stained Liz Claiborne. Then she arranged herself on
one of the queen beds and touched the phone's
Skype icon. Twenty seconds later, Marcus's face was
on the screen, his sleepy eyes focusing beyond his
aquiline nose with that adorable little bump on its
bridge.

"Oh, no. Did I wake you?" She made it sound like
a shock.

"No, no." Marcus was at the laptop on the little
desk in his bedroom. "Just turning in. Is everything
all right?" He was bare-chested, and since he always
slept in the nude, Amy wondered if the rest of him
might be bare, as well.

"Everything's fine. I have a few minutes before Fanny walks in. She's downstairs, at the bar, pointing her rose at any man who'll pay attention."

"Pointing her rose? Is that a euphemism?"

"What? Ew, no. Don't be gross."

"Okay . . ." Marcus scrunched his brow in concentration. A second later he laughed. "She put the camera in a fake flower? Where? In her hairdo? That's funny."

Amy sighed. "It scares me that I never have to explain my mother's behavior to you."

"Some women would find that endearing."

"You're right. It's endearing."

"Not very convincing."

"How's the office?"

"The office is fine. Tell me about your day."

Amy went on to tell him about the coffin-like business class, the tourist sights, the disturbing mural, and their tango hall encounter with Jorge and his financial angel. It felt good to review the details of her weird, exhausting day. It helped normalize it. "Oh, did you call the real estate agent? Sara's friend?"

"Yes." The speed and certainty of Marcus's reply gave Amy a feeling, 60 percent maybe, that he was telling the truth. Give or take 10 percent.

"Good. I know some brokers don't like dealing in rentals."

"Well, this guy specializes in them. I told him Village or the East Village. A one bedroom in a prewar or a brownstone. He's not optimistic. He says we'd have more luck on the Upper West Side, above Ninety-Sixth. He also has some listings in Queens. A lot more space."

"Queens?" The notion of moving out of the Barrow Street house suddenly seemed extreme. It was one thing to move a few blocks away from her mother and all her childhood haunts. But across the river? In Queens? "Isn't that a little far from the office?"

"There's also Hoboken," said Marcus. "Just across the Hudson."

"Really? Is this guy licensed in New Jersey?" Meaning the real estate agent. "He can't show us stuff there unless he's licensed."

"I don't know. He mentioned New Jersey."

The odds of Marcus telling the truth about contacting the agent had just gone down from 60 percent to around 40. But it still gave Amy something to think about. It was tough, tough and annoying, to be priced out of your own neighborhood. And how badly did she really want to move?

"Well, keep looking," she said, which she hoped would translate into "Start looking." "If you find anything promising, send me the link. I don't know how much Internet access I'll have, but I'll try my best."

CHAPTER 6

Amy loved train stations. She was too young to have seen the magnificence of New York's old Penn Station, except in photographs, but Grand Central had always been her ideal, a cathedral of travel, with thousands of people traipsing its marble floors, some rushing home, some starting out on trips across the continent or around the world—saying sentimental good-byes or escaping or commuting while half awake. Lives that crisscrossed in a pattern unchanged for a hundred years.

Constitución Station was also part of that tradition, with a Beaux Arts canyon of vaulted ceilings, skylights, and creamy monumental pillars at every corner. According to Pablo's running account of all things historical, the station had been built by the British, who at the time owned the Great Southern Railway. But the block-long building looked more French than English, and not at all like anything South American.

Their instructions were to wait at the top of the stairs on the train level. The Abels had arrived early with Pablo, and Amy would have been content to stay in one place, to lean back against the railing with her paper cup of steaming espresso and do a little people watching. But Fanny wasn't in the mood, and she wrangled Pablo into helping her roam the huge station and explore.

Amy's last words to Pablo before he was dragged away were said in a whisper. "Don't let her buy cigarettes."

By the time she'd disposed of her coffee cup, other guests had gathered. Three well-dressed, impeccably groomed women clattered up the stairs together, chattering in animated Spanish. Amy hadn't thought that her fellow travel professionals might be Spanish speakers, but it made sense. This was their territory. Meanwhile, Alicia Lindborn hovered at a nearby kiosk, trying on sunglasses. And the two men she'd noticed in the hotel's breakfast room walked in together through one of the street-level doors. Amy's heart sank.

From the moment she'd seen them this morning at breakfast—or rather heard them—she'd recognized them as competitive travelers, those most annoying of creatures, professional or amateur, who spent half of every trip talking about how special all their previous trips had been. ("I'm glad we did Salalah before it became trendy." Amy had no idea where Salalah even was. "The sunrise balloon ride is a cliché. But there's a local who can take you up in his glider." "We had to reserve a table exactly nine months in advance. But the food!") And then, when they would reunite over drinks that evening, they would compete over who'd just had the best day. ("The sunset over the marsh changed my life." "Yes, we wanted to do the sunset, but there was this legendary one-hundred-year-old guitarist performing his farewell concert in the medieval chapel. Transporting!")

Amy had been praying that these bores would not be among Jorge's travel experts. But of course they were. The British offender was blond and neatly bearded, like a thirtysomething Brooklyn hipster. Thin and wiry, with at least one tattoo. It was a spider web circling his left elbow, and Amy made a mental note never to ask about it, since the story would probably involve a Hanoi bar, an exotic beverage, and a transvestite Buddhist monk. Right off, he seemed more pretentious that the other, but that might just have been his accent.

His companion/competitor was shorter—five feet six inches?—and boxier, midforties, with a square face and close-cropped gray hair. He probably wasn't overweight, not that much. But there was something about him, some lumbering aspect, that gave that impression. "My best meal in Buenos Aires was at a hole-in-the-wall pizza joint, believe it or not. Only the locals know it. I had to bribe a taxi driver to take—"

The short, lumbering man halted in mid-sentence, which seemed unusual. An unwritten rule of the game was that you didn't stop bragging until your opponent interrupted. "Well, if it isn't TrippyGirl." He splayed his arms with a limited range of motion and pointed himself in Amy's direction. "Good to know you're not totally imaginary."

"Not imaginary at all," Amy answered. "At your service." She suddenly had a good idea who this lumberer was. If he was the man she thought, then he might well object to the notion of Trippy being the half-fictional spawn of her mother's imagination. "And you are?"

"Todd Drucker. *TD Travel.*" He halted but kept his arms extended, as if embracing her shoulders from two feet away. "O'Bannion promised you'd be joining us. It's the main reason I came."

His opponent stepped forward. "That and a free trip and the fact that traveling's his job." The man smiled warmly and extended his hand. "Edgar Wolowitz. *London Times.*"

She shook it. "Amy Abel."

"Todd has informed me of your blog, Ms. Abel. I haven't had the chance to read it, but I do confess to being quite jealous. Marvelous idea." He certainly didn't talk like a hipster.

"Call me Amy. I didn't realize Mr. Drucker was a fan."

She expected Mr. Drucker to respond with a modest-sounding "Please, we're all fellow writers. Call me Todd," but he didn't. Instead . . . "Oh, I read *TrippyGirl* religiously, every episode, the same way I used to devour the Sunday comics as a child."

"Are you comparing my work to a comic strip?" Amy adjusted her Randy Jackson black frames and tried to maintain her smile.

"Is that wrong?" said Drucker with a faux grimace and a shrug. "Sorry. I thought you would love comics. You know, bright colors, two-dimensional characters, outrageous situations. And no one for a minute believes that they're real."

"My exploits are real." Given the heat of the moment, it was a lie she had to tell.

"Really?" Todd cocked his head. "Really? You don't think that I know what the Jersey City PATH train looks like? I live in Jersey City."

"My camera was stolen in Russia. I didn't have a good shot to illustrate the story."

"So you admit to posting a fake photo?"

"I was illustrating my predicament. I know it's not the kind of travel writing you do."

"She has a point," said Edgar Wolowitz. Amy noticed his thin gold wedding band and somehow felt more at ease with this British version of a hipster. "Travel memoirs have more leeway," he added. "Not everyone gets to write hard-hitting news pieces on the ten best hotel pools in the world."

"Perhaps." If Todd Drucker was ruffled by this jibe, he didn't let it show. "I do have to say I'm looking forward to witnessing your exploits. Should be exciting." He touched a stubby finger to his chin. "Hmm, don't tell me. A torrid affair with a gaucho and his lariat, followed by a murder on a Patagonian glacier."

"Just wait and see," said Amy. And she was actually relieved when, out of the corner of her eye, she saw Fanny approaching from the arcade of little shops. "Oh, look. Here's my mother."

"You brought your mother?" said Drucker, raising a single eyebrow. "You're kidding."

Fanny was carrying an earthenware gourd, stirring the contents with a shiny metal straw, then taking a sip. "You must try this," she ordered her daughter and thrust the steaming gourd up toward her nose. "Pablo says it's better than coffee and cigarettes combined."

Pablo followed in Fanny's wake, apologizing with a tiny wave of his hands. "It is our secret to health. One of my tourists said to me it is like a steroid green tea."

Amy had to think. "Green tea on steroids." The gourd was stuffed with a greenish-brown mass of leaves and twigs.

"Yes, exactly." Pablo took a thermos from under

his arm, popped the lid, and poured another few ounces of hot water through the gourd's shrubbery. "You need to mash it to release the flavor." He pulled out the straw and showed her. It was curved near the top, like a permanently fixed bendy straw. The bottom ended in a small bulbous sieve, which you used to mash up the herbs and then suck in the tea without drawing in too many of the twigs. Fanny did as she was told, then offered the gourd up again to Amy's nose.

"They do love their maté." Todd Drucker managed to sound both bored and impatient. "It's a type of South American holly, and they've built a whole culture around it. Rules, traditions, folklore. It's a little bitter until you get used to it. You may want sugar."

"I prefer it straight," said Fanny. "Come on." The gourd remained under Amy's nose, steaming up her Randy Jacksons, until she took it with both hands and sipped.

It tasted pretty much the way Amy expected a shrub to taste, and yes, it was bitter, although she didn't want to give anyone the satisfaction. "Good," she managed to say and handed the gourd back down to Fanny.

"This, I take it, is TrippyMother," said Edgar with a polite half bow. "Edgar Wolowitz. And our fellow traveler Todd Drucker."

Fanny stopped playing with her gourd long enough to take part in the introductions.

"Are you here to keep Trippy out of trouble?" Todd asked her with a condescending twist of the head.

"Out of trouble?" Fanny's tone remained neutral.

"I expect you'll be a calming, more mature voice of reason," said Todd. "That's what I meant."

And here Fanny bristled. "So you think I'm what? Some ancient, boring chaperone?"

"Not chaperone exactly, but . . . Well, I assume you read your daughter's blog—all her escapades and wild sex and impulsive behavior. You'll be keeping an eye on her."

"What makes you think she's the one who needs an eye . . . kept on her?"

For a few seconds Todd didn't get her point. When he did, he broke into a hearty laugh. "Yeah, right. You're the one we have to look out for."

Fanny retracted her chin as if she'd just been punched. "Why is that so funny?"

"No reason, Mrs. Abel. Sorry. Just makes a great mental picture."

"Really?" Fanny extended her chin. "And why is that picture so funny?"

"Well . . ." The travel writer probably had a blithely sarcastic reply on the tip of his tongue. He didn't seem the type to back down, at least not verbally. But the reply never arrived. What did arrive was the echoing blare of a tango band. All the lingering people by the staircase—Todd and Edgar, the Abels, Alicia Lindborn, and the three Spanish speakers—turned toward the nearest archway that opened onto the nearest train platform. So did half the denizens of Constitución Station.

Jorge O'Bannion stood in the middle of the archway, decked out in top hat and tails, his arms flung wide like a ringmaster welcoming his spectators into the big top. Ten yards behind him was the tango band, which looked suspiciously similar to the band that had played last night at the Iglesia del Tango, complete with the eighty-year-old accordionist.

Wordlessly, the eight luxury explorers gravitated up to and through the archway, exchanging solemn sideway glances as they merged. Amy couldn't help feeling an instant, almost eerie bond, as if they were all about to share in some life-changing adventure. To a certain extent, she felt this way at the beginning of every tour. But in this case, with the old Victorian station and the tango band and the shiny Chilean ringmaster . . . And behind the ringmaster were the photographers, one video and one still, capturing the moment for future brochures and PR releases and Web sites. Amy wished she'd worn something nicer. Fanny had already handed off her maté gourd to Pablo, taken the sports camera out of her bag, and joined in the photographic frenzy.

A moment later the train cars came into view. Amy couldn't see the engine at the other end, but from the fog enveloping the track, she assumed it to be a steam engine. The carriages themselves were straight from a Turner Classic Movie. Marlene Dietrich could have been gazing out of one of those fogged windows that were edged in beveled glass. Cary Grant could have been checking out his reflection in the polished brass fittings. The carriages did not look identical— different lengths, slightly different heights, undoubtedly rescued from various long defunct lines. But the wood was a uniform dark brown, lustrous, and rich.

"Welcome, my friends, to the New Patagonian Express," boomed Jorge, then repeated himself with equal volume and intensity in Spanish. "It is my honor to welcome my most distinguished guests." Again translated. "These glorious carriages, magic carpets from long ago, are prepared to transport us to a bygone world of luxury and adventure." The ringmaster had just finished a much longer Spanish version of this when his attention was diverted by a man in a semi-official-looking brown uniform who was scurrying down the platform from the direction of the engine. "Eight days of wonder, carrying you to the Eighth Wonder . . ."

When the uniform could no longer be ignored, Jorge held up his hands, begged them "Excuse me" in Spanish, then turned to face the new arrival. Everyone waited while the men pivoted away and whispered back and forth. The uniform pointed toward the front of the train with one hand, then with the other hand. Jorge's hands stayed closer to his body, but his head moved, shaking and nodding, lowering to his chest, then up to the vaulted steel and perhaps the sky beyond. At one point the discussion seemed to get quite heated.

"My dear friends." Jorge O'Bannion turned to face them, once again all smiles. "I deeply regret that there is a situation here beyond our control. My very capable engineer informs me that we have encountered the shortest of delays. Your luggage awaits in your compartments. Unfortunately, you cannot yet go into your compartments due to safety concerns, not that your possessions won't be perfectly safe. It will be a delay of a mere half hour."

"Safety concerns?" asked Todd Drucker, speaking for everyone.

"No concerns," said Jorge. "Just a station regulation whenever repairs are being made." When Jorge repeated his explanation for the three Spanish speakers and got to the words *media hora*, the uniformed engineer made a face and waggled his head.

"*Una hora*? One hour, then?" He watched the waggle morph into a dubious shrug. "One hour, maybe a little more. And there's no possible danger, not to worry. *No hay peligro.*"

Despite his assurance, everyone looked concerned—except Fanny. Her eyes were alight with anticipation, and she leaned up to whisper toward her daughter's ear. "Is this how it begins?"

"Nothing's beginning," Amy whispered back. "Everything's going to be fine." And she tried to will herself to believe it.

CHAPTER 7

One thing that regularly took Amy by surprise was just how big the world was. Big and often empty. She had visited plenty of these wide-open spaces. In some cases she was mentally prepared. The famously desolate deserts, of course. The row after infinite row of snow-peaked mountains. The lakes that resembled oceans, complete with tides and waves and landless horizons. But she had never stopped to think about the endlessness of South America. Even more amazing was the fact that it was right there, just below, hidden in plain sight, lying in the shadow of her own familiar, well-traveled continent. And so much of it.

The safety concern seemed to have something to do with the train's engine, some steam valve or gauge; even hundred-year-old technology remained unfathomable to Amy. All she knew was that the delay had lasted four hours and that Jorge O'Bannion had been torn between trying to provide four hours' worth of distraction for his grumbling guests and sneaking away to bark anxiously into his cell phone. Fanny had used some of the time to buy her own thermos for hot water, more yerba maté for her gourd, and to rail against Todd Drucker (Toad Drucker, as she kept calling him) and his rude assumptions.

The first part of their steam journey took them south of Buenos Aires, through the typical gradation of suburbs—upper-class ones, all gates and high walls and manicured trees behind the walls; followed by middle-class ones, with fenced yards and dogs; followed by slums, with crumbling facades and patched roofs and more dogs and properties too close to the tracks for safety or comfort. Afterward came open spaces dotted with scruffy fields and factories. And then, far off to the left of her window, Amy glimpsed the first of the seaside resorts, with high-rise hotels defining what was undoubtedly an unseen coastline.

Their progress was slower than the normal traffic along the southern rails. The soft chug of the engine lulled them into a mellower mood, like a lullaby played out on a time machine. Only the occasional whoosh of a passing diesel engine broke the reverie. Once or twice, when their own track was preempted by the speed and schedule of a real train, they were forced to pull into a siding and wait until the intruder from the future had passed, and the world was once more safe for the Patagonian Express.

As they'd boarded in Constitución Station, Amy had counted nine carriages. Some were rather standard-looking affairs, such as the old caboose and the dining car. Others were much longer, like the one containing their sleeper.

Theirs was a good-sized compartment, done in a heavy-paneled Edwardian style with velvet and leather and with tulip wall sconces for lighting. Against each side wall was a twin bed that lifted up and back to produce a couch. The two most improbable luxuries, things that shouldn't be on any train anywhere, she thought, were (a) a bathroom with a claw-foot bathtub and (b) a bedroom fireplace. Amy assumed that the fireplace was nonfunctioning, despite the authentic kindling and birch logs laid out in the hearth. She had spent her first five minutes on board talking her mother out of lighting a fire.

A door at the far end opened up onto a semiprivate lounge with a bar and comfortable seating for four around a circular mahogany table. Beyond that was another suite, where one of the Spanish women was in residence and which was part of the same elongated carriage. They wondered aloud if that one also had a fireplace and if she was going to try to use it.

Dinner on the first evening was in the dining car, the menu choices being a poached sea bream or the omnipresent Argentine steak or some vegetarian dish. Amy and Fanny both ordered the fish.

The dining space was equipped with enough red-striped armchairs facing enough white linen–covered tables to comfortably seat forty, which gave all eight of the guests the opportunity to stay in their own little cliques and not mingle. Amy felt both relieved and vaguely disappointed. Travel was supposed to be all about new people and new experiences, wasn't it? And here she was, making conversation with her mother, splitting her attention between Fanny's annoying growing expertise with the maté gourd and, through the table-side window, her view of the Argentine pampas.

The steam-driven locomotive chugged on at a relaxed clip, which somehow made the landscape seem even more vast. The pampas were these immense, cool pastures of green, which took on a slightly purplish hue in the shadows of the late-day sun. Peppered here and there, always at a lonely distance, was a farmhouse or two, usually with red roofs. And then the smaller brown dots of cattle moving gently from one zone of empty green to another. Not a human being in sight.

"You should be careful with too much maté," said Pablo, shyly pointing to Fanny's gourd. He had stepped up to their table, and Amy motioned for him to sit down and join them as they waited for dessert. She moved a little closer to the window, and he squeezed in an armchair next to hers. "There is caffeine in the herbs, you know."

"Good. It's probably the only thing keeping me awake," said Fanny. Between the long day of travel and the rocking rhythm of the train, exhaustion seemed finally to be catching up with her. "But I get your point." And she set her gourd and thermos aside. "It's not a drug, is it? I mean, I'm not going to be getting any crazy visions or heart palpitations?"

"I don't think so," said Pablo. "But everyone is different."

"At least it keeps me from smoking." Fanny shot her daughter a sly, crooked smile.

"That's your excuse?" said Amy. "And what are you going to use to get off maté?"

"I was thinking heroin."

Their guide's eyes widened.

"She doesn't mean it," Amy assured him. "Just kidding."

"Good," said Pablo. "There are enough problems without that."

"Problems? Is everything all right with the engine?" Amy was voicing the concern that had been nagging at her since the start. She felt self-conscious even mentioning it. "I don't mean to be a worrier."

"The train engine? Yes, yes, all fine," Pablo said with the confidence of a man who probably didn't know very much. "They say it was a bad valve that needed replacing. It runs on oil, not coal, like in the old days. All very modern, although we still have steam. Steam is more romantic than diesel, yes?"

"Very romantic," said Fanny, stifling a yawn.

Pablo made small talk with them until their desserts arrived. It was *dulce de batata*, he explained, a kind of sweet potato jam served with crackers. "Delicious," he added, just in case they doubted it. Then he left them to prod the dark gelatinous mounds with their sterling silver spoons.

Fanny took a tentative bite, pronounced a hearty "yum" for all to hear, then leaned across to her daughter. "I think we may want to save up, dear. You know, store the credits away in the old calorie bank for another day."

"Agreed," said Amy, pushing her *dulce* away and stifling her own yawn. She was already mentally preparing for her snug single bed, gently rocking in the shadow of their unlit fireplace.

By the time her mother pulled back the velvet to welcome the day, the landscape beneath their wheels had changed. The endless green pastures had given way to a dry, almost desertlike plateau. The gray-brown earth was streaked with purple-green outbreaks of thorny bushes. Now and then a line of wooden fence posts would stretch across their view in a series of odd angles, the posts connected by a few slackened strands of barbed wire, keeping out nothing, since there seemed to be nothing to keep out or in. And above it all in the far, far distance was a line of snowcapped mountains.

Once again, they ate in the dining car, at the same table—a breakfast of pomegranate juice, cold cuts, cheese, and a croissant, plus strong coffee for Amy, the ever-present maté gourd for Fanny—and finished just in time to see the train pulling into the ancient town of Carmen de Patagones, on the banks of the Río Negro. This, Amy knew from the itinerary, would be the stop for the day, their first chance to escape the mesmerizing rocking of the past fourteen hours, to stretch their legs, and to do a little sightseeing.

Amy couldn't remember the last day of touring she'd done with her mother. Buenos Aires didn't count, since Pablo and Alicia Lindborn had been along, acting as unwitting buffers. But now, as the Abel women wandered the sleepy, winding streets that wove from the train station down to the river, Amy was surprised to find that it wasn't so bad. When separated from the cares and distractions of everyday life, Fanny could actually be good company. Funny and relaxed and ready for anything.

From the outset, they'd been determined to find some kind of memorable souvenir in Carmen, which was probably the least touristy town Amy had ever encountered. In fact, it was hard for her to imagine what the main industry of the town was or ever had been, or even a possible reason for its existence for the past two hundred-plus years, except perhaps that it was situated on a river.

For her souvenir, Fanny settled on a Peruvian wool hat with earflaps, a pompom, and a silver, mirrorlike

Batman insignia sparkling over the forehead. As they exited the store, she stuffed the hat into her oversize purse and heaved a disappointed sigh.

"I think it's cute," Amy said. "Batman goes Peruvian disco."

"That's not why I'm sighing. I'm just disappointed." Reaching into her purse again, she rummaged, then pulled out her camera by its glittery red strap. "Outside of an inconvenient little delay, absolutely nothing's happened. No murder. No threats. I hate to say it, but you're losing your touch."

"Is that why you came?" Amy asked. "To see someone get killed? To record it for your blog?"

"You make it sound so heartless. No, I just thought there might be an adventure. That jerk Toad Drucker is accusing us of making things up."

"Very perceptive man."

Fanny gave her a look. "You laugh. But I promised my readers a South American adventure. I can't just make one up. Well, I could, but not with Drucker hovering over us like a vulture. Unless I help create a little something."

"No. You are not going to concoct an adventure."

"Of course not." Fanny thought for a moment, nodding her head. "It doesn't have to be a murder, you know. It can be a simple kidnapping or a jewel heist. Or a revolution. How stable is this government, by the way?"

"I know you're perfectly capable of starting a revolution, Mother, but please don't."

"I'm just asking. Are you hungry for lunch? I know there's food on the train, but I don't want to get back on. Is there a restaurant in this town? Or are we going to be reduced to knocking on the door of some shack and washing dishes in exchange for a few handmade tacos? Do they have tacos here? Or is that just Mexico?"

Amy was in the process of thinking up a witty answer, although much of her attention was consumed by keeping her footing on the uneven cobblestones. And that was when they heard the explosion, echoing through the meandering stone streets. It was a single blast, with more resonance than one would expect from a leftover firecracker. "Oh, my God!"

"About time!" Fanny crowed with something like glee. The camera was already in her hand. She fumbled for the ON switch, then held the camera out in front of her. "Which way to the station?"

"It doesn't have to be the train," Amy argued. "It could have been an engine backfiring or a firecracker."

"How much do you want to bet?" And before her daughter could take the bet, Fanny was on the move, the small square camera in front of her like a flashlight. Amy raced to catch up.

Within two blocks, they didn't have to guess anymore about directions. Doors had opened onto the street, and half a dozen locals, maybe more, were making their way across the little town, chattering and exchanging questions. Amy and Fanny simply followed—all the way to the train station. Other locals poured out of other streets, joining the parade, chattering more, and going faster. Fanny tried to catch as much on video as possible.

The engine, Jorge O'Bannion's antique steam engine, was the finish line of this informal race. The machine was where Amy had last seen it, off on the siding by the old water tank, looking perfectly normal—except for the splintered brown wood toward the rear of the engine, and the gaping hole, and the two men lying on the gravel by the tracks.

"Do you think it's a murder?" said Fanny, knowing that she was recording herself and trying to keep the excitement out of her voice.

CHAPTER 8

Marcus tried Amy for the third time, and the call went once again to voice mail. He kept his phone out of sight, below the lip of his polished concierge desk, hung up without leaving a message, then watched the three-minute video one more time. The footage had been extensively edited and crudely dubbed with an overexcited narration from Fanny.

Life at the Ritz-Carlton Battery Park was not as hectic as it had been a few miles north at the Ritz-Carlton Central Park, especially now that he was working evenings. He had traded shifts with Xavier for two weeks so that he could keep Amy's Travel open for business while the Abel women were away. But even during the day, Battery Park was nothing compared to Central Park.

Up there he'd once had to deal with a Saudi Arabian oil wife who had lost two pieces of luggage filled with her sexy lingerie collection. Apparently, sexy lingerie, some of it almost comically, Frederick's of Hollywood sexy, serves a critical function behind the closed doors of the Saudi Arabian kingdom.

Marcus had had to arrange to replace the hundred-plus items based on very detailed descriptions transmitted to him by a male assistant who had received them from a very reluctant female assistant. Some of the items, Marcus had discovered, could be purchased locally, in Chinatown of all places. But for others, diagrams had been made, seamstresses engaged, and everything had had to be completed by sunset of the following day.

Down here it was mostly business clients, Wall Streeters and international financiers. Their demands were small and easily handled. Last week a pair of Silicon Valley soon-to-be billionaires had asked for courtside seats with Spike Lee at a Knicks game. That had taken all of three calls to arrange: one to Spike Lee's manager, a second to Spike Lee's favorite charity, offering a sizable donation, and a third received from Mr. Lee himself, who needed a little persuading that these two geeks would not act too geeky at the game and would never speak to him unless spoken to. Easy by comparison. Almost boring.

Marcus adjusted his earbuds and played the *Trippy-Girl* video again. It began with a shakily filmed race through the streets of a picturesque South American town. Then it cut to the train station and pushed through the gathering crowd. Next was a close-up of the train engine's boiler, steam still escaping through a small, open petal of ruptured steel. Fanny's off-camera voice explained about the faulty valve that had just been replaced the day before in Buenos Aires, about the inexplicable explosion and the multiple injuries, two as it turned out. This was all very suspicious, she claimed breathlessly.

The train station's manager appeared next, saying a few things in garbled, half-decipherable English.

Then the video cut to the two injured men as they received first aid on the platform, the older identified as the engineer, the younger as a tour guide named Pablo. The engineer, it seemed, had been adjusting the new valve, which became suddenly and inexplicably jammed during a boiler test. The explosion had resulted in his temporary deafness and second-degree burns from the steam. Pablo, who had been there to help the engineer with the test, was more seriously injured. Marcus couldn't figure out what the injuries were exactly, but they didn't appear to be life-threatening. The boy was conscious and was trying to reassure everyone that he was okay.

This was followed by another close-up of the open steel petal and Fanny's voice speaking almost rapturously about "so-called accidents" and mysterious plots and the tips of sinister, metaphorical icebergs. "This time there were no fatalities. Who knows what will happen tomorrow?" It ended when an older man with black, wavy hair put his hand over the camera lens, looking distraught and pleading with them "by all that is holy" to stop the filming. A nice dramatic touch.

Marcus scrolled past the video, read the rest of the blog, which was big on hyperbole but short on details, then put aside his phone just in time to help a hotel guest—fiftyish, well dressed, and well maintained, Australian from the sound of her—who asked if he could help her get hold of a shrunken head as a gag gift for her husband's birthday tomorrow.

"He's a psychiatrist," she explained. "A headshrinker we call them. I guess you call them that, too."

"Does it have to be real and human?" asked Marcus, without skipping a beat.

"No, it does not. Good God, no. But it should look real." A thoughtful pause. The psychiatrist's wife eyed Marcus with some newfound respect. "Could you really get an actual human head?"

"Life-sized, no. Shrunken, probably."

"Let's stick with a fake."

"I can have it for you by morning."

It felt good not to be in a moving bedroom.

The boiler explosion, whatever its cause, had failed to delay the Patagonian Express by more than a few hours. The engineer had recovered enough to be back on the job. And by some miraculous stroke of luck, Jorge O'Bannion had managed to track down a replacement engine in the town of Viedma, just across the Río Negro. The antique steam engine had been restored for a pharmaceutical magnate who was planning to move it to his estate, to replace the miniature train that circled his extensive grounds, a train that his five children had apparently outgrown. Jorge had reported all of this with a straight face, and Amy assumed it had to be true. At great expense, the New Patagonian Express had taken out the required insurance policy and had rented the shiny silver engine, pledging to return it in pristine condition to the Viedma station in exactly one week.

After a second gently rocking night on the rails, and with no further incident, they had crossed the border into Chile and had wandered along a river valley to arrive at Glendaval station, an ancient stone whistle-stop, little more than a platform and a shed, half a mile from Glendaval, the first of the O'Bannion estancias. The ranch was picturesquely nestled between an apple orchard on a gentle hillside and an emerald lawn manicured by a flock of white sheep.

The estancia itself, Timothy O'Bannion's original sheep-herding manse, was everything his grandson had promised. It reminded Amy of a Montana hunting lodge, the kind owned by Internet billionaires pretending to be cowboys, except that this was undoubtedly the real thing. Long planks of polished mahogany led the way to a soaring stone fireplace in the great room. Two curving staircases, one on each end, brought you up to a gallery on three sides, off of which were the main bedrooms and corridors, which were floored in a gorgeous golden teak and led off to other bedrooms.

The staff from the train joined the staff already working at the lodge. The train's chef and his assistant, the waiter and the bartender, the cabin attendant and Nicolas, the new guide, continued their responsibilities in the new setting. Amy marveled, not for the first time, at how hard people in the hospitality industry worked, usually with smiles on their faces, as if this was somehow their vacation, too.

It was still early in the day when Amy and Fanny settled into their room near the back and changed into their versions of ranch clothes. They had all eaten a late breakfast on the train, and everyone was looking forward to their first dude ranch excursion. Fanny stood in front of their full-length mirror, buttoning her light cotton sweater and securing the camera onto the Peruvian Batman wool hat with the flashy bat mirror and the earflaps and the pompom.

"Are you really going to wear that?" Amy asked.

"Don't you like Batman?"

"I'm not talking about the hat."

"What? You mean this?" Fanny tried to tighten the

red head mount strap and succeeded only in making the camera slip off center. She straightened it as best she could. "If I hadn't had this, we never would have gotten that video." Fanny had spent much of the previous evening hopped up on maté, editing the footage on her tablet. Amy had been hoping that this sheep ranch at the end of the world wouldn't have Internet access. But it did, a slow satellite signal, best accessed from a rocking chair in a corner of the great room. As soon as they'd arrived, Fanny had planted herself there and had rocked as the video churned its way onto the World Wide Web. "I'll bet you anything we go viral."

"I wouldn't be surprised," said Amy. "You practically promised them a murder."

"I did no such thing. I might have suggested the explosion was suspicious."

"Mom, you laid in music from *Psycho*."

"I like the music from *Psycho*." Fanny turned from the mirror to an end table where her gourd full of yerba maté was steaming away. She mashed the metal straw around the bottom, then took a long, powerful sip. "Ahhh! Good stuff."

"You should be careful," Amy warned. "You've been jittery all day."

"It gives me energy," said Fanny. "I feel I could do ten more explosions."

"Please don't."

When the Abels stepped out onto the main porch, the three Spanish speakers were already on their horses. Amy had heard their names once, on the first day, during the introductions, but had forgotten them almost instantly. The women continued to huddle together, do everything together, with unsmiling faces and furious chatter. Fanny had nicknamed them the

Furies, after the three angry sisters of Greek mythology. Alicia Lindborn was being assisted into her stirrups by a thin, weathered ranch hand with a step stool. Edgar Wolowitz, the bearded British hipster, had already mounted and was loosely holding his reins, looking tweedy and relaxed.

The last of the guests, Todd Drucker, stood by the side of his tall steel-gray horse, waiting for the step stool to become available. His eyes locked on Amy's as soon as she emerged from the lodge. "Brava," he said, applauding slowly and sarcastically. "I was a skeptic, Ms. TrippyGirl. But it seems like danger does indeed follow you. I haven't witnessed so much adventure since I had that flight delay in Newark. Is this a sign of things to come?"

"You've seen the blog," Amy ventured. "Already?"

"It was the first alert that popped up on my phone." He raised his hands and waved his stubby fingers in mock alarm. "Oh, the horror! A steam blast and second-degree burns."

"Pablo suffered more than second-degree burns," Amy said, correcting him. "A wrenched back and who knows what. He's still in the hospital." Amy and Fanny had, in fact, gone to see Pablo in the Carmen de Patagones hospital, a newish two-story facility on the outskirts of town. They'd been the only ones from the tour to visit, and he'd appreciated their concern. Fanny took a minute's worth of video of him, just in case.

"Are you sure he wasn't crippled?" Todd asked. "Or murdered? I can't wait to see what you turn this into."

"We're not turning it into anything," said Fanny. "I just record."

Todd looked at Fanny for the first time since

they'd emerged on the porch. "Oh, no." His laugh was genuine but mirthless. "So you're the culprit. I knew it didn't sound like Amy's voice. A second TrippyGirl. Heaven protect us."

"Senora Abel? Senorita? Welcome." It was Nicolas, Pablo's replacement. Like all good guides, he knew how and when to intrude and change the subject. "Have either of you ridden before?"

"Once," said Amy. "A pony at a birthday party."

Edgar Wolowitz chuckled. Fanny didn't say anything but nodded like the expert rider she wasn't.

Amy regarded her steed, a docile-looking chestnut mare with a slight bow to her back, and decided that she needed a name. Hortense. For the next few hours it would be Amy and Hortense, two kindred souls joined at the saddle.

"Don't worry," said Nicolas with a comforting grin. "I'm told these horses are very gentle."

Yesterday in Carmen de Patagones, Jorge O'Bannion had made a few frantic calls. The result was an ever-grinning Nicolas, who had joined the tour early this morning, when the train stopped for passport control at the border crossing from Argentina into Chile.

The new guide reined his dappled palomino back and forth along the gravel drive, as if not yet quite in control. "Are you ready to see our famous Patagonian nature? We have majestic condors and guanacos, maybe a puma, if we're lucky."

He pointed to the weathered ranch hand, who had finished with Alicia and was now moving the stool over to Todd. The unsmiling man fit the image of a South American gaucho, wearing a crimson poncho, a flat Buster Keaton hat, and fantastic thigh-high boots, which all the women, including Amy, eyed with envy. "Oscar has spent many years here," said Nicolas. "He knows the best spots. We'll be on good trails. Very safe." Like Pablo before him, he repeated everything in Spanish.

Nicolas didn't strike Amy as the typical nature guide. He was older than Pablo, in his early thirties. Taller and paler than his predecessor, Nicolas wasn't what you could call overweight, but there was a slight doughiness, which reminded Amy more of a grad student than an outdoorsman.

"Will Mr. O'Bannion be joining us?" asked Alicia, turning her horse toward the stables to check.

"I'm certain he wants to," said Nicolas. "But he is busy arranging things, I think."

Nicolas had saved the shortest of the horses for Fanny, who insisted on mounting it without the step stool. Amy was surprised at how easy it looked when her mother simply threw herself at something, whether it was a life-affirming challenge or a stirrup on the side of an unsuspecting horse.

Oscar took a minute to make sure everyone was adjusted. Nicolas went from horse to horse and snapped a canteen onto each saddle. "Specially made," he said, showing off the custom design and lettering. "The New Patagonian Express. You can keep it as a souvenir." Then the guide and the ranch hand swung up onto their mounts. Wordlessly, Oscar led them down the gravel path, through the apple orchard, and up a winding path into the hills.

It was a beautiful summer afternoon, sunny but with a light breeze. Amy had heard that a breeze was as calm as the air ever got in this part of the world. Patagonia was famous for its winds, buffeting and harsh for weeks at a time, the kind that often drove people eccentric, the kind that could, on a bad day, make a plane fly backward. So the locals said.

The horses knew every rock and gully, and they trailed Oscar's horse without complaint. At the top of a small bluff, the path opened onto a rocky plateau with panoramic views of the snowcapped Andes, which seemed to almost circle the valley. Oscar and Nicolas rode side by side now, with the local man pointing out things that needed amplification and translation. The green and red bushes weren't bushes, but firetrees, kept stunted and sturdy by the unending wind. The periwinkle-blue buds were edelweiss. Yes, like the song, but a South American variety. The green birds that looked like parrots were indeed parrots. The thing that looked like a furry ostrich on the next hill was a Darwin's rhea, named after the great man, who had wandered these valleys 150 years ago.

Amy was proud of herself and of Hortense. She had gotten into a riding rhythm, rocking her weight back and forth with each step, leaning forward for the uphill sections and back for the downhill ones, keeping her feet solidly in the stirrups. Her mother, one horse ahead, was not doing as well. The shortness of Fanny's torso might have been part of the problem, denying her some needed leverage. But she was also distracted by the head-mounted camera, keeping it straight and focused, trying to find something exciting to look at. Amy wanted to ride up beside her and tell her just to enjoy the moment, but she knew better.

"What is that bird?" Fanny called ahead.

Nicolas turned to see her aiming her camera at a huge black thing with separated feathers, like fingers sticking out on the end of each wing. The wingspan was enormous, perhaps three times the length of its body. The bird flew high above, floating lazily from one thermal to another.

Nicolas didn't have to confer with Oscar. "That is our Andean condor, bigger than your condors in California. They are also like vultures, you know, eating dead things on the ground."

"Dead things?" asked Fanny. "You mean like bodies?"

"Animal bodies, yes," said Nicolas with an ingratiating grin. "We do not have human bodies in the wilderness."

Fanny shrugged. "You don't know that for sure."

The horse parade had stopped to watch and point and listen to the guide.

"You sound disappointed," Todd said. "Did you want the bird to find a murder victim? Would that make you happy?"

Fanny pierced him with a scowl. "If I need a murder victim, I'll make one myself."

The condor disappeared behind a ridge, allowing the parade to continue its journey across the plateau. Fanny kept one eye on the sky. Edgar and Todd were ahead of her now, and even with one eye, she could see them whispering and laughing, with Todd taking the occasional glance back at her, then turning to Edgar again and whispering and laughing.

"Toad," Fanny muttered.

"Just ignore them," Amy advised.

Fanny ignored them as best she could. "Oh, look, Two more condors." She pointed to the new pair, hovering by the same ridge where the first one had disappeared. This time a few heads nodded, but no one stopped. "And another one," she announced a few seconds later. "Look, look, look!"

By the sheer force of her enthusiasm, Fanny once again stopped the parade. By now there were six condors dipping below the same ridge, then popping up again. Nowhere else in the sky had they seen a condor except for now at this spot.

"Must be something fresh," said Fanny. After reaching up to her head, she clicked on the camera and switched over to her announcer voice. "We are horseback riding in the Patagonian wilderness, witnessing something extraordinary. See those magnificent condors by that ridge? They are messengers of death, come to feast on nature's destruction."

"Mother," moaned Amy. "Really?"

"Say what you want, dear. I can edit you out."

"Not to worry. It is probably a goat," said Nicolas. "Or an old guanaco or a skunk. Perhaps not a skunk."

"Enough." Todd rolled his eyes, exasperated rather than amused. "Trippy, get your mother under control. This is not how you want to run your business."

"Mother!"

Fanny wasn't listening. "We should go over and see. Can we do that?"

Nicolas took a moment to confer with Oscar in Spanish. "Oscar wants to know why," he said in English.

"Because it's nature. And this is a nature excursion." Fanny was nearly shivering with anticipation. "Let's go."

"It is not as close as it looks," said Nicolas. He translated for Oscar, who shook his head.

Amy tried to reach out for Fanny's reins. "You may have had too much maté."

"Maybe." Fanny glanced down, videoing her own trembling hands. "Or maybe it's something worth seeing. Being at the right place? Isn't that what Trippy's about?"

"Can you go into withdrawal from maté?" Amy asked everyone. She had almost grabbed her mother's reins when Fanny saw her and instinctively pulled away. The jolt startled Fanny's horse, who raised his head with a frightened neigh. Fanny reacted with a neigh sound of her own.

Amy was not quite sure how it happened, whether Fanny started the gallop on her own or the horse started it. Perhaps it was both—Fanny and the horse combining their wills to rebel against the group. Whatever the cause, the horse neighed again, twisting its head in panic. Then it took off, tore across the last hundred yards of plateau, and stumbled down into the wooded valley. Everyone else just sat there, stunned.

"Mother!" shouted Amy into the dust. "Don't be an idiot. Come back." But Fanny was already out of sight and out of earshot.

"Did she do that on purpose?" asked Alicia Lindborn.

Oscar was the first to recover. Not speaking English, he'd taken longer than the others to understand that this wasn't something planned. But he was a gaucho, used to emergencies. He said a few fast words to Nicolas, pointed to the two-way radio clipped to his vest, and kicked his horse in the haunches. Man and horse followed the previous trail of dust over the rocks and down into the valley.

"What do we do?" asked Amy, the fear rising in her voice. "Do we follow?"

"I don't know," said Nicolas. "Will your mother come back?"

"I don't know."

"She might get herself lost," said Edgar, a statement that didn't help anyone's state of mind. "I mean, she might."

"We will find her," said Nicolas. And then he pulled his own two-way radio from its clips, turned it on, and pressed a large button. "Senor O'Bannion? Mr. O'Bannion. Hello, sir. I am afraid we have a situation." He said all this in English, perhaps in an effort to keep Amy feeling calm and in the loop.

It wasn't working.

CHAPTER 9

It was the gaucho who took control. Spanish speaking, nearly silent Oscar. He had returned no more than five minutes after galloping off—without Fanny, looking frustrated but calm. The woman's horse was experienced, he told them. It would return to the stable. The only danger would be if the small lady had been thrown and was lying hidden and injured somewhere. The search would be better with all of them, he said. They would divide into two groups, one of Spanish speakers, headed by Oscar; the other of English speakers, headed by Nicolas. Jorge O'Bannion would wait by the stables and contact them if the horse returned.

The Furies seemed totally unfazed. They scowled no more than before, chattered no more or less than before, and willingly followed Oscar down the plateau and to the north side of the valley.

Nicolas led his group of four—Amy, Alicia, Edgar, and Todd—down the same path, then branched out to the east. Each party would swing around the plain, each rider staying within shouting distance as they called out Fanny's name and checked every ravine along the way. Both groups would swing around to the spot where a few condors were still visible in the sky.

"I apologize," said Todd Drucker, just before he broke off to the right of Amy and her horse. Amy was about to accept his apology when he finished his thought. "I had no idea your mother was so unstable."

"She's not unstable. You rattled her, and her horse bolted." But by the time she got the words out, the smug little publisher was already trotting down another trail.

Amy did exactly as she was told. This was always her reaction in emergencies. If you did what you were told, then it was not your fault. You were to proceed methodically, keep your eyes moving between near and mid-distance, alert for any color or movement. You kept shouting the name, kept aware of the rider to your left and the one to your right. Except that this was her mother's life at stake, and "fault" didn't matter. All that mattered was finding Fanny and hoping she was all right. Any second, Amy thought, the news would squawk through Nicolas's radio, and everything would be fine.

But the call didn't come. And as much as Amy tried to concentrate on the task, she couldn't help glancing up at the condor or two still there. Were they hovering over the same place as before? Did they have anything new and fresh suddenly within their sights? She didn't even want to think about that.

When the two-way radio finally squawked, Amy

reined in Hortense and listened through the breeze. Seconds later a message was shouted from one rider to another. "They found her horse," Nicolas said, then passed the news down the chain. "They found her horse."

"But not her?" Amy shouted.

"But not her." Nicolas waved a bandanna, gathering the other four to his side. "Oscar says the horse came to them. Uninjured. By itself," he added. "We're changing our course farther north. If we don't locate her by the time we meet up with the others . . ."

"Then what?" asked Amy.

"Then we circle back to the estancia and call the rescue and the carabineros. That's what Mr. O'Bannion tells me."

Amy was too numb to argue. She simply did as she was told: moving her eyes, keeping the right distance, shouting the name. Not her fault. Every few minutes she would wrap the reins around her saddle horn and use both hands to wipe the dust from her glasses.

The scrub was getting thicker now, making it harder to see ahead or to the sides. Maybe fifteen minutes later, she caught sight of movement in the northern distance, not far off. Then the sound of voices. Shouting voices. Were they happy shouting voices? Amy made pretend that they were. Getting closer now. Nicolas was on his radio again. They really sounded like happy shouting voices. They did.

And they were.

Amy and the searchers from the east converged on a clearing of brush and grass. The five from the north had already dismounted, gathered around a rock outcropping. Oscar had just unbuckled his canteen and was unscrewing the lid. Amy dismounted without giving it a thought, pushed through the search party, and saw her mother seated on the rock, her sweater torn, her face dirty, maybe bruised, looking distracted and exhausted. But alive. Amy knelt down, flooded with relief. She hugged her mother and felt her wince under the grip.

"Sorry, sorry, sorry," she said and almost instantly let go. "Are you all right?"

"I'm fine," Fanny said, then took a few gulps from the canteen Oscar had just handed her. "Sore. Nothing broken, I think."

"What the hell were you doing?" Amy asked as nicely as possible given the circumstances. "I was worried sick. You see what I meant about not bringing you along? Sorry. I didn't mean that. I'm just so glad you're safe."

"It wasn't on purpose," said Fanny. "The horse took off. By the time it stopped, I was down in the valley and all turned around. I couldn't see the ridge. I tried a few times. But the only landmark I could see was the condors."

"What are you saying? You followed the condors?"

"It was the only thing. Plus, I was curious. Weren't you curious?"

"No, Mom. I was worried sick."

"Well, I followed the condors, and I found them. You'll never guess what they were eating. Hopping around and pecking. It was horrible."

"A skunk?"

"A dead woman. I threw my canteen at them, but they just came back. They're not as majestic close up, believe me."

"Did you say *woman*?"

"There were three or four condors and some little ratty . . . I think foxes. I tried to get a closer look, but my horse got spooked and took me away. At some point I fell off."

Had Amy heard right? "You found a body?"

"Isn't that wild? I tell you, Toad Drucker is going to poop himself when he sees."

Amy took a deep breath and looked her mother straight in the eyes. "You're sure? A human body?"

"Of course I'm sure. It's all right here." And with that, Fanny reached up to her Peruvian Batman hat. "Oh, no!"

The tour was at a standstill. Fanny had taken another few gulps of water and had repeated her story for the English-speaking public. Nicolas had translated it for Oscar and the Furies, then had got on the radio to Jorge O'Bannion, still in Spanish mode. The guide's expression remained neutral as he relayed the news, but Amy had a feeling that he was nearly as skeptical as Todd Drucker.

For his part, Todd seemed both amused and outraged. "You chased down condors, found a murdered woman. . . ."

"I didn't say *murdered*," Fanny countered. "Dead."

"And you just happened to lose your camera, so there's not any proof. I'm new to the *TrippyGirl* experience. Is this the usual way? Disrupting everyone's hard-earned vacations? Exaggerating little hiccups? Finding corpses no one else can find?"

"You can find it," snarled Fanny. "We'll all find it. It can't be far."

Edgar Wolowitz agreed. "If there is a body, then it's our duty."

"That's true," said Nicolas. He had just gotten off the radio with O'Bannion.

"If I may . . ." Alicia Lindborn was the oldest member of the party, half a decade or more north of Fanny. To the untrained eye, she might have seemed pampered. But good eating habits, a strong will, and lots of Pilates gave her a kind of steely energy that Amy herself was lacking right at the moment. "If the animals are eating the body, then we need to find it."

"Oh, yes," said Todd. "Before it disappears like a mirage."

"It's not a mirage," said Fanny.

Alicia looked to the sky, shielding her eyes with a manicured hand. "The sun won't be setting for a few more hours, so I suggest we get back on our horses and do the right thing."

Nicolas returned to his radio. "Mr. O'Bannion says no," he reported a minute or so later. "I mean, he strongly advises that we go back to the estancia. He has already called the authorities. Oscar?" A few rapid-fire exchanges with Oscar in Spanish. Then . . . "Oscar knows where the condors were. He can show the carabineros when they come."

"Oscar knows the spot where they were?" asked Fanny.

"Absolutely," Nicolas assured her. "He was watching the whole time."

"Good." Fanny clapped her hands. "He can take us there now."

"No," said Nicolas. "That's for the carabineros."

"But we're just a few minutes away," said Alicia. "I

think we owe this to the poor woman, whoever she was."

"Or wasn't," muttered Todd.

"Excuse me." Nicolas went back into Spanish, speaking into the radio, then to Oscar privately, back and forth, then to the Furies. When he lapsed into English, it was in a deliberate, patient tone that indicated how little patience he had. "You are right. Please drink your water. I will pass around some nuts for anyone who is hungry. Then let us all remount and find her."

No one was in the mood for a snack. A few took slugs from their canteens. Oscar ran his hands over the flanks of Fanny's horse, checking it for injuries and scrapes, then gently murmured into the animal's muzzle. He turned to say something to Nicolas.

"Oscar will ride your horse," the guide said, translating for Fanny. "Do not worry. His horse is very nice also."

"Why?" asked Fanny. "Is he asking the horse where to go?"

Nicolas shrugged. "That wouldn't be the strangest thing today."

The guide and the ranch hand helped the women and Todd Drucker into their saddles. The constant breeze had picked up. Now it gently howled, more noise than wind, like a sleep machine on a bedside table. And following Oscar's lead, with Nicolas in second positon and the witness, Fanny, in third, the parade rode out of the clearing and back into the brush.

Amy believed her mother, of course. More or less. But she couldn't shake a certain unease. She pulled Hortense up alongside Fanny's horse, close enough to whisper. "Is there anything you're not telling me?"

Amy was accustomed to Fanny's hurt expression but could never tell, even after a lifetime, if it was fake or real. "My own daughter!"

"Yes, I am," said Amy and left it at that.

Silent Oscar did whatever magic he had to do. A compass appeared from a pocket of his woolen vest and disappeared back inside. The late afternoon sky was consulted, even though there were no longer any condors cutting through the blue expanse. Brambles and branches were checked. Twice during the ride, Oscar got off his horse, Fanny's old horse, to examine some faint lines on the ground. When he remounted the second time, he said something over his shoulder to Nicolas.

"Did you cross a river?" Nicolas asked, translating. Fanny had not even seen a river and relayed the information back up the line.

After a few more minutes . . . "This looks very familiar," Fanny called excitedly back to her daughter. But to Amy it all looked the same.

After Oscar led the way into a broad, long clearing near the foot of a sandy cliff, he dismounted for the third time and tied his reins to a tree. The wind was stronger now, creating eddies of dust around the horses' hooves, like tiny tornadoes. Oscar looked around slowly, revolving 360 degrees and nodding to himself. "Aquí estamos."

Fanny knew what he meant. "This isn't the place. It can't be."

"Why?" asked Todd, standing painfully up in his stirrups and using his left hand to massage the left side of his buttocks. "Because there's no corpse? What a surprise."

"Yes, because there's no corpse. She was here. I mean there."

The response was a general groan from the other riders, an upwelling of irritation. It was impossible for Amy to pinpoint the primary source of the groan since she'd been part of it herself.

"This can't be the place," Fanny shouted.

Nicolas was off his horse, too, walking at Oscar's side as the ranch hand took a branch from the ground and poked through the brush and grunted in a steady, soft monologue. "Condors were here," Nicolas repeated in English. "Their droppings and feathers. Foxes too."

"Maybe you saw a dead animal and thought it was a woman," Alicia suggested.

"It was a woman," said Fanny. "A real woman in a red top and black trousers. We have to keep looking."

Nicolas conveyed her objections to Oscar. The gaucho remained unimpressed. He continued to forage with his branch, enlarging the concentric circles of his search, overturning small rocks, and separating the thickly knit branches of the firetrees.

"She's not under a rock," Fanny growled.

Oscar continued. And soon enough, his branch hit something. Something not rock or earth, but metallic. He bent down and, by using his shoe and his branch, managed to spread a prickly yellow bush enough to reach inside. What he brought out glinted in the late-day sun.

"It's a canteen," said Nicolas. Everyone could see it was a canteen. "Mrs. Abel, you said you threw your canteen at the condors, yes?"

"That could be anybody's canteen," said Fanny. "A

rancher's or a backpacker's. Maybe it looks like the canteen I threw, but . . ."

Oscar handed the aluminum container to Nicolas, who brushed his hand over something engraved on the side. He held it up. "It says 'The New Patagonian Express.' "

CHAPTER 10

The next morning they were off in the Land Rovers, Nicolas and Oscar and six of the eight guests. According to the itinerary, there would be breathtaking panoramic views and a hike along the rim of a pristine glacier. At the end of the hike they would be greeted with a gourmet picnic lunch, laid out in a meadow of blossoming wildflowers. Amy was disappointed about missing this, of course. But the worst would be when they returned for their afternoon rests and she would be forced to listen to the competitive travelers waxing rhapsodic about this transformative experience and debating how it compared to other transformative experiences that Amy had undoubtedly also missed in her lifetime.

She could have gone with them. Technically. But that would have meant abandoning her mother to the sergeant, which would not have been fair to the sergeant. The man and his two officers had arrived late last night, after driving for hours from the nearest settlement with a police outpost. Today they'd been up since dawn, with Oscar, investigating the scene at the foot of the sandy cliff. Now the sergeant was back at the estancia and, after all he'd been through, didn't deserve to face Fanny alone.

Their meeting was in Jorge O'Bannion's office, a log cabin a hundred yards or so behind the main building, on a rise nestled in the apple orchard. O'Bannion had been very understanding about the whole thing. It was certainly not Fanny's fault if she'd seen or thought she'd seen a body. Finding the spot again was the right thing to do. His only regret, he said, was that Mrs. and Ms. Abel would be missing out on the morning excursion.

O'Bannion retreated into the front room, the cabin's outer office, leaving Amy and Fanny alone with Sergeant Ramirez in the larger living-room space. The man wore a brown uniform with a beige shirt and a brown tie under a bomber-style jacket ladened with patches, epaulets, and a name tag. He was perhaps a few years younger than O'Bannion but with less hair to show for it, just a few wisps of fluffy white around the temples. His roundish face held a permanent expression of wary sympathy, probably standard-issue equipment.

"You like maté?" he asked, pointing to the earthenware gourd and the matching thermos on the table by Fanny's chair. "It is unusual for *norteamericanos* to enjoy it. Do you mind?" And with that, he opened the leather satchel at his feet and brought out his own burl-wood maté gourd with silver rims around its lip and its base.

"I just filled my thermos," said Fanny and handed it over. "Here."

"Thank you," said Ramirez with a courtly nod. Fanny watched as he took a few ounces of yerba maté from a pouch in his jacket, slipped them in the burl-wood bowl, added some steaming water from Fanny's thermos, then brought out a gold- and silver-striped straw from his pocket.

"I like your straw."

"It's called a *bombilla*," said Ramirez. "Usually there are rituals with maté—how long to wait, who drinks first, how the gourd is passed from person to person." He inhaled the steam from his bowl. "It is a very social part of life. But given our situation . . ."

"Your English is very good," said Fanny.

"My family sent me to the U.S. for my education. I disappointed them by coming home."

"I'm sure they weren't disappointed. So, what did you find out?" Fanny asked it matter-of-factly, as if she were the one conducting the interview.

Ramirez didn't seem to mind. "There had been condors, yes. And foxes. We know something dead was there."

"What about clothing? You'd think the birds would tear off pieces of her clothing. . . ."

"We found no clothing."

"How about meat?" asked Fanny. "Sorry to be crude, but they didn't appear to be delicate eaters."

The sergeant pressed his herbs with his *bombilla* and took a first, tentative sip. "The birds and foxes are scavengers—thorough eaters. You saw them, granted. But it may have been an animal they could carry off. Perhaps a hare?"

"What if a whole bunch of them grabbed onto a person and lifted at the same time?"

He shook his head. "That is not how they work."

Fanny took a moment to sip from her own gourd. "Maybe they changed methods since the last time you checked."

Sergeant Ramirez smiled, until he realized that Fanny wasn't joking. "Condors do not change."

"Then she wasn't dead, and she just crawled away."

"Half eaten?"

"Not half eaten. I stretched the truth. A few nibbles. Even I could crawl with a few nibbles gone."

"Scavengers do not eat live things."

"Maybe they changed methods."

Sergeant Ramirez put down his gourd and uttered a sigh, the first of many to come. "My men searched a two-kilometer circle around the location. No one crawled away."

"Then someone moved her."

"Moved her? Why?"

"To bury her."

Ramirez mulled it over. "Possible. But the land is hard, and we found no evidence of burial."

"Then to hide her. He didn't want the body to be found."

"Why?"

"Why, why, why. Any child can ask why over and over."

"Very well. How? Let's pretend someone wanted to keep her death a secret. How would he make her disappear? Our vehicles could barely get to that spot. Between the time you say you saw her and the time you returned was how long? Half an hour?"

"Closer to an hour." Fanny wrinkled her nose. "Forty-five minutes?"

"And in that time, someone came in, took the woman, and carried her away."

"Exactly." Fanny took a few moments to sip, more of a slurp than a sip. Sergeant Ramirez did the same. Amy sat off to the side and watched, happy not to have to be a part of this. "How about footprints?" asked Fanny, putting aside her gourd.

"Yes, many footprints. Yours and mine and everyone's. What did this woman look like?"

"It happened so fast." Fanny closed her eyes. "Slim, I think. Not young. Walking shoes. She might have been hiking, but I didn't see any equipment. No backpack. Her top was red, unless that was just the blood. Black pants, not jeans. Light-colored hair, not too long. Has anyone disappeared who fits this description?"

"That is another problem," said Ramirez. "No one has disappeared. We telephoned the resorts and campsites for two hundred kilometers. All the farms and estancias. Not that there are many."

"We are a little remote," Fanny had to admit.

"If someone was missing, then my other questions would not matter so much."

"I suppose you need a missing person in order to have a corpse." Fanny's tone was reluctant.

"Exactly," said Ramirez. "So how can I ask the Chilean government to keep looking for a body that doesn't exist except for what you saw? You and no one else."

That was pretty much the end of the conversation, even though it went on for another few minutes. Sergeant Ramirez did his best to be diplomatic, but there was nothing more he could do. If someone was reported missing in the next few days, he might have cause to reopen the case. Fanny's reaction was to say that she didn't accept his decision. But her outrage was lackluster compared to her normal outrage.

And so they sat there, facing each other in the log cabin's living room, Fanny and the sergeant, quietly drinking maté through their *bombillas*. Amy had a feeling that neither one would move, not until the thermos was empty. She had said next to nothing during the whole interview, and now, with nothing even to listen to, Amy pushed back her chair, touched her mother on the shoulder, and made her way to the outer office.

Jorge O'Bannion was at his desk near the front window, staring glassily at his computer screen. The businessman looked older now, slumped in his chair, his suit a little crumpled, his wavy dark hair disheveled, as if he'd run his hand through it more than a few times. She could see the bald spot, which must have been artfully, carefully combed over on all their previous encounters.

"How's it going?" she asked and immediately regretted it.

"Miss TrippyGirl," he said, sitting up and waving for her to join him. He spoke in a near monotone, his voice sounding tired and resigned. "I never took time to read these before. Fascinating." He turned the monitor so she could see.

"Oh." It was a very familiar Web page, for Amy at least. Well designed in comforting blues and greens, with tabs on the right for the blog entries, it had been created by one of the Abel cousins, a graphic artist just out of school. Banner ads along the top and bottom linked up with all the best travel sites. "You never read *TrippyGirl* before?"

O'Bannion shook his head. "My publicist I hired in New York said you were important. She didn't say how or why. Apparently, things happen when you two travel."

Amy felt horrible, as if all this were somehow her fault. On the other hand . . . "I think I tried to tell you at one point."

"At your house when you mentioned murder? I should have listened."

"In my defense, it's not like I ever caused a murder." Her voice lightened. "And we don't have one now. Look on the bright side. Great weather. Exciting excursions."

O'Bannion chuckled. "Exciting, yes. A delay in Buenos Aires, an explosion, two injuries, a woman who sees dead bodies. I don't want to be rude, but do you believe your mother's story?"

Amy had been awake half the night mulling over this question. Given the bare facts, it seemed almost comically coincidental. Todd Drucker had ridiculed Fanny's overheated blog post about the explosion. Fanny herself had mentioned how some excitement, even a murder, might be helpful, just to shut him up. Then she stormed off and decided to invent a body in the wilderness. On the other hand, her mother was not stupid.

"You're taking a long time to answer."

Amy nodded slowly. "I believe she saw something. Fanny likes to exaggerate, but she wouldn't make it up. Even if Drucker did make fun of her."

"Last night at the bar, Mr. Drucker . . . You should have heard. Drinking my best scotch and railing on about how dangerous you were for the travel business. Delusional. Attracting the wrong kind of attention. Creating chaos from nothing."

Amy didn't know what to say. "I am so sorry."

"Me too. Good scotch is hard to get in Patagonia."

Well, at least he could laugh about it, she thought. "What will you do if this doesn't work out?" It was a very personal question. But the mood of the moment seemed to make it okay. "What if their reviews aren't glowing? Or they don't spread the word and make all their clients sign up? My reviews will be glowing, of course."

O'Bannion looked past his computer and focused on the orchard just outside his window, then on the valley sloping below it. His tone was wistful. "My grandfather named this place Glendaval. He had memories of the Glendalough Valley near his family's home in Ireland. He talked about it always, how much prettier it was. How much better the soil and the weather. But he never went back, even when he had money." He straightened in his chair. "There's a wildness here that's not just about the lack of houses or people. Our air here no one else breathes. Our flowers couldn't live elsewhere. It would be too easy, and they'd die. The wind is like a brother. Our only civilization here is what we have made. I could be smart and sell to the national parks or some resort chain run by Europeans. I could move to Valparaiso and live like a millionaire forever."

"But you're going to stay. Even if you run out of money."

Jorge turned back from the window. His eyes glanced across the blue and green of the monitor, then settled on something shiny, half hidden by the edge of the printer. It was a pendant looped into a silver chain. A turquoise oval with a tiny sunburst of silver inlaid in the center. Amy saw it, too.

"That's beautiful," she said. "Is it old?"

Jorge seemed taken aback, as if her glimpse of this was a glimpse too far into his soul. "I was going through boxes in the old house. It was my mother's favorite. I thought maybe to make a present to Lola Pisano. My investor."

Amy thought back to the wealthy, possessive woman with the mole. They'd met for only a few moments in the Iglesia del Tango, but Amy felt she knew enough about the woman to have an opinion. "I think she'll love it."

"Me too."

"Why isn't she here?"

Jorge treated her to an uncharacteristic roll of the eyes. "I think maybe I'm lucky she's not. Maybe at the next estancia she will come, and everything will run wonderful and smooth."

"Maybe," Amy said hopefully. Jorge smiled back. And then, like a cold wave of reality, the living-room door opened and Fanny emerged with her gourd and empty thermos, followed by Sergeant Ramirez.

"So if I find a missing person, you'll start taking my story seriously?"

"Yes, Mrs. Abel," said the sergeant, then exhaled his final sigh of the morning. "That would be a good start."

CHAPTER 11

"The glaciers off Tierra del Fuego are much more impressive," Todd Drucker said.

"They're certainly larger," agreed Edgar Wolowitz. "But for absolute blueness, nothing beats the Perito Moreno. You've been there, of course."

"Of course," answered Todd. "Although I would argue that Glacier Bay in Alaska has a deeper blue. We helicoptered into the middle of it last summer. I might still have a photo." Before Edgar could make the transition to another, better glacier—in Iceland, perhaps, or Tanzania—his opponent was tapping his phone, trying to pull up proof of his superiority.

Amy nursed her post-lunch cup of Earl Grey and eavesdropped from across the great room as the travel writers faced off for the next round of competitive touring. Despite their nitpicking about which of the world's diminishing number of glaciers was still worth a visit, the consensus from the entire group was that the excursion had been enthralling, an unforgettable, not particularly difficult hike to a lake glacier where they'd been the only humans, perhaps the only humans to visit it all week. Or all month.

Alicia had been most impressed by the picnic lunch waiting for them at the end. "I don't know how the drivers managed to get there and get everything set up. We were literally in the middle of nowhere, with hot soup and delicious sandwiches and a wine bucket chilled with ice from the glacier." Then, as if to dispel any criticism . . . "I'm sure they didn't chop off the glacier itself. That wouldn't be right."

Amy had never seen a glacier. It had always been on her must-see list. But there were plenty more of them in Patagonia, she told herself. There was still time. For right now, she would console herself with the chilled salmon salad she'd just had for lunch and with the prospect of this afternoon's visit to . . . Amy picked up the daily schedule, which had been slipped under their door during the night.

"Whoo," said Fanny as she plopped herself down on the sofa next to her daughter. "This touring and dealing with murder at the same time . . . My hat's off to you. It's harder than it looks."

"We're not dealing with murder," Amy whispered, trying to encourage her mother to use her indoor voice. "No one has said that word. At most we're dealing with a death."

"What do you mean, at most? Are you saying you don't believe me?"

"No." And then, to avoid any misunderstanding, she added, "I mean, yes, I believe you."

"Then we're dealing with a death. A death that no one reported and that someone went to great lengths to cover up. At the least we can call it mysterious, probably criminal."

"Possibly criminal. Look, Mom. I don't want to

spoil your fun. But I missed a glacier this morning. This afternoon we're off to visit . . ." She picked up the schedule and found the paragraph. "A local homestead where a gaucho family will give you an unforgettable glimpse into a way of life unchanged for a hundred years."

"Sounds charming, dear."

"You've never dealt with this before. I have. My approach is to ignore it as long as possible. If this turns into a real crime, we'll find out soon enough."

"Interesting. But let me put this another way." Fanny lost her smile. She scooched a little closer and finally lowered her voice. "This is not a lark, sweetie. We, you and I, are the brand known as TrippyGirl, and we are trying to save ourselves from the impending doom known as Toad Drucker. I've given this a lot of thought. Maté's good for your thinking."

"I'm not sure you should be making decisions when you're jacked up on maté."

Fanny ignored her. "If I'd known the body was going to disappear, I never would have made such a fuss. But I did. And it disappeared. And Toad Drucker was suspicious from even before any of this. So what do you think he's going to do if we never find it?"

"If you never mention it again, maybe it'll go away."

"And if it doesn't? He's a toad with a magazine and a Web site and an evil personality. If he ridicules us, then everyone who thought it was cool to follow a half-real, half-fictional adventurer is going to lose interest."

"Not necessarily."

Fanny snorted at her naïveté. "Our book editor is a perfect example. What's her name? Little Rumplestiltskin."

"Sabrina."

"The girl practically fainted when she realized I was Trippy. I never really read our contract, but I'll bet she can find a way to cancel the book."

"Can she really?"

"Let's say she can. The result will be bad publicity and no book. Then our advertising falls off, et cetera, et cetera. Before you know it, we're homeless. But, hey, go ahead and visit your gaucho family. They'll probably have some tips about building trash can fires and living off of street rats. Tips we'll be able to use."

"Okay, okay." Her mother did seem to have a point. "We'll investigate a little. But you can't blog about any of this."

"Why not?"

"Because you don't want to dig your hole any deeper. Plus, if there is a crime, then the bad guys can read your blog and know what we're up to."

Fanny seemed flattered. "You think the bad guys read my blog?"

"Yes. It's number one in San Quentin. So no blogging. You promise?"

"Okay, I promise." Fanny held up her hand in a pledge.

Amy checked her other hand for crossed fingers. "Good. So where do we start?"

"The sergeant gave me an idea. We start by identifying our victim. This ranch is the closest place to where I found her. There are employees here. Maids, cooks, bartenders. Also maintenance people. If one of them is missing, we can find out."

"We should do that this afternoon," agreed Amy. "How about other people in the area? I can talk to them."

"Good idea." Fanny was pleasantly surprised that her daughter had gotten on board so quickly. "What other people?"

"Well, there's a gaucho family living nearby. They may have a wife or a daughter who was out tending the sheep yesterday and didn't come home." Amy repressed a smile, taking off her blond tortoiseshells and wiping them with the napkin from her tea service. "I should go visit them and ask."

Fanny cocked her head quizzically. "You think some Little Bo Peep might be our victim?"

"It's a legitimate line of inquiry. The gauchos must live as close to the scavenger site as we are here."

"Amy Josephine Abel." She was using her mother voice. "If you're not going to treat this seriously . . ."

"I *am* treating it seriously. It won't take two of us to make sure all the maids are accounted for. Meanwhile, I can check on the neighbors."

"Fine," Fanny said, drawing out the word into three syllables. "I'll stay here. You go learn how to make lariats and weave blankets and shine the spurs on your boots."

"I will do that."

The excursion met at 4:00 p.m. out in front of the lodge. Amy was surprised to find herself the only English speaker there except for Nicolas.

"Ms. Lindborn is resting until dinner," the young guide explained when she asked. "And the gentlemen are trying to get the Wi-Fi to connect them to their offices at home."

That left Amy and the Spanish-speaking Furies to join Nicolas in the Land Rover. Amy sat shotgun and volunteered to get out every now and then to open the barbed-wire gates and close them again. For a place with such wide-open spaces, there seemed to be a lot of fences and gates.

The ride was perhaps fifteen minutes long, interrupted by three gates and an equal number of radio conversations. Each time there'd be a choice between two rocky trails, Nicolas would press his intercom button, fire off a question, and wind up driving down the rockier, less hospitable trail. "Sorry," he mumbled in English. "My first time here."

"You're doing wonderfully," Amy assured him. "We're lucky you were free on such short notice. Did you have to drive all night from Buenos Aires?"

"I'm Chilean," said Nicolas, keeping his eyes glued to the dusty road. "I applied for the job originally, but Senor O'Bannion chose someone else. My references, I guess, are not so many. I decided to do a holiday instead. I was in Bariloche. Do you know Bariloche? Lake district. Very like Switzerland they say. Good skiing in winter."

"I've never been." Amy was always embarrassed by the number of places she'd never been.

"I don't think I was the first guide he called. Lucky for me, Bariloche is not far. Four hours by car to the border crossing." He pointed through the now-grimy windshield. "Time for your help again."

The final barbed-wire gate led them to the final fork in the road. But this time Nicolas didn't need his radio. The homestead was in sight, just off to the right.

Amy had been expecting something a little more charming and rustic. But the gaucho home was a patchwork of small prefabricated sections, with a sliding glass door at the back and a roof of corrugated metal. An equally small barn was made from the same material and stood at the far end of a white-washed corral, along with a lean-to and two outbuildings. What it lacked in charm, it made up for in neatness. Everything was tidy and clean, right up to the corrugated roof.

Three figures were waiting in front of the cheerfully painted blue door, two women—one older, one younger—flanking a familiar male figure. It was Oscar, of course. Who else would have a typical Patagonian homestead open for view by the owner of the Glendaval estancia? Oscar wore pretty much what he had worn yesterday, except for the hat, which was not the Buster Keaton flat hat but a more casual beret. The women, apparently his wife and daughter, were dressed in more folksy costumes: long red pleated skirts, white stockings, white blouses, and a strange type of plaid bib, like a Scottish version of a lobster bib.

Nicolas and the four women descended from the Land Rover. The Furies were quick to approach the family and introduced themselves in their usual furious way. Nicolas stood by Amy's side, ready with a translation, as needed.

"Is this a native costume?" she asked.

Nicolas in turn asked Oscar, who seemed not to be holding any grudge from yesterday's adventure. "It's traditional, yes," reported Nicolas. "From Wales. But not what they wear every day."

Amy didn't quite understand. "Do you mean whales, like the animal?"

"Like the country," said Nicolas. "Oscar's last name is Jones. You find many groups in Patagonia. German, Portuguese, Croatian. In the eighteen hundreds, people all over Europe dreamed of a better life. The corrupt schemers took advantage and sold them property in this paradise of South America. Whole towns would come over to farm and build new settlements. It was a big shock for them to arrive here."

Amy glanced around at the rugged, isolated beauty of the plains. "I can imagine."

"Most of them did stay," Nicolas explained. "They were isolated and made their own governments, far from the kings and the unfair laws. And they kept their ways. Some places in Patagonia are still like Europe. They teach the languages and have the holidays. There are towns here more Welsh than any place in Wales."

"So Oscar speaks Welsh?"

"His parents did. Here he doesn't get much chance to speak it."

Oscar Jones and his family invited Nicolas and the tourists inside. And suddenly Amy found herself in the rustic atmosphere she'd been expecting. The main room, a combination living room and kitchen, was paneled in dark, rough, overlapping wood slats. The chairs looked old and homemade, with small sheepskin rugs as their only upholstery. A black iron woodstove stood against an exterior wall and seemed to fulfill the double purpose of heating and cooking. Amy didn't know if it was lit or not, but the whole house had a warm, almost peat-like aroma. The floor was a brown tile, rich and deep in hue, the kind that a New York designer might want for a Manhattan country-style pantry.

The Joneses stood in a formal row. Oscar introduced his wife, Maria, then turned to his daughter with obvious pride, a hand on her shoulder, and made a longer, more impassioned introduction. The girl turned her face away and blushed.

"Her name is Juanita," Nicolas said, translating,

"and Oscar is very proud of how smart and hard-working she is."

Amy shook hands with each of the Joneses, re-vealed her own name, and accepted Maria's offer of a maté gourd. She knew from experience that refusing whatever you were offered upon entering a home any-where in the world was the same as refusing their hos-pitality. She stirred and sipped and smiled and set it aside.

"Would you like to see how they spin wool?" Nico-las asked, speaking for Senora Jones. The woman was shy but welcoming, with graying brown hair parted down the middle, thick features, and a sturdy bear-ing. *A wilderness beauty,* Amy thought, *who might have once known better things.*

Everyone, Amy and the Furies, expressed their ex-citement, and Senora Jones led them outside to a corrugated tin lean-to, protected from the prevailing winds. For the moment, Nicolas stayed inside, drink-ing maté with Oscar.

Amy had seen enough spinning demonstrations in her life, so she didn't mind when the other women jockeyed their way to the front, each with a dozen ques-tions about the wool and the carding process and the spinning wheel and whatever else they were pointing at. She took a step back, physically and mentally, and began to wonder how she was going to do it. She'd promised her mother. But how in the world could she start asking about a theoretically missing woman? She didn't even speak their language.

"Are you *norteamericana*? USA?" The voice was soft, only slightly louder than a thought.

Amy turned. A few feet behind her was the daugh-ter, still wearing her plaid bib. She was a younger ver-

sion of the mother, late teens perhaps, still holding
on to the hope of youth.

"I am. New York City."

"Oh." Juanita Jones looked impressed. "I have a
cousin who went to New York City. He says it is very
busy all the time."

"It's not quite that bad."

"I don't mean bad." She smiled and showed off
white and perfect teeth. "Do you mind if I practice
my English? People at the estancia help me. Someday I will work at a hotel in Santiago. Not like a maid.
My father wants more for me. My mother says it is all
the same, just making money. But my father says I
can do more."

Amy was impressed. Not every father, gaucho or
not, would be so supportive of his daughter. "It is
good to have big goals, Juanita."

"He says I can work at a front desk, speaking English to *norteamericanos*. How do you call yourselves?
North . . ."

"We call ourselves Americans. It's wrong, I know,
but simpler." Amy was practically beaming. "And to
answer your other question, yes, I would love to help
you practice your English."

The spinning wheel was spinning now. Senora
Jones and the Furies were huddled, fully engaged
with the making of thread, allowing Amy and Juanita
to slip around the side of the lean-to, then away to
the edge of the corral.

Juanita climbed up on a railing and settled back
against a fence post. "People say I'm smart. I work
hard. I want to do things. Do you know how you are
lucky this way, to be born who you are and where you
were born?"

It was a sobering thought, plainly and beautifully put. "I'm very lucky," said Amy. "I don't think about that enough. And I'm lucky to meet you, too."

Juanita nodded gravely, removed her touristy Welsh bib, and folded it into her pocket. "So let us talk English."

Over the next ten minutes or so, their practice session was intense and targeted. Amy introduced words into the conversation like *disappeared* and *missing*. Also the words *woman*, *local*, and *friend*.

At first, Juanita treated it as a vocabulary challenge, like a quiz in a language primer. "Do you know any girls who are missing?" "Yes, I know many girls who are missing. One has brown hair. One has red hair." But then Amy made it clear that these were real questions, ones that needed honest, thoughtful answers. Juanita nodded and played along. "No, I don't know any girls who are missing."

Things got interesting for Amy only when she introduced words like *anything unusual* and *stranger* into the session. Also the word *auto*.

"Isn't 'auto' the same word in both languages?" asked Juanita.

"Yes," her English professor agreed. "But most North Americans say 'car.' Now what about this car that you saw?"

CHAPTER 12

When Amy returned to the lodge at a little after six, the sun was still high in the sky. Fanny was not in their room but had left a note on Glendaval stationery, inviting her daughter to change into her bathing suit and join her in the wood-burning hot tub. Amy felt self-conscious traipsing into the great room in a hotel bathrobe and slippers. But the maid who was dusting the mounted head of a puma understood English enough to point her in the right direction. Amy found the hot tub out on a stone terrace, nestled in a crook off the main level, out of sight of the driveway and everything else except the sheep meadow and the mountains.

"You've never been in a hot tub in your life."

"You say that like it's an excuse not to try." Fanny was up to her neck in steaming water, barely able to keep her head afloat, but smiling and determined to enjoy herself. "Alejandro the waiter says they can't always fire up the tub, because of the wind, but that today was good. By the way, Alejandro says the staff is all present and accounted for. My first day of investigating, and it's a dead end."

"Hey, if solving mysteries was easy, everyone would do it."

Their hot tub was made of cedar, circular like a barrel cut in half, with seating for six and two platforms for getting in and out. The side away from the view held a twenty-foot-high smokestack and a spigot in the tub for adding cold water and controlling the temperature. Amy could smell the burning logs and assumed that somewhere just below them was a roaring fire, along with all the appropriate safety precautions.

"We're like lobsters in a pot," joked Fanny. "Come on in."

Amy did as she was told, making a point of finding a seat away from the smokestack. Her glasses immediately steamed, and she had to choose between a foggy view and a fuzzy view. She chose fuzzy and placed her Perry Ellis frames on a platform, beside the two glasses of chilled white wine. The tub's temperature was surprisingly uneven, with a pocket of chilly water under her feet. She sat down and moved her legs around to even it out. "Nice."

"So tell me about gaucho arts and crafts. Did you make a cute little lanyard, maybe with bolos on the end?"

"No lanyard. But I had a conversation with the gaucho daughter. A remarkable girl."

Fanny handed her a glass of wine, and they toasted. "Tell me."

"Mmm." The first sip reminded Amy just how much she liked Chilean wines.

The English lesson had at first produced no re-
sults. Juanita had grown up with few friends. Sad but
not unexpected. She was homeschooled, pretty much
self-schooled from books. Once a year her father
drove her more than two hours into town for the national exams, and they would stay overnight. That
was the highlight of her existence, the promise of a
life that Oscar wanted for his little girl. Now that the
estancia had been restored, things were improving.
She was starting to make friends with the Glendaval
staff. Maybe one of them would teach her how to use
a computer.

Then yesterday Juanita took her horse to the estancia just for a ride. She didn't talk to anyone, but
on the way back home in the late morning, she noticed an unfamiliar auto—sorry, car—on the main
road. It was a regular black car, not a Jeep or a truck.
And it had Chilean plates. But Juanita was riding
across a field, and she lost sight of it.

"The bottom line," said Amy, "is that someone
drove in on the morning we arrived." She paused to
enjoy her second sip of the white. "Well before you
found your body."

"Did the car drive out again?" asked Fanny.

"Juanita doesn't know. But we should ask the staff
about visitors. Also, I can go online and check towns
within driving distance. If there are any car rental
places, they'll have a record."

"A record of someone renting a black car somewhere in Chile? There must be dozens."

"Maybe this car was never returned. It could be sitting in the wilderness or wrecked in a gully the police
haven't looked at. In that case they'd have a record,
and we'd get a name. We can also talk to the car services. Ask if they dropped off a customer in the vicin-

ity. If this was a woman on a trip by herself, she might not be reported missing for a while."

"I suppose that's something," said Fanny.

Amy was annoyed by her mother's lukewarm reaction. "It's the only something we can expect. The body itself is gone. What else is there?"

"There's my camera," said Fanny, brightening at the thought. "We can borrow the horses and try to find it. I had some great footage. It'll prove I'm telling the truth."

"We are not doing that. Remember the last time you went horseback riding?"

"It was an expensive camera."

"The police have already been over that ground. What we need to find is the person in that car."

"I suppose. Do you think we're getting any warmer?" asked Fanny.

"No, I don't." Then Amy realized what she meant. "Oh, the hot tub. Yes." It was indeed starting to get uncomfortably warm, even around her feet. "Can we turn down the fire? How do we do that?"

"They explained, but I didn't understand. Let's try turning on the cold water." And she twisted the spigot by the smokestack. A torrent of water flowed in.

"No. No more." Amy turned it right off. "If the level gets any higher, you'll drown."

Fanny turned it back on. "Then we'll start bailing with our wineglasses."

"Or we could just get out."

"Ahhhhhh." Fanny's groan would have been more dramatic, but that would have entailed opening her mouth all the way and taking in a lungful. "I don't know why I take you on vacations. You're no fun at all." Then she downed the rest of her wine and began to bail.

* * *

Their second night at the Glendaval estancia was scheduled to be their last. Amy spent the hour or so before dinner looking at a map and trying to contact car companies in Puerto Cisnes, Puerto Aysén, Chile Chico, all the way down to the larger town of Puerto Natales. Two of the towns didn't have rental cars at all, one had a car service, but no one there spoke English or French or Italian or cared to make sense of Amy's garbled attempt at Spanish. Puerto Natales did have a combination of car service and car rental agency. The manager there spoke English. He assured her that all their cars and drivers were accounted for and that they had had no recent trips to the Glendaval region.

Fanny didn't fare any better. She spoke again to Alejandro and to the bartender. She even enlisted Nicolas to translate her inquiries to a respectable-looking maid who had been there for a week before their arrival, cleaning and polishing. Other than delivery trucks, no one had come up the drive to the lodge. There had been no outsiders that they knew of. No one was missing, and no one new had arrived.

In the morning there was one last excursion, a short drive in the Land Rovers to a cave at the foot of a rare Patagonian waterfall. Breakfast was cooked on an open fire under an opening toward the rear of the cave—eggs, ham, fruit, pastries, and coffee—and laid out for them on a table-sized rock facing the sheet of water as it cascaded into the lagoon. After breakfast, they exited the cave on the dry side and walked around to where two men in skiffs were waiting to row them around the waterfall's lagoon. The rowers pointed out a family of guanacos, camel-like cousins to the llama, that had come to drink from the shallows.

By noon they were back at Glendaval station, the lonely stone whistle-stop, standing on the platform, drinking tea and coffee and maté as the porters loaded their luggage back into their compartments. A hose from the station's tower had just finished feeding water into the borrowed silver engine.

Amy stood at her mother's side. They hadn't spoken seriously all morning, just the usual exchanges about how cute and unafraid the guanacos were and how lucky they'd been with the weather and "Did you remember the toothbrushes?" But waiting here, barely tasting their coffee and maté, Amy could tell that Fanny was thinking the same thing she was. How could they leave? They certainly couldn't stay. That wasn't a possibility. But given their situation, with Todd Drucker lurking twenty feet down the platform, with *TrippyGirl's* credibility on the line, with a dead woman unaccounted for in the Patagonian wilds, how could they possibly leave the scene, crime scene or not, never to return?

"I'm sorry," Amy said, barely aware that she'd said it.

Fanny made a face. "I always said you should've studied Spanish in high school. But no, you were too artsy. It had to be French."

"What?" Amy blinked, for a moment unsure if she'd heard correctly. "That is so not fair. It wouldn't have made a difference."

"I know."

"Even if I could have talked to every car place in Patagonia in perfect Spanish, I don't think it would have helped."

"I know. I just said it so you'd feel as bad as I do."

"Aw, thanks, Mom."

"It was my exaggerations that got us into this mess. I don't blame you, sweetie. I was just venting. Forgiven?"

"Forgiven. But next time it's my turn to vent."

They fell back into silence, not an awkward silence this time, but not a happy one. And then the silver engine itself vented, letting out a whoosh and a plume of steam from each side of the boiler, just above the cowcatcher. Amy laughed out loud.

Fanny had to think about it for a second; then she laughed. "I guess everybody needs to vent."

The engine's venting petered out into nothing, to be replaced by the steam whistle. It was a piercing, elongated howl, like the call of a thousand-pound tea kettle coming to a boil. Everyone on the platform put down their drinks and smiled in anticipation. Amy and Fanny, too.

CHAPTER 13

"It's what we call a prewar convertible two-bedroom." Hanna Jorengsen stood in the middle of the cramped apartment, spread her arms wide in a display of spaciousness and somehow managed not to hit any walls. Then she pointed to the alcove. "Just put up a screen and it's like a separate room. The kitchen is prewar, so the appliances are all original. There's a police station right down the street, so the block is incredibly safe, if you don't mind a few sirens. And in the summer you can open the living-room window and use the fire escape as a terrace. Very *Breakfast at Tiffany's*. Ooh!" Her hands flew to her heart as she remembered the absolutely best part. "Do you like Indian food?" Her client assured her that he loved Indian food. "Good. The *Delhi Belly* just below you has had some ventilation issues, at least in the past—full disclosure. But their food is fabulous. You'll grow addicted to the smell."

Marcus had seen three apartments this morning with this agent, and he had two more agents lined up for tomorrow, one in Hoboken, one in Queens. It wasn't the best use of his few hours off. But he had promised Amy he'd look, and this promise he intended to keep. "When is the apartment available?"

Hanna seemed a little surprised by his interest. "Um, right away."

"Right away?" Marcus look around again. There was clothing strewn over every chair, half-eaten garbage draped over every flat surface, and dog-eared college textbooks piled in every corner.

"They'll be gone as soon as you sign the lease. Once they get rid of their junk and you get your stuff in here, it will look so much . . ." Hanna took a big breath and threw up her hands. "Okay, okay, it's a dump. Even I know that. Maybe if your budget was twice as big. The place I showed you on Mercer . . ."

"I like this place," said Marcus.

Hanna seemed confused. "Are you sure? No one likes Indian food that much."

"No, this is a possibility." Marcus took out his phone and began to snap. "Let me send these to my girlfriend. She'll be back next week, and we'll set up an appointment. Sometime in the evening?"

"When the *Delhi Belly* is open for business? I'm not sure I'd recommend that."

Marcus set up a tentative time for the following Tuesday and promised he'd be in touch to confirm. As Hanna closed up, using three keys to secure the two dead bolts and the handle lock, Marcus bundled up against the February chill. Then he escorted the real estate agent past the "soon to be repaired" elevator and down one flight to street level, where she headed south to another showing in Chinatown and he headed west.

It was a relatively short walk by New York standards, across the Village, then across Bleecker Street to the storefront on Hudson. The opening time of the travel agency, printed on the door, was 10:00 a.m., but he'd been a little lax with the schedule. Amy had toyed with the idea of hiring a temporary assistant. But the Patagonian trip had materialized so quickly, and they'd be away less than two weeks. And, to be honest, walk-in traffic was not such a big part of their business.

Except for the lookie-loos, Marcus had to remind himself.

He was just crossing Hudson when he saw them, two twentysomethings, both blond with highlights, hermetically attached to their phones, one of them texting, the other taking a pouty selfie in front of the Amy's Travel sign. They paid no attention to him as he approached—always disheartening ego-wise—until they realized he was arriving with keys to the store.

"Is this where TrippyGirl works?" asked the shorter, slightly more intelligent-looking one.

Over the past few months, Amy and Fanny had played with several different answers to this question. At first they'd denied it. "Trippy who?" they'd ask. When they'd got tired of this, they tried the simple truth, that Trippy didn't exist. But those who had made the pilgrimage to Hudson Street didn't want to hear the truth. It had become easier to say, "Yes, Trippy works here, but she is off on another adventure. Please keep reading the blog." This had become more complicated when Fanny started posting the occasional photo of her daughter and the visitors would recognize her. Fanny had tried telling them that this wasn't Trippy, but Trippy's older, stay-at-home sister. That hadn't always worked. Amy's current strategy was to hide in the bathroom whenever she saw someone who looked like a Trippy fan come through the door.

"Trippy's in Patagonia," said Marcus, glad that he could for once tell the truth.

"We know," said the taller one. "But we thought she might be back. What happened after the explosion? We have to know."

"Your guess is as good as mine." Again the truth.

Marcus invited them inside and turned on the Alvarez charm. The girls expressed keen interest in a Trans-Siberian Railway expedition run by a British company and taking off from Moscow in July. Special, 15 percent off. But Marcus knew, at the end of the day, they would never sign up for a train with a shared bathroom and no place to plug in their hair dryers. He sent them away happy, with a few more selfies around Amy's desk and three Club Med brochures.

The landline rang just as Marcus was making himself comfortable at Fanny's desk. "Amy's Travel." He added, "How may I direct your call?" just for fun.

"Marcus? It's Sabrina, Amy's editor from Banyan. How are you?" Marcus was fine. "I just read Trippy-Girl's blog from Patagonia. Is there any way I can get in touch with her?" Marcus knew all about Sabrina. They'd spoken once before but not in person.

"You can leave a message on her cell or send an e-mail," Marcus suggested. "But I don't think her train has phone or Internet access."

"I suppose not. Have you talked to her since that explosion? Is she okay?"

"She e-mailed me. Don't worry. Is there anything you want me to tell her?"

"Well, this is hard to say. I don't know how to ask." Sabrina proved her point by hemming and hawing and leaving several seconds of dead air. "Ummm. Do you think the explosion was real? Your honest opinion."

"Yes, it was real. How could they fake that? Why would they want to?"

"Good. Sorry." Sabrina's laugh sounded tight-mouthed and nervous. "Banyan was very excited when Amy and Fanny mentioned this trip. More *TrippyGirl*! More adventure! And the fact that some big-name travel people were going, that was great. We thought."

"But . . ." Marcus strung out the word.

"It's just that Fanny, dear funny Fanny, admits to stretching the truth. Not that we have anything against that. Hemingway did it. Do you think something dangerous is really going on?"

"I don't know. Why?"

"No reason. We're just preparing some pre-promotional material for *TrippyGirl's World*. If there is another crime connected to their trip, a real crime, then great. We can promote the hell out of it, kind of a teaser to pique interest. But if there's no crime . . . I mean, if it's just Mrs. Abel filming some small-town accident and making the rest up . . . You understand?"

"Then you'd like for her to stop."

"We would love for her to stop. Actually, we'd kind of have to insist on her stopping. Not that we don't support *TrippyGirl*. We support her one hundred percent."

Marcus got it. "But there's a line between a fun, tongue-in-cheek exaggeration and an outright lie."

"Yes. Not that I'm sure exactly where that line is, but we have to stay on the right side of it. Wherever. And let me say again that we support *TrippyGirl* one hundred percent."

That is discouraging to hear, thought Marcus. *When people insist more than once that they support you one hundred percent, that's the time to worry.*

The lounge car, like the dining car, could comfortably seat forty or more. Plush chairs and horsehair-stuffed sofas lined the walls of the elongated space, which was artfully broken up by sets of mahogany pillars and arches interspersed with side tables and table lamps. The slightly peach-colored hue of the lamp shades was an old designer trick, one that helped even the most aged skin seem a little more vibrant.

"I like this room," said Fanny, not for the first time. She settled in beside her daughter on the sofa, then turned an eye to the rest of the car. Todd Drucker was in an arch-secluded alcove, reading a book. Across from him, the neatly bearded reporter from the *London Times* leaned his tattooed elbow against the window ledge, taking in the changing, slowly moving scenery. Two of the Furies sat in their usual huddle, one of them crocheting and one writing in a book, probably a diary. "Are people avoiding us," Fanny asked, "or is it just my imagination?"

"People are avoiding you because of your imagination." That was what Amy wanted to say, except that she actually believed Fanny's story, so it would have been clever but not fair.

"Don't feel bad, Fanny dear." It was Alicia Lindborn. "I couldn't help overhearing. May I? Thanks." The elegant blonde seated herself on the sofa across from them and leaned in. "Ordinary people, they have trouble dealing with visions. I've seen it over and over. People get nervous, and they don't know what to say."

Amy herself didn't quite know what to say. "You think what my mother saw was a vision?"

The matriarch of travel leaned in farther, allowing the moonstone on her gold necklace to dangle into the aisle. "When you've been to as many places as I have, ashrams in India, sweat lodges in New Mexico, living in a plural marriage with a shaman in the Amazonian rain forest—that was the sixties, of course—you learn that there's more to existence than just the physical world."

"More than the physical world?" Amy asked

Alicia smiled. "Oh, there's a whole other realm of existence. You can tap into it in a variety of ways." She began to count them on her fingers. "Peyote, for example. Mushrooms, delirium from dehydration, LSD. I could go on."

"Please go on," said Fanny.

Both of the Abels were transfixed. This was the last thing they had expected to hear from a woman who did her best to resemble a pulled-together, if aging Realtor. Amy cleared her throat. "If I can speak for my mother, and I hope I can, she doesn't use any of those."

"But she does use yerba maté, which comes from the rain forest. My ex-husband, the shaman, and I used to chew on the leaves. I remember clear as day. One morning I was chewing leaves, sweating in a hammock, bored out of my mind, being eaten alive by mosquitos. It was at that moment I had the most crucial vision of my life. I dreamed of going home, marrying rich, and starting a travel empire. I knew at that moment, no matter the cost, I had to divorce my

Peruvian prince and his other wife, who was a good friend by this point, and return to my old fiancé in Philadelphia. Again, it was the sixties."

"Fascinating." That word was quite a compliment, coming from Fanny, who very rarely found anyone else fascinating. "What do you think *my* vision meant?"

Alicia had to give it some thought. "Did this corpse look like you? Perhaps it signifies the death of your youth. Or your relationship with Amy? Do you ever fantasize about someone, and I don't necessarily mean Amy, being pecked apart by vultures?"

"Can't say I do," said Fanny. "But let me think about it."

"Wait." Like her mother, Amy had been leaning in. Now she pulled back. "So you really didn't see a corpse? Honestly, Mom? You put everyone through this because you had a maté-induced vision?"

Fanny raised her eyebrows. "It's one possibility."

"Please! You never had a vision in your life. You're the most practical, levelheaded. . . . No offense, Alicia." Amy grabbed her mother's arm for emphasis. "I know you, Mom. You think that by saying it was a hallucination, you can get out of this. An easy out. But that doesn't change what actually happened, does it?"

"I thought you liked avoiding confrontation. A vision is a lot less confrontational than a corpse."

"You did not have a vision."

"I could have." Fanny sounded deeply hurt. And with nothing more to say, she turned to the window and stared out into the passing prairie.

"Mom, stop pouting."

"Oh, dear." Alicia sank back into her horsehair cushion. "I'm sorry if I started something between you."

"It's not your fault." Fanny spoke into the window. "If my own flesh and blood doesn't believe I'm special enough . . ." There was a pause and a little intake of air. "Like right now. Where you just see desert grasses and rocks, I see more. I see our host, Jorge O'Bannion, on a motorcycle, riding beside the train and waving at us. I'm not sure what that means."

Amy turned to face the window. "It means he's on a motorcycle, riding beside the train and waving at us." Under any circumstances, it would have been an unusual sight, the patriarchal, fifty-something gentleman straddling a maroon motorcycle with the word *Indian* emblazoned in silver on the gas tank, bumping over a dirt side road, keeping pace with the train. To add to the surreal sight, one of the Furies was in the machine's sidecar, bouncing and holding on for dear life.

"You see it, too?" Fanny asked. "Or are you just pretending so that you don't feel left out?"

"We all see it, Mother."

"True," Alicia confirmed. She crossed to their window and waved at O'Bannion. Amy and Fanny joined her in waving. "Jorge keeps an old motorcycle at the Glendaval ranch. He brought it on board to take to his second ranch. He said he wanted to try this on one of the slow, level patches."

"Are you sure?" asked Fanny. "All three of us could be having the same vision—although you'll have to admit I saw it first."

By this point, the other guests had gathered by the left window. Most had their phones or cameras out, snapping and waving. Even the dyspeptic Todd Drucker was whooping and snapping, leaning up to the glass and trying to line up a selfie with O'Bannion and the Fury in the background.

The chase between the two machines went on for several more minutes, until the side road began to get rougher and the tracks began to twist and climb into the Andean foothills. Then the engineer played three blasts on his steam whistle, applied the brakes, and brought the procession to a halt.

At that point the train was halfway around a curve, placing the caboose within view of the lounge car. Amy opened a lounge-car window and leaned out. She could see O'Bannion riding back to the last car, where two crew members were waiting to help him, his passenger, and the Indian back on board. When the two riders walked through the car a few minutes later, everyone stood to applaud.

It would turn out to be the second most memorable event of the day.

CHAPTER 14

After the motorcycle chase, the terrain changed, as the forever distant mountains finally grew closer. Their semiarid plateau had evolved into foothills, and the foothills opened onto the occasional chasm, with a tall bridge of ancient wood spanning the gulf. One moment Amy would look out to see a herd of goats grazing on a stubbly meadow mere yards away. The next moment she would be stunned to see the meadow disappear. Nothing would be visible below, as if the whole world had been pulled out from under them.

For the rest of the day, the Patagonian Express limped along, the tracks groaning under the unaccustomed weight. Amy didn't even want to think about the groaning bridges.

For nearly an hour, as the luxury train skirted the edge of the Andes, it was forced to go backward, to zigzag its way down a hill that would have otherwise been too steep. Amy had experienced a zigzag only once before, in Peru, on the ride from Cuzco to Machu Picchu, but that had been a newer train and newer tracks, on a part of a well-traveled route that was within hailing distance of an emergency crew if something went wrong.

The process was for the engine to pull the entire length of the train down onto a side track. Then a worker would get out, switch the rails at the rear, and the engine would start again, in reverse, pushing the train gently down a different set of tracks to the next switchback, using its brakes more than its engine. Amy counted four of these zigzags. And as intrigued as everyone seemed by the outdated technology, they breathed a collective sigh of relief when the engine finally picked up steam near the bottom of the valley.

Despite O'Bannion's boast about the great lengths the government had gone to in repairing the tracks, the result was a hodgepodge—new sections, old sections, old bridges, and dark, dripping tunnels. There were perilous ledges where the windows brushed against a mountain on one side and opened onto oblivion on the other. Nightfall didn't make it any more comforting. The darkness came down like a curtain, with no moon, while up ahead there was only the single beam of a steam engine that had been rebuilt in Argentina to carry guests around the confines of a billionaire's estate.

Amy and Fanny had a light meal that evening. From what they could see around them, the others shared a similar loss of appetite. *But isn't this what travel was supposed to be about?* Amy asked herself. She had always complained about how easy and prepackaged travel had become. ATMs were everywhere. The Internet was everywhere. Elevators took you down the cliffs to a once-hidden grotto, where you could buy grotto T-shirts with your MasterCard. Wasn't it wonderful that she could still experience the thrill of adventure, a sense of the dangerous unknown—and also have a bathtub and a fireplace in her compartment? All she had to do was survive.

Fanny ordered a post-dinner brandy, for the nerves, and convinced her daughter to join her. They had just taken their first warming sips when the train ground and squeaked and bounced to another stop.

"Oh, dear," said Fanny under her breath and took another sip.

Everyone was in the dining car except for Jorge O'Bannion, and they all fell silent. No one uttered another word, not until the lights flickered off and the electricity went out, plunging their world into darkness.

"This could be better," said Edgar with typically British understatement.

"Just great," growled Todd. A few seconds later and his face was illuminated by the glow of his cell phone. Three other cell phones, including Amy's, lit up, providing soft white accents in the otherwise black carriage.

No one wanted to panic. More exactly, no one wanted to be the first to panic. Their whispering hum of worry grew steadily. What could have gone wrong? The train must have a generator for emergencies. There was a satellite phone on board, wasn't there? Someone remembered it being mentioned in the brochure. Does it get very cold here at night? How many extra blankets were on the train? Would the toilet still work? I knew I should have used the toilet before dinner. And where the hell was Jorge O'Bannion?

This last question was answered first. A flashlight beam played behind the glass of the connecting door. Then the door opened. Senor O'Bannion raised the beam to show his face. His expression was serious, almost comically ghostly in its highlights and shadows. "Ladies and gentlemen, I fear that we will be here for a while." He repeated himself immediately in Spanish.

"How long of a while?" demanded Todd.

"We'll be here for an hour at least. Unavoidable." O'Bannion pointed out the left side window. Half a dozen high-beam flashlights flitted around the dark emptiness. "My men are out there, working as fast as they can."

"What's wrong?" asked Amy. "Is it the engine? Is it something on the tracks?"

O'Bannion wiped his forehead with a handkerchief from his breast pocket, but he didn't answer.

Amy went on. "Is there a bridge out? Is it a rock slide?" The romance of being in the middle of nowhere with no other trains coming and no maintenance crew was quickly losing its luster. "Is anyone coming to help?"

The Furies must have been feeling left out, because they suddenly erupted with questions of their own.

Todd pointed out the window and tried shouting over the din. "What are your men doing out there?" It seemed like a good question. What problem could possibly be solved outside, twenty yards off to the side of the dining car?

The owner of the New Patagonian Express stayed calm. He found a spot to prop up his flashlight, in the crook of a currently useless wall sconce, then arranged himself in its narrow beam. Taking his time, he arranged the handkerchief back in his breast pocket, then cleared his throat.

"I must ask you to please forgive me. This may not

be the best idea. But I knew no other way to demon-
strate to you the absolute beauty, the frightening
isolation of my Patagonia. For what is beautiful isolation, I ask myself, without a little awe, a little fear
of the unknown?" He checked his watch for the second time since walking into the dining car. "Please
forgive me," he repeated. "But I think we should all
go outside."

Two of the crew, the engineer and a waiter, were at
the rear door with flashlights, ready to escort the passengers into the blackness. Whatever panic might
have been welling up had now morphed into curiosity. Amy was at the end of the line, and as she approached the door, she could have sworn she heard
one of the Furies ahead of her say, "*Fuego*," Spanish
for "fire." For a moment she envisioned stepping out
and witnessing their silver engine engulfed in a fire-
ball.

"Ooh, fire," said Fanny, just in front of her.

It was a cozy campfire that they saw, newly lit and
just beginning to throw a glow onto its surroundings.
No one was working on the train or the tracks. There
were collapsible chairs and cushions in a circle, plus
dozens of candles, with a porter busily setting them
all aflame. Silver buckets were mixed among the
chairs, full of ice and champagne. The engineer put
down his flashlight and picked up a tray of caviar-
stuffed canapés. The chef was by the fire, tuning his
guitar. At the outer edge of the circle was a telescope,
pointing up to the southern sky, which was alive with
the brightest stars Amy had ever seen. A hand-painted
sign hanging from the tripod showed a fanciful portrait of the man in the moon, orange on a background of bright blue.

Some people caught on faster than others. Edgar

had been smiling from the last few sentences of O'Bannion's speech. For Amy it was the telescope. One of the Furies was on her second glass of champagne before her companions could convince her that this wasn't an emergency, after all, that O'Bannion had fooled them, that he and his staff had deliberately stopped at the most remote spot on their journey just as a special, unexpected treat.

"Welcome to the real Patagonia," the ringmaster announced in both languages.

Fanny settled into a cushioned camp chair by the fire. Their mischievous host poured a little more brandy into her snifter, and side by side they waited for the chef to commence his concert. This left Amy free to wander the perimeter, edging tentatively out into the void. Were the mountain peaks in this direction or the other? She couldn't see the emptiness, just the incredible stars above, bright clusters she'd never seen before and a band of stardust brighter than the Milky Way. The breeze was picking up, and Amy imagined that the wind had traveled forever to get here, unimpeded, across hundreds of miles, just to fly into her this very second.

"The stars are different here. Do you want to see?" Nicolas stood by the telescope and beckoned to her. She left the black void and joined him.

"Your boss really had us going."

Nicolas didn't get the jargon.

"He had us very scared. The delay, the explosion, the condition of the track. When we stopped and the lights went out, I thought we were stranded. For days."

"But you are not. It was a game designed for the rich." Nicolas spoke softly from the heart, as if the darkness and isolation gave him the right to be so candid. "Tonight you will sleep in your comfortable beds, on your way to even more comfortable beds, while we take care of your every need. Your existence is charmed—in our eyes."

Amy wasn't sure if he'd meant to be condescending or not. Either way he had a point. "Compared to the rest of the world, I guess."

"Compared to here—in Chile, Argentina. Now is not so bad. But the history of our world has been violent, cruel without reason. As a tourist, you see what we want you to. You don't see what came before. Our ways are quaint. The tango. The gauchos. That's the word? Quaint?"

"You're making me ashamed to be a tourist."

"I apologize," he said without seeming to mean it. "Tourists bring money. Some, like you, are very nice. But they remind us life isn't fair. We don't always want to be reminded."

Amy wasn't offended, just uncomfortable. She looked around them for a change of subject. "I think I would like to see those stars, not that I can't see them already."

"The biggest telescopes in the world are built in Chile. Astronomers come here for the altitude, the darkness, the lack of pollution." He made a sad, ironic face. "My telescope is a little smaller."

Nicolas's telescope was white with black bands, about three feet long, the kind that Amy had seen but had never used on the balconies of luxury resorts. He gazed down through the eyepiece, changed the angle and the focus. "We have constellations you have never seen."

"Beautiful," Amy agreed, then examined the sky

for anything that might look familiar. Three bright stars in a row caught her eye. "That one looks like Orion, only bigger."

Nicolas looked up from the eyepiece and followed her finger. "That is Orion. But it's upside down."

"It looks bigger upside down. Oh, is that the Southern Cross?"

"It is." Nicolas was obviously pleased. "Those four stars, like the Savior's cross. It has safely guided our sailors and explorers for centuries."

"Like our North Star. And it points directly south?"

"Uh, no. Almost." He stretched his arm and pointed. "You draw an imaginary line from the top to the bottom of the cross, then go four and half times that length and draw another imaginary line to the horizon. That is south."

Amy frowned. "Four and a half lengths and imaginary lines? Seems a lot of work."

"What do you mean, work?" ·

"For the explorers. I mean, it's not south. More like southeast. How did it get the name Southern Cross?"

"Because it is the Southern Cross," Nicolas insisted.

"Absolutely," said Amy and began to look around for another change of subject. "Did you paint the sign?" She indicated the hand-painted moon hanging from the telescope's tripod. "It's charming." Somehow the word *charming* came out sounding like *quaint.*

Nicolas smiled and nodded. "Senor O'Bannion asked us to create special touches. There were some wood pieces and house paint in a shed at the estancia."

"You can do that with house paint?" She was impressed. The man in the moon was purposely primitive and delicately done, with a wry, twisted grin and an unmistakable twinkle in the shape of his eyes. "You should be an artist."

"I studied art at the conservatory in the capital, Santiago. One day I will go back."

"You should. Absolutely. Follow your dream."

His reply came softly, almost a whisper. "Dreams are not for someone like me."

"Dreams are for everyone." Amy cupped a hand around his shoulder. "I know money can be a problem, Nicolas. Everywhere. But if you love art like you say . . ."

"My dreams don't matter." The disdain was back in his voice, giving a harder edge to his whisper. "What matters is family. Obligations. Right and wrong. If I manage to survive, then maybe I will. . . ."

"If you manage to survive?"

"I didn't mean that."

"Manage to survive what?"

Nicolas took a long, deliberate breath, then bent down once more to gaze through the eyepiece and focus. "I mean that we could all die at any time."

"That's not what you said. Why did you say that?"

Nicolas didn't have a response. He just stood there, looking down through his telescope at the southern stars until Amy gave up and wandered away.

CHAPTER 15

When Amy finally stumbled out of bed, still woozy from the brandy and the late night, it took her a minute to realize that the New Patagonian Express wasn't moving. It took her another minute to realize that she wasn't all that alarmed. Jorge O'Bannion's magical surprise party had gone a long way in convincing her, convincing all his guests, that the tour was once again under control.

The hour delay that he'd warned them about, flashlight poised under his chin, had become over two hours of laughter and stargazing, drinking and telling multilingual tales around the campfire. The highlight had been a talent show by the train's crew. The chef had played his guitar, accompanied by the engineer, who had blown across the tops of his pan-pipes. No one had brought an accordion. But the waiter and bartender had shown off their skills with a bolo and a lariat, and everyone had joined in on Chilean folk songs that seemed to have fifty verses apiece. Toward the end, Jorge had imbibed enough brandy to permit Edgar to ride his beloved motorcycle in a huge circle around the scrubby plains, with Todd in the sidecar, the dual headlamps roaming the outer reaches of the darkness.

Fanny had always been an early riser, no matter how late she'd fallen asleep, so Amy now had the compartment to herself. She washed her face, brushed her hair, slipped on a white resort bathrobe, and stepped out into the small semiprivate lounge separating them from the next compartment. It was empty for the time being, but as always, there were thermoses of hot coffee and hot water waiting on a side table and a carafe of fruit juice. The velvet drapes were tied back, and Amy was pleased to see the reason for their stationary state. They had arrived.

Outside the window stood a stone train depot, similar to the whistle-stop at Glendaval, although this one was larger and seemed more dilapidated than the first. The waiting room, for example, was more than just a place away from the wind and rain. It was outfitted with a fireplace and a chimney, but a chimney that, to Amy's eye, leaned precariously toward the train and the tracks.

Several crew members wandered the platform. Two at the caboose end were unloading Jorge O'Bannion's Indian motorcycle and sidecar, lifting them onto the back of a pickup truck. Just inside the waiting room, Amy could see Jorge himself engaged in an intimate conversation with a thin woman in a tropically floral dress and a stylish black fedora. Beneath the fedora was a helmet of ash-blond curls. Instinctively, Amy looked for the large mole just below the left cheekbone. It was there.

She could tell from Jorge's body language that he was overjoyed at Lola's presence. Amy watched as he reached into the pocket of his long coat and pulled

out something silver and blue. *It has to be the pendant,*
Amy thought, *his mother's favorite on a silver chain.* He
presented it to the woman, who looked at it apprais-
ingly and then, without much fanfare or apparent
emotion, slipped it over her head. Jorge straightened
it around her neck.

"The woman with Jorge. Is that Lola Pisano?" Amy
didn't know which startled her more, the fact that
the woman from the adjoining compartment, one of
the Furies, had so silently entered the lounge or the
fact that she was speaking English. Accented but very
good English.

"I think so, yes. I met her once in a tango bar, just
for a minute."

"*Bueno.*" The Fury moved past Amy to the window
and tilted her head for a better look. "Jorge promised
she would be here. She is known not to be sociable."

"Excuse me," said Amy, turning to her new companion, feeling a little shamefaced. "I know we were
introduced days ago. Amy Abel, from New York." She
held out her hand. "I had no idea . . ."

The woman took Amy's hand in both of hers.
"Gabriela Garcia, Buenos Aires. I apologize if I was
rude. My friends don't speak English, and I didn't
want to abandon them. After the first day, it felt easier just to say nothing. Laziness on my part." She was
the shortest, most ordinary looking of the Furies, the
one with the fastest tongue and the sternest expression. Her speech was slower now; her expression all
smiles. "Good to meet you again. I'm the owner of
Hemispherio Travel."

Amy smiled back. "I've heard of you, of course. Well,
not you personally." Hemispherio was a legendary
name. At one point, she recalled, the company had

owned a dozen hotels and a small cruise line. She didn't know exactly what had happened. The recession, perhaps. Even in its reduced circumstances, it remained a force in South American travel. In fact, as soon as it became public knowledge about Trippy-Girl's Patagonian trip . . . "I must thank you. Your company is buying banner ads on my Web site. *Trippy-Girl.*"

"*Trippy?*" Gabriela shook her head. "I'm afraid I hire out my marketing to others these days. Are we getting good value from your *Trippy* site?"

"*TrippyGirl.* I hope so."

"Arturo, my husband, was the genius. He would have memorized every number and fact. He would have called you at all hours and driven you a hard bargain. But you would have loved him."

"It sounds like you loved him."

"I still do," Gabriela said softly. "But he took business too seriously. The work and the worry. In the end it killed him." Before Amy could express her condolences, Gabriela's attention wandered back to the scene through the window. "She doesn't look pleased with him, does she?"

Amy changed her own angle to see. Jorge and Lola were in almost the same spot, their intense, solemn faces close together. Jorge reached out to adjust the pendant. Lola allowed this, grudgingly perhaps. "He's a charming man," Amy said. "But you're right. She doesn't look pleased."

"Why is this so expensive, Jorge?" Gabriela said in a high, mocking imitation. "Why are you giving away trips? You know how much it cost to rent that engine? I will have to sell my terrible, tasteless jewelry. Please don't touch my mole."

Amy blurted out a laugh. Was this what conversation was like when the Furies chattered among themselves? She could kick herself for not learning Spanish. "Poor Jorge. I don't mean to be nosy, but is Hemispherio going to promote the New Patagonian Express?"

Gabriela made a face. "If no one dies. There's a good market for adventure travel that looks dangerous but is not."

"If no one dies?"

"Other than what your mother saw. Imaginary deaths do not matter." Her smile had morphed into a hard smirk. Once again Gabriela Garcia was one of Furies.

"Do you really think she imagined it?"

"Whether she saw a rabbit or a guanaco or nothing, your mother likes to be the center of attention. She has provided my friends and me with much entertainment."

"Oh." Amy felt her cheeks turn red. "Do you want some coffee?"

"Just a small cup, thank you. Then I suppose we need to pull ourselves together for our next safe adventure. Cross our fingers."

An hour later, after Amy had drunk her coffee, indulged in a long shower, and made herself presentable, she packed up her suitcase and bag and left them in the compartment, next to Fanny's already packed luggage. Then she joined Alicia, Gabriela, and one of the other Furies in the second vehicle, Toyota Land Cruisers on this leg instead of Land Rovers, heading to the O'Bannion family's second estancia. Amy sat shotgun and did her best to ignore Gabriela and her friend's aggressive chatter in the back. She concentrated instead on the breathtaking scenery. In just a few minutes they would arrive at Torre Vista, where breakfast would be waiting on the wide veranda.

Fanny had been careful not to wake her daughter. Amy hadn't been sleeping well. She took things so seriously, Fanny thought, despite her general inclination to ignore problems. Or perhaps because of it. Ignoring things could be very stressful.

Fanny had been alone on the train platform, enjoying her first gourd of the day, when the dusty black Mercedes pulled up. Through the tint of the windshield, she'd been able to make out the form of a woman behind the wheel, adjusting the rearview mirror, then adjusting herself, setting her hat at a jaunty angle, running her fingers through her hair. Before she could open the door, Jorge O'Bannion had been at the Mercedes, opening it for her, saying something solicitous and nervous. Fanny would have loved to eavesdrop but had been prevented by the distance and that pesky language barrier.

By the time the first Land Rover drove up, Edgar, Todd, and one of the Furies had joined her on the platform. The ride was short, and Fanny spent it glued to the window, transfixed by the unique sawtooth tops of Torres del Paine. It was the most famous, most iconic sight in all of Chile, on the cover of almost every tour guide.

Seated beside her, Todd Drucker was engaged in a monologue about how the mountain looked magically different from every angle, with some of the best angles, showing off the glaciers and lakes, being visible from places like this, well outside the national park. The seatmates were on their best behavior, and no one mentioned the real or imagined corpse.

The views were even better from the veranda of Torre Vista. The estancia was a long white stucco building. A row of second-level dormers, each with a postcard-size balcony, was edged in red tile, as was the roof, giving the old estancia a clean yet timeless feel. The building's location, like the one for Glendaval, was perfect, with the front veranda framing glorious views of the jagged granite peaks. It made her feel good that the sheep ranchers of a hundred years ago, despite their hard lives, had taken the time and effort to lay out their houses to take advantage of the scenery.

Fanny was just getting settled in their suite, which occupied two of the many red-tiled dormers. She opened one of the dormer doors just to air things out and kept her eye open for the second Land Cruiser, the one that would bring her slugabed of a daughter. But it wasn't a Land Cruiser that created the next little dust storm along the winding road. It was the black Mercedes.

Fanny stood in the window and watched the car stop directly in front. Jorge O'Bannion emerged from the passenger side and walked around to the trunk. Seconds later the driver joined him. She pointed imperiously to the luggage and walked alongside the Chilean gentleman as he carried the three Louis Vuitton bags up the half flight of veranda stairs and out of Fanny's line of sight.

Something about the woman had struck Fanny as familiar—something about her half-hidden hair, her build, the sharpness of her features. Fanny's natural curiosity was enough to send her scurrying out of her suite and down to the entry hall. Seeing the new arrivals just inside the door, she caught her breath, slowed her pace, and adopted a casual, disinterested air. "*Buenos dias.*"

O'Bannion looked momentarily startled. "Senora Abel, good morning. We are about to set the *desayuno*—our full gaucho breakfast—out in front, so that everyone can enjoy the view. I don't believe you have met my good friend Senora Pisano." Then he said something similar in Spanish.

Fanny instinctively turned on the charm. "Wonderful to meet you. You must be Jorge's partner. He's mentioned how much he depends on you. Such a pleasure to finally meet." She plastered on a grin and waited for the flattering translation to have its effect.

Lola Pisano didn't reply. She simply adjusted the collar of her jacket and turned away—but not before Fanny noted the mole, the size and shape of a dirty quarter.

"You'll have to excuse us," O'Bannion apologized. "The flight from Buenos Aires to Santiago, then to Puerto Natales, then the car ride here. Exhausting."

"Which is why your train concept is so brilliant," said Fanny. "Guaranteed to succeed."

"I'm certain we will all talk soon," O'Bannion said in his courtly way, then picked up the three pieces of luggage and began lugging them off to the ground floor's right wing. The couple disappeared down the hall just as four members of the staff emerged from the depths of the estancia, rolling out fragrant carts of food and pushing them toward the open double doors to the veranda.

Fanny was barely aware of the activity coursing around her. She barely heard the polite cries of "*Disculpe*" as the staff begged her pardon for being in her way. From the vantage point of the bedroom balcony, she had sensed something familiar about this woman. On actually meeting Lola Pisano that sense had grown—and solidified into something quite amazing. Inexplicable and amazing.

"I think Alicia was right," Fanny mumbled to no one but herself. "I think I may have had a vision."

CHAPTER 16

"**A** watched pot never boils," as they say. And a watched-for Land Cruiser never comes up a Patagonian road. *Of course neither of those is true*, Fanny reminded herself as she paced and watched and waited. *The pot eventually does boil*. And the second Land Cruiser, containing Amy, Alicia, and two of the Furies, did come up the dusty road from the station.

"Morning, dear," she said as her daughter bounded up the veranda's steps and gave her a peck on the cheek.

"Did you sleep well?" Amy asked, full of energy and anticipation for the new location. "I slept like a log for once. Isn't this stunning? Oh, good. They have eggs and toast. And pickles, of course. Why do some cultures love things like pickles for breakfast? You would think digestive tracts would be the same the world over. Oh . . ." And here she lowered her voice and checked around. "I have news about the Furies. You'll never guess. One of them, the short one . . ."

"That's nice, dear. But I have to talk to Alicia."

"Alicia? Why Alicia?"

"Never you mind why. Go have breakfast and plan your day. I'll be with you in a few."

"Mother, what are you up to?"

"Nothing." Fanny did her best to avoid the penetrating gaze. "And try the pickles. Live a little. A billion or so Chinese can't be wrong."

Alicia Lindborn could be found on the far side of the buffet, already hovering over the selection of tea bags, at last choosing a green tea. Fanny forced herself to take a few calming breaths and waited until the travel matriarch had added the water to her cup and entered into the dunking part of the ritual. Amy, she saw, was by the coffee carafe, eyeing her suspiciously but well out of earshot.

"Alicia, good morning. Gorgeous day, although they say the rain can appear at a moment's notice." She leaned in. "What exactly do you know about visions, particularly maté visions?"

Alicia paused in her tea bag dunking. "Fanny, are you saying you had a vision? The dead woman?"

"That's what I wanted to ask. The vision you talked about, when you knew you had to leave your Peruvian husband. Did it seem real? Like the vision was really happening?"

"It did," said Alicia, taking a few steps to a more secluded corner. Fanny followed her. "But honestly, I may have had more going on than maté. We used to mix it with shrooms and a quarter tab of LSD. It was the sixties."

"But the vision felt real."

"It felt real."

"Was it like looking into the future? Seeing something that hasn't yet happened? And do you think you could have changed what happened next? That's the important question."

"You mean changed the future?" Alicia had never thought of it that way. "I guess people have visions but never act on them. I could have stayed in Peru, I guess. Nothing was stopping me."

"And if I, just for argument's sake, saw a death that hadn't happened yet, I could maybe change it? Keep the death from happening?"

"It would be worth a shot." Alicia retrieved her tea bag, wrapped it across her spoon, and deposited it onto a colorful little ceramic tray. "This woman in your vision, you think she's still alive? How do you know? Have you seen her? Alive? No condor bites?"

"What?" Fanny shook her head. "Oh, no. It was just a hypothetical. Forget I even asked."

"So she's not alive?"

"I don't honestly know." Fanny adopted her most sincere expression, perfected after years of practice. "But if I do see her, then I'll know. Maybe I can keep her alive."

Alicia didn't look convinced. "This is like science fiction, you know."

"No." Fanny scoffed. "I hate science fiction. I was just curious. Like people who have premonitions about plane crashes and tell you not to get on a certain flight. I would just tell this woman not to be outside alone with condors."

"Right." Alicia added a spoonful of sugar to her green tea and stirred. "Can you promise me something, Fanny?"

"I can promise. That part's easy."

"Can you promise to call on me if you need help? If you do find this woman and you need help in some way, please let me know."

"That I can promise. Why not?"

By the time Fanny rejoined her daughter, she had the first part of her plan in place. "So what was the big secret with Alicia?" asked Amy. She was sitting on the steps, balancing a plate of eggs and sausage on her lap. A pickle had been pushed to the far side of the plate and remained untasted.

"We were discussing my vision."

Amy's eyes darted around. "Indoor voice."

"Sorry." Fanny complied and sat down beside her. "After much deliberation, I decided it wasn't a vision. Just an inexplicable corpse from nowhere that disappeared."

"Much more logical. Good." Amy chewed and swallowed. "Did you see today's schedule? There's a boat ride out to a glacier, maybe even kayaking. The Tyndall is one of the biggest glaciers in Patagonia." When Fanny didn't respond immediately . . . "What?"

"I don't know if I can go. I'm feeling a bit under the weather."

"That's too bad. What's wrong?"

Fanny thought fast. "I had a pickle, and it didn't agree with me."

"Oh." Amy stared daggers at her own pickle. "Do you need Pepto? I have some in my kit."

"No, thanks. But I may just hang around here today."

"Do you want me to stay with you?" Amy said, trying to hide her reluctance. "I will."

"No, no. You've been dying to see a glacier. Who knows? I may join you. It depends on how I'm feeling in an hour."

What it really depended on, Fanny knew, was what Lola Pisano was planning for the day.

Just as breakfast ended, Fanny was buttonholing Nicolas in the entry hall and asking a few questions. Minutes later her pickle attack flared up, and she had to beg off the glacier excursion. This just happened to coincide with the news that Jorge O'Bannion and his investor would also be missing the excursion. Amy told her mother she understood and promised to bring back plenty of photos.

Fanny loved house tours. Her favorites were the improvised ones where she'd be at a dinner party and wander off, presumably looking for a bathroom just down this hall or up those stairs. It wasn't really snooping, she rationalized. It was an unescorted glimpse into their lives. Just as this wasn't snooping right now. She was merely wandering the Torre Vista facilities, going from the renovated public spaces, through the half-renovated spaces, to the un-renovated private spaces.

With the rest of the guests gone, plus Nicolas and several others, she felt free to take her time. The remaining staff would be busy with their jobs and wouldn't necessarily know how to deal with a roaming, clueless, entitled *norteamericana* who refused to understand the most basic sign language for "Stop," "Forbidden," and "Do not enter." If anyone persisted, then she could fall back on her real mission. "I'm trying to find Senora Lola Pisano? Do you know where she is? The woman with the polka dot on her cheek?"

The farther Fanny penetrated into the estancia, the more fascinating it became. There was a section of cellar, under the kitchen, which was crowded with dusty furniture and toys from a hundred years ago: an old hobbyhorse on a stick, rattan chairs without the rattan, dolls with worn-off faces, and locked trunks that refused to open, no matter how hard she pried at them.

On the second floor, away from the views, the house seemed relatively unchanged from the family's glory days. Expensive but peeling wallpaper. A moth-eaten Persian rug, probably silk, that ran the length of a corridor. On the walls were old framed photographs of stern-looking ranchers and their wives. Others of men on polo ponies. The more recent of the faded portraits displayed a more relaxed attitude—children on their mothers' knees, visiting politicians and celebrities. What was Mickey Mouse doing in this one photo? Fanny put on her reading glasses and squinted. The grinning, confident man with the mustache, posing with the oversize Mickey doll, looked like a young Walt Disney. Had Disney ever visited Patagonia? Apparently so.

Fanny had just put away her glasses when a movement at the other end of the corridor caught her eye. She was not by nature superstitious, quite the contrary. But the recent suggestion of her psychic abilities, combined with the dusty, shadowy corridor and the fact that she'd watched *The Shining* two weeks earlier on Turner Classic Movies . . . "Lola?" she whispered. "Lola Pisano?"

The figure at the end of the corridor seemed to know the name.

"Are you the real Lola? Or are you just a vision? I

didn't mean *just.* Visions are important." Fanny started to walk slowly toward it. "I come in peace."

The figure said nothing but glanced from side to side, almost as if trapped and looking for an escape. And this was enough to convince Fanny that it was real.

"Senora Pisano," she said with relief and put on her warmest smile. "We met earlier today. Fanny Abel."

The figure said something in Spanish and took a step back into the shadows.

Fanny came closer and now recognized the mole and the hair. She lowered her voice to a conspiratorial whisper. "I have something to tell you. You're in trouble, dear. I don't mean to alarm, but I'm pretty sure I can see into the future, and you're dead. Nod if you understand English at all. No? Okay." She took a breath and racked her brains for any memory of the language. "*Muerto,*" she said. "*Usted.* In *poco* time. I know this sounds ridiculous. *Ridiculo. Pero no salir fuera* by yourself. *Non sola.* Or with anyone you don't trust absolutely, because the *muerto* I'm talking about could be an *accidento* or maybe murder. I wish I could be more *specifico.*"

Lola's expression seemed to reflect an alarmed kind of curiosity. She fingered the turquoise pendant on the silver chain around her neck. And then she replied in the most commonly used word in the English language. It was also the most commonly used word in Spanish, French, Chinese, and just about any other language. "Eh?" In this case, with this inflection, the universal translation was "What the hell?"

"Please listen. *Por favor. Muerto.* I'm not kidding. *Peligro.* Is that the word for *danger?* I've seen it on signs."

Lola seemed to think about it, then turned to the door behind her and shouted, "Jorge, ven aqui. Ahora."

Almost instantly the door opened and Jorge O'Bannion appeared, bathed in a glow from the room behind him. "Fanny. Hello. What are you doing?" Then a torrent of words to Lola in Spanish.

"Hello," Fanny chirped, wriggling her fingers in a wave. "I must have gotten lost. Big house. I know I should be off with the others, but I ate a bad pickle, so I'm here by myself. Just wandering around."

There was another torrent of Spanish back and forth. "Lola wants to know what you said to her. You said *muerto*? Death?" He looked concerned.

"*Muerto*? No, I meant maté. I'm trying to find maté. I ran out." It took Fanny a second to realize why she'd lied. Not that lying was bad. It was almost second nature. But if there was any possibility of Lola's future death being a murder, then she should be suspicious of everyone. Even Jorge. "I need to settle my stomach after the bad pickle."

"Maté?" O'Bannion chuckled and translated. Lola still looked confused. "There is plenty of maté in the kitchen. Let me take you there."

He was about to close the door behind him when Lola touched his arm. They spoke, this time quickly and softly, as if they were solving a problem. Whatever she said last, he agreed to with a smile.

"Lola wants to know if you will do us a favor."

"A favor?"

"It takes but a moment. Senora Pisano has graciously, and very wisely, decided to extend the funding for the New Patagonian Express." Then he bent at the waist and kissed his investor's hand.

"Why, that's wonderful. It's a great tour," Fanny said in Lola's direction. "Congratulations."

O'Bannion was beaming in his reserved, gentlemanly way. "We wrote up an extension to our current agreement. We were just about to track down a maid as our witness. But since you are here, perhaps you can do us the honor."

"Sure," said Fanny. "But I don't read Spanish. Is that a problem?"

"That's what we were discussing. You do not need to read it, just attest to the fact that Lola and I both signed." He swung open the door, revealing an old-fashioned study trimmed in dark leather and mahogany. Except for the laptop computer lying open on the desk, it would have been the pride of any nineteenth-century tycoon.

"Sounds reasonable," Fanny said and led the way inside.

It was a simple procedure. A printer, discreetly hidden in a corner, was already spitting out three copies of a two-page document. Jorge explained the essence of the agreement, which seemed straightforward enough. O'Bannion was giving Lola or her company, Fanny wasn't sure which, an extra 20 percent stake in the New Patagonian Express Corporation in exchange for some astronomical number of Chilean pesos, which Fanny seemed to recall went for about seven hundred to the U.S. dollar. After the others had signed all three copies, Francis V. Abel initialed the bottom of each page one and affixed her signature to each page two, on the line labeled *testigo*.

"Wonderful," said O'Bannion, sounding almost giddy. "Thank you both." He slipped the documents into a manila folder, then stepped around to a sideboard where a chilled bottle of champagne was peeking out from the top of an ice bucket, flanked by three champagne flutes. "I know it's early in the day, but, ladies, please join me in a toast."

"It's never too early for champagne." Fanny didn't really believe that, but she thought it sounded sophisticated.

CHAPTER 17

"Mom, you should have come. The weather was perfect. And the glacier was so blue. And huge. We got to kayak right up beside it."

"You sound like those competitive tourists you hate so."

"Sorry. But it was such a great day."

The vehicles had returned about an hour ago. The seven kayakers and their guide had barged through the entry hall, looking wet and tired and happy. They had disappeared up to their rooms to change. Now they were down in the lounge, holding celebratory cups of spiked hot chocolate and reliving their adventure by the warmth of the fireplace. Fanny had been waiting for her daughter in a comfortable chair in a book-lined corner, glancing through a picture book of Patagonian wildlife.

"There was this waterfall coming right off the glacier. Nicolas pointed it out, but I guess Todd didn't hear. His kayak went straight for it. Drenched. He didn't quite capsize, but it was touch and go, because of the undertow, I guess, pulling him closer. Edgar went to his rescue, and so did Alicia, which was amazing. She's such an inspiration. They grabbed his towline and . . ."

"I assume Mr. Toad was all outraged?"

"Actually, he took it pretty well. Afterward, he thanked everyone and didn't blame Nicolas. We all joked about it."

"Maybe Toady Drucker isn't so bad."

"He never once mentioned *TrippyGirl*. Of course, you weren't there to goad him on."

"It's nice to know I was missed."

"Wait. I didn't tell you about the penguins. Oh, my God. After the glacier, Nicolas led the kayaks around to the land side, where there was this whole flock of penguins, small ones, digging in the ground and making their nests. More than a flock. Hundreds, like a city. We got out and walked around. They weren't afraid at all or even curious. Just going about their business. But let me tell you, they were stinky. Truly the stinkiest birds ever."

Fanny had to smile. "Look at you, the outdoor girl."

Amy nodded. "Not like me at all, I know. Usually, it's museums and culture and history. Anyway, I wish you'd been there."

"If only I hadn't eaten that pickle."

From across the lounge, Edgar called out Amy's name and held up a bottle of Johnnie Walker Black, pantomiming an offer to top off her hot chocolate.

"Go play with your friends," said Fanny. "I'll join you in a minute." Then she watched as her little girl practically skipped across the room. It was good to see her excited by a trip, like in the old days, before the murders started following her around.

Fanny's afternoon hadn't been nearly as invigorating. Two and a half flutes of good champagne had left her sleepy and with a headache. She awoke from her late-morning nap with a head full of misgivings. Her pitiful attempt to warn Lola Pisano had only emphasized her problem. Fanny had never considered language as a barrier to communication. But when your idea was as complex as "I had a vision of you being eaten by condors in the middle of nowhere, so please be careful," it wasn't so easy. Especially when you were shouting the word *muerto* and the woman was already wary of you.

Her first instinct had been to ask Jorge to translate. But even if Jorge was innocent of any plan against Lola, Fanny didn't want to risk the ridicule that would rain down when she explained about her vision. For the same reason, she had rejected using Nicolas. Or anyone else. For a while, she had considered doing it herself, hunting down the strongest Wi-Fi signal and using Google Translate to create her note of warning. But, in the midst of her bubbly fog, while trying to think of exactly how to word such a message, she had got bogged down.

Amy was at the coffee table by the fireplace, hunched over a phone with Edgar and Todd, laughing and covering her mouth over some video one of them had shot. She'd had an exhilarating day, the kind that she used to have with Eddie, the kind that had made her fall in love with travel. The last thing she needed was for her mother to inform her that the woman in the Patagonian wilds was the same woman who'd just arrived here at Torre Vista.

For right now, Fanny's plan was simple. She would keep an eye on Lola Pisano. If the Argentine heiress left the estancia, Fanny would find some excuse to go with her. If Lola somehow left on her own, Fanny would reveal her vision to the others and organize a search party. More than that she couldn't do, at least not in her current condition.

"Excuse me." It was one of the Furies, not much taller than Fanny herself, entering her line of vision. "It's my fault that we have not been properly introduced." She bowed her head slightly, which seemed to be the local equivalent of the American handshake. "Gabriela Garcia."

"Fanny Abel." She pointed to the chair across from her. "Please. Amy told me we had another English speaker among us."

Gabriela refused the chair. "I wasn't being unfriendly or pretending not to speak English." She hesitated. "I just want to ask . . . Have you seen Lola Pisano, Jorge's friend?"

"Lola?" A slight chill ran down Fanny's spine, although she didn't quite know why. "Do you know Lola Pisano?"

"We've never met," said Gabriela. "But I want to introduce myself. Her late husband had been a business associate of my late husband. We're both from Buenos Aires, but she doesn't spend much time in public."

"Because of the hairy mole? I've noticed that she tries to hide it."

"Wouldn't you? And to make it worse, we *porteños* are quite vain. We may not do as much plastic surgery as Brazilians, but almost. A thing like that you would think is fixable. It draws the eye and makes people uncomfortable." Gabriela continued to hover over Fanny's chair. "You have seen her, then?"

Fanny checked around the room, just to make sure. "No. But I'm sure she'll be at dinner."

"I will keep an eye out, as they say. Pleasure to

meet you, Mrs. Abel." And with that, Senora Garcia wandered back toward her friends, who were at the bar with Nicolas and the cute little bartender who worked in the stables during the day and whose name Fanny could never quite recall.

That evening in the dining room, Fanny kept an eye focused the doorway. She expected Lola to walk in on Jorge's arm. But the O'Bannion patriarch entered alone, making the rounds to all his guests and settling in with Alicia Lindborn at a table for two. Fanny and Amy were sharing a table with Edgar and Todd. Their conversation was agreeable and light—all about travel, of course, and travel's most common pairing these days, wine.

"I don't understand," said Todd in a cordial but officious tone. "You come all the way to Chile to drink a cab. This is the home of the Carménère, for heaven's sake."

"Not a cab. A cab-merlot blend," said Edgar, holding up his bottle for inspection. "More complex than a Carménère, less of a summer wine. We'll let Fanny be the judge." He waved for the waiter to bring two more glasses. Fanny didn't object. She wasn't much of a wine drinker. Martinis were her poison of choice. But she liked giving her opinion. Plus, the wine would help calm her down, she thought, help her to keep things in perspective. After half a glass of each, she sided with Todd and voted for the Carménère.

The wine continued to flow, and the subject of *TrippyGirl* never once came up. Despite several more arguments about Malbecs and Syrahs, a portion of Fanny's attention stayed focused on the empty doorway at the edge of her vision. But the doorway remained empty, even after the late Patagonian sun finally edged behind the jagged peaks.

The fruit and cheese plate was followed by the dessert wine and the final course, *suspiro limeño*, an overly sweet caramel concoction that had nothing to do with limes or lemons. And still no Lola. It was only toward the end that Fanny realized she wasn't the only one focused on the missing woman. Every minute or so, Gabriela would turn to look. That was to be expected. But also Edgar and Todd, Fanny noticed, and Alicia, who was seated with Jorge but kept scanning the room. The two other Furies were the exception and remained oblivious to everything but the *suspiro limeño*.

As for Amy, she seemed animated and happy, blissfully unaware of the empty doorway and whatever meaning it might hold.

For once she was up before her mother, thanks in part to last night's battle of the wines. Amy could tell from the depth and volume of the snoring that Fanny had another hour at least before joining the conscious world. Amy used this time to visit the bathroom quietly, put on her black skinny jeans and an oversize plaid shirt, one that had mysteriously gone missing from Marcus's closet. She lamented the fact that she'd brought only four different pairs of glasses. For today, she chose the Lafonts. Again.

At first glance, as Amy came down the stairs, the lounge seemed empty. Outside the windows, daylight was having trouble arriving. Low, fat clouds scudded across the sky, leaving the room in undulating shades of reflected gray, and she wondered where the light switch might be, something you rarely had cause to wonder about in a hotel's public spaces, where someone was almost always there before you. But just as her Top-Siders hit the last step, the lights went on.

"Good morning." It was Gabriela Garcia, wearing a similar outfit of a plaid top and skinny jeans, standing by a row of switches. "Is it so early still?"

"Morning." Amy reached into a pocket and checked her phone, which during the past few days had been functioning as nothing more than a watch and a camera. "Eight-oh-six."

"Everyone must be getting a late start." Somewhere deep behind the lounge they could hear dishes clinking and doors being opened and closed. "What is on the agenda?"

Amy had the daily schedule folded in her back pocket, but she didn't have to look. "The Monastery of Monte Carmelo. It's never been open to the public. But Jorge has a cousin who's the main monk there, so he arranged a visit. They're supposed to have these wonderful mosaics brought over from Spain and reconstructed piece by piece. Quite worth seeing." Amy could tell that Gabriela wasn't paying attention, even though she'd asked the question. "Anyway, that's today. Did you get a chance to speak to Senora Pisano? Mother said you were looking for her."

"I was hoping to see her this morning," said Gabriela. "Before we go off for our fun."

"I don't know about fun in a monastery." Amy took a few steps toward the large picture windows and angled her neck up. "We may have some weather."

"There is always weather, no?"

"Sorry. I mean bad weather. Is there someone outside?" She had seen movement under the clouds. Something on the porch? Just beyond the porch?

Both women headed for the front double doors to see for themselves.

On the porch, by the steps, was Jorge O'Bannion. On the dirt path just beyond him was a horse, large and black, well built, like a thoroughbred. On the horse was a charcoal riding blanket. On the blanket was an English saddle. On the saddle, looking poised and determined, was Lola Pisano, dressed in a red jacket, black trousers, and a scarf protecting her ash-blond hair. Upon seeing the two new arrivals, she reacted, pulling the horse in a tight little circle, kicking up dust in the growing breeze.

"Ms. Garcia. Ms. Abel." O'Bannion seemed thrown, suddenly on edge. "My friend was about to go out. I am trying to persuade her not to. Storms come and go very quickly in Patagonia."

"Senora Pisano," said Gabriela, raising her voice into the breeze. From the tone of what she said next, Amy deduced it was a request. *The word* hablar, Amy noted. *To speak. I need to speak to you?* She mentioned her own name, too. Gabriela Garcia.

Lola's response was a dismissive shake of her head and a tug of the reins. The horse emitted a short guttural neigh, and before anyone could react, Lola kicked it in the sides, and they were off. Horse and rider went trotting, then galloping away on the dirt road toward the hills.

"Lola," shouted O'Bannion. "Lola!"

"What happened?" Amy asked. The moment was eerily reminiscent of what had happened with Fanny and her horse, except that this time it was on purpose. "Should we go after her?"

O'Bannion paused as horse and rider went over a small rise and down the other side, disappearing from view. "I don't know why she did that."

"She doesn't want to confront me," Gabriela announced in English. A hard, satisfied look played across her face, pulling down the corners of her mouth. "The coward."

"Confront you about what?" asked Amy.

"Her husband's legacy," Gabriela said but didn't elaborate.

Amy repeated her first question. "Should we go after her? Jorge?"

O'Bannion turned back from the road and climbed the steps to the estancia's porch. "Lola is an expert rider. She'll be back soon." He raised his eyes to the sky. "Before the storm, I hope."

Amy and Gabriela just stood there, transfixed, as Lola and her mount reappeared above another small rise, then disappeared behind it.

"Why is everyone out here?" The double doors had been left open. Fanny was in a resort bathrobe, simple white terry cloth with PATAGONIAN EXPRESS stitched in gold on the pocket. The one-size-fits-all dimensions made her look like a little girl playing in her mother's housedress. She was barefoot, just beginning to wake up.

"Nothing," Amy said, unsure if it was really nothing or not. "Lola went out for a ride."

Fanny stared out into the storm clouds, the wind forcing her to grip the robe tight around her. "Alone?"

"Alone, yes." Jorge O'Bannion tried to sound reassuring. "She's an excellent rider."

"She's going to die." Fanny's hands gravitated slowly up to her cheeks. "The poor woman's going to die. And it's all my fault."

CHAPTER 18

"Let me say it again. You did not have a vision."
They were in the leather armchairs in the
lounge, side by side, Fanny still in her bathrobe, facing one of the picture windows. The predicted storm
had turned the day to night, ricocheting off a half
acre of red tile roofs in millions of tiny explosions.
Even though the room was empty, Amy kept her
voice low.

"It's the same woman," Fanny insisted. "Unlike
you, I never met Lola before. But the second I saw
her, I knew. The mole, the hair, her general build.
What was she wearing? When she rode off today,
what was she wearing?"

Amy had to think. "I don't know. A red jacket and
black pants? I wasn't paying attention. And a scarf."

"Ha!" Fanny looked triumphant. "I didn't envision
a scarf. Maybe she loses it. But my woman was definitely in red and black. That's what I told the police.
It's engraved in my mind."

"A lot of people wear red and black. Now, if you'd
said chartreuse and pink—"

"Don't be glib, little girl." Fanny took a break, adding hot water to her maté gourd and stirring it. This was already her second time draining and re-filling the gourd, and the herbal brew wasn't helping her nerves. "Everyone ridiculed me when the body disappeared. Well, a vision explains that. Right?"

"Mom, there has to be a logical explanation."

"This is a logical—"

"Another logical explanation. One that's logical."

Fanny took another swig. "Four days ago I saw a corpse no one else saw. Then the same woman shows up alive. Then she rides off into the Patagonian wilderness, never to be seen again."

"Never to be seen? It's been fifteen minutes."

"In a thunderstorm. Any living person would have come back."

"Maybe she's on her way. Maybe she found a cave or a cottage and is waiting it out."

Fanny exhaled. "It's my fault for not warning her. But I don't speak Spanish, and your friends plied me with wine. We have to go out and find her."

"Find her where? She could have ridden in a dozen directions."

"Jorge should be out there. Instead, he's in the din-ing room, pouring coffee and talking about monas-teries."

"Which shows how unworried he is." Amy placed a comforting hand on her mother's knee. "You take a shower and get dressed. No trousers for the women and something with sleeves. That's what the itinerary says."

"They're telling us how to dress?"

"For the monastery. I guarantee, by the time we pull ourselves together, Lola and her horse will be back."

"You have no basis for that guarantee," Fanny said somberly. "But I appreciate your naively positive attitude."

At Amy's insistence, they went up to their suite. A few minutes later, while Fanny was in the bathroom and Amy was straightening up, the pounding on the tile roof ceased. The storm was over, and a breeze was starting to clear the skies. Neither of the Abels mentioned the vision again, not until they came down the staircase, properly dressed, and saw the front doors once again wide open.

Outside, they found Jorge O'Bannion, Nicolas, and the estancia's stable hand off to the right of the main building, by the white-fenced paddock and the adjoining stables. The hand was examining the flanks of the black thoroughbred, checking for cuts or injuries. The horse looked exhausted, its head lowered into a water trough, taking big lapping gulps. The riding blanket and saddle were still in place, but off-kilter, pushed forward and to one side.

"Where's Lola?" Amy asked as she rushed over to the paddock. Fanny was a few yards behind, refusing to rush. "Is she all right?"

Nicolas was the one to come over and answer. "Everything is fine. Nothing to worry about."

"Now you have me worried. Is Lola hurt?"

The young guide caught O'Bannion's eye, and the older man shrugged, his shoulders heavy. It looked like he'd put on ten years in the past ten minutes.

"It came back without her." It was Fanny speaking, calm in an almost fatalistic way.

"Yes," said Nicolas. "The horse came back without her."

* * *

For the second time in four days, the Patagonian Express was put on hold. The excursion to see the monastery's mosaics was canceled, and everyone began searching for a woman in the wilderness.

The Torre Vista search had several natural advantages over the Glendaval search. They were closer to the Torres del Paine National Park, meaning the police were closer, less than a two-hour drive. A helicopter was also available, a Bell 407, normally used to take wealthy fly fishermen to the remotest rivers and fjords. And, perhaps the biggest advantage, this was a real woman who'd gone missing, the widow of an Argentinean tycoon, seen by three reliable witnesses riding off into a storm and not coming back.

The guests could do only so much to help. Edgar Wolowitz, the youngest and fittest of the men, mounted a horse and joined O'Bannion and the stable hand in riding through the ravines that were inaccessible to most motor vehicles. Todd and Amy joined the tour drivers in the two Land Cruisers, acting as lookouts while their driving partners maneuvered the trails and tried not to get stuck in the brand-new gullies carved out by the downpour. All three teams stayed in radio contact. Back at Torre Vista, Alicia set up a command center on one of the tables in the dining room, keeping people connected and crossing off the searched sections on a map. If they didn't find her, Alicia would have the map ready for the police, a little head start, when they arrived. The other guests, Fanny, Todd, and the Furies, did their part at the estancia by agreeing to fend for themselves and not complain.

"I feel so helpless." Gabriela was looking over Alicia's shoulder. Without her compatriots at her side, she was speaking more and more English. "The red

X, is that the estancia?" It was a large topographical map, the one that had been framed and on display in the lounge. Removed from behind its glass, the map was disfigured with a red *X* almost exactly in the middle, with three multicolored lines expanding from it in different directions.

"That's us." Fanny stood over Alicia's other shoulder, holding a fistful of Magic Markers, ready to hand to Alicia. There was no reason for them to be hovering, but it felt better than doing nothing. "The blue line is vehicle number one, the red is number two, and the green is the horses."

Gabriela studied the lines. "Only one green line? There are three horses. They should split up."

Alicia kept focused on the lines, as if expecting them to move on their own. "The horses are on the most rugged trails. The last thing we want is for another rider to get lost or injured."

Lost or injured, mused Fanny. *The fools are not even thinking dead, but that's how it's going to wind up.*

"What about this area?" Gabriela pointed a pink-lacquered nail at the unlined section just to the north of the estancia.

"There are no trails on that side," Alicia said. "And she rode the other way. If they don't find her before the authorities arrive, I'm sure that'll be next."

All three continued to stare at the map. Then the two-way radio on the table next to it squawked. "Vehicle one."

Alicia answered. "Torre Vista. Over."

"Hello, Torre Vista." It was Amy's voice, sounding competent and calm. She said something to her driver in Italian, then translated for Alicia. "We're crossing the arroyo. *Come si dice in inglese?*" Slight pause. "I guess *arroyo* is the same in English. Over."

"It means 'a dry gully,' " said Alicia. "Which arroyo? Over. There are a few in your area, judging from the topography. Over. And they're not labeled. Over." Alicia was still getting used to her "overs."

"This one is flooded at the moment. But we're getting across. Dante says we're just east of the salt ponds. Half a kilometer." Dante's Italian had been a lucky discovery this morning, as the teams were getting organized. The Chilean-born son of an Italian mining engineer, he was a nature conservation student in Santiago, working for the summer as a driver. "Over."

The salt ponds, a haven for orange and pink flamingos, where Dante was supposed to have driven them today, after breakfast, were labeled on the map. "Found it," said Alicia. Fanny handed her a blue marker, and Alicia extended their line to the southwest, crossing a thin line that could have been an arroyo or a stream, depending on the season. "Any sign of her?" She waited for an answer. "Any sign? Over."

"Dante saw some horse droppings, but he says they're a week old. She probably didn't come this way. Has anyone picked up her trail? Over."

"Not so far. The police are coming soon, so maybe we should have everyone circle back around and come in. I'll suggest it to Jorge. Over."

Amy said that it sounded like a good idea. She also sounded discouraged. "Over and out."

When Fanny looked up from the map, she was surprised to see that Gabriela Garcia had quietly left the room.

The arrival of the Chilean authorities was a disappointment. At least Fanny thought so. The entire force consisted of a Toyota SUV and two officers barely out of high school, both of whom seemed very proud of their neatly pressed uniforms. Alicia and Fanny met them on the porch and did their best to explain. It was an instance in which Gabriela's language skills would have been helpful. Fanny had asked around the estancia, pantomiming the woman's description and saying her name, but Gabriela Garcia was nowhere to be found.

Alicia led the boys into the dining room and displayed the map. If they were impressed by the diligence of the searchers, they didn't let on. If they at all understood what the lines and the X stood for, they also didn't let on. When Jorge and the other horsemen returned a few minutes later, the language barrier was broken. But it hardly improved matters. The gist of the conversation, which Fanny and everyone else would soon learn, was pretty much as follows.

According to the officers, tourists do die. It is a sad truth, but in the thousands of acres in and around the national park, backpackers and mountain climbers, even horseback riders, go missing, and the rural police who oversee the area do not have the resources to make extensive searches.

Jorge O'Bannion was furious. His agony and frustration were clear. This wasn't a tourist. It was Senora Lola Pisano, the widow of a powerful Argentine tycoon. But whatever cachet the word *tycoon* might have brought to O'Bannion's case, it was undone by the word *Argentine*. So, the woman was a tourist, after all, the officers said, and not even from the United States but from that socialist-leaning country next door that was always trying to argue over territory and make life difficult for the good people of Chile. "Do you really think our country should spend its limited budget trying to find some Argentine widow who had stupidly ignored an approaching storm?"

The neatly pressed officers did their job. They dutifully looked over Alicia's map and listened to Jorge and the drivers, one of them a local, describe the territory and the most likely unsearched spots where a rider could have been thrown. After that the officers drove away, supposedly to conduct their own search, then fill out the paperwork. Everyone assumed that they would be back in their homes before sundown, in time to have their wives press their uniforms for the next day.

"So that's it?" Fanny asked. She and Amy had stepped outside and were walking the gravel path around the stables and the newer garage, built in the same white, barnlike style. "We're just going to give up?"

Amy wrapped a light gray shawl around her shoulders and kept an eye peeled for horse droppings camouflaged in the dark gravel. "Jorge rented the helicopter for tomorrow morning. But there's only so far they can look. The woman was on a horse, not a jet plane."

"But she has to be somewhere."

"What do you suggest? We can't stay indefinitely. Poor Jorge has a tour to run. All his time and investment, and Lola's investment. Todd Drucker is already complaining. He was counting on seeing that monastery."

To Fanny it still sounded heartless. "Did Jorge talk to her relatives in Buenos Aires?"

"He's probably hoping he doesn't have to."

"Why did the stupid woman ride off in the first place? You were on the scene."

"I know." Amy's sigh was almost a growl. "They were speaking Spanish."

Fanny rolled her eyes. "I don't quite get your mental block with that language."

"Lola and Gabriela were exchanging words."

"Very observant. In Spanish."

"In Spanish. I don't think they knew each other, not personally. There was some animosity about their late husbands. Gabriela wanted to confront her, but Lola just rode off." Amy could sense her mother's disappointment. "Why she rode off isn't important."

"It is important, dear, if Lola was murdered."

"Inside voice!" Even though they were outside and no one was in sight, Amy pulled her mother by the arm, edging her around the side of the garage. "How could she be murdered?" she whispered. "First off, Lola's not officially dead."

Fanny whispered back, "Visions don't lie. She's dead."

"And second, who could have killed her? From the time she went away, everyone's been looking for her. In groups."

"It could have been one of the staff," Fanny reasoned. "They weren't in groups. Or a local rancher. Or a drifter."

"Did you actually say 'drifter'? How about a hobo? Maybe it was a Patagonian hobo."

"Remember what your father used to say? 'You can't win an argument by making fun of people.'"

"He used to say that to you."

"Still a valid point." Fanny pivoted on her heel and was about to start back for the estancia when they heard the approaching car, from around the front of the garage, slowly pulling up from the road onto the noisier gravel.

The sound of a motor vehicle wasn't unusual. But given the hour, given the fact that the emergency had pretty much brought work to a halt, and given the subject they'd just been discussing—about someone out in the wilderness killing Lola Pisano . . . The Abels inched themselves back against the side wall of the garage and waited.

Someone had just driven inside. From this angle they couldn't see, although it had sounded like one of the three brand-new Land Cruisers, the mainstays of the Torre Vista motor pool. The engine was switched off. The door opened. If the driver was heading to the estancia, he or she would be walking through their line of sight.

"We're just being paranoid," said Amy, barely audible even to herself. Common sense told her it was probably a gaucho who'd been out checking fences or whatever else gauchos did. But this time common sense was wrong.

The driver who emerged from the mouth of the garage was Gabriela Garcia. The Argentine businesswoman checked her surroundings quickly, then moved furtively toward the estancia, gaining confidence in her stride only as she rounded the corner and came into the lights of the long porch.

Amy and Fanny said nothing, not until they had walked into the garage themselves. There were three Land Cruisers lined up in two rows, plus Jorge's sidecar, looking lonely without its motorcycle partner. Amy went up to the first Land Cruiser, which was still throwing off heat from its run. The keys were in the ignition. She checked. The keys were in the ignition of all the vehicles in the garage.

"When did you last see Gabriela?" she asked.

Fanny was standing guard at the door. "Just now."

"Before then."

Fanny scrunched her face into a wrinkled ball. "We were looking at the maps. She asked why no one was out searching the woods north of the ranch. Alicia told her it was because Lola rode off the other way."

"And that's the last time you saw her?"

"Yes. Until just now."

CHAPTER 19

The two rural carabineros returned early that evening, but only to report their failure, get O'Bannion's signature on a form, and assure him that, according to their experience, most missing persons, or their remains, did show up eventually.

Dinner was a subdued affair. Most of the guests and the staff were exhausted, physically and mentally, by the events of the day. An hour after, Amy couldn't even remember what she'd eaten. No one stayed up late to chat in the bar or to enjoy a game of gin. In the lounge, Todd Drucker and Edgar Wolowitz did play a round or two of competitive traveling. But they quickly agreed that on all their previous trips they'd never engaged in an activity like this and that it was probably in bad taste to compare it to anything.

The next morning, the mood in the dining room had returned to a semblance of normalcy. The Furies were chattering, Fanny was slurping maté, and Nicolas was once again apologizing to Todd about the lack of orange juice with breakfast.

"The nearest orange trees are in Brazil," the guide explained patiently. "The fruit itself is not popular, so it's hard to get. Please try the guava. Or grape. You enjoy the local grapes, yes? Just like wine."

The mood grew subdued again when helicopter rotors were heard, passing low over the estancia. Jorge O'Bannion stood and looked up to the beamed ceiling as if he could stare through it. Even the Furies stopped to listen and think. Gabriela took advantage of their lull to make a trip to the buffet for another cup of coffee.

"Do you think they'll find her?" Fanny asked. She'd been waiting for this moment. As soon as she'd seen Gabriela break off from her friends, she grabbed a coffee cup from her table and rushed over, pretending to be in need of a refill.

Gabriela considered the question. "A helicopter covers more ground. On the other hand, how much ground could Lola have traveled?"

"What did you think of the police yesterday? Did you talk to them?" From her years of experience as the mother of a teenage girl, Fanny considered herself an expert in the loaded question. And this one, she thought, was pretty well loaded.

"I didn't meet them, no. My friends say they were not helpful."

"They weren't helpful," Fanny agreed. "I tried talking to them when they got here, but they pretended not to understand. If only you'd been around to translate. I tried to find you."

"I went up to my room with a headache. The stress of the day."

"I know from headaches," Fanny said. "Aspirins don't always help, do they? I've spent hours in bed. Is that the way it was with you, dear? Hours in bed? Not going outside at all?"

"All yesterday afternoon," Gabriela confirmed. "I went out for a little while before dinner."

"You went out?" Fanny tried to sound disinterested.

"A little walk before dinner. Why? Did I miss anything?"

Fanny told her no. She hadn't missed anything at all.

The rotors passed over twice during the breakfast service, about half an hour apart. The third time they didn't pass but came in for a landing.

By the time the large blue and white helicopter settled down on the meadow in front of the gravel drive, everyone had gathered on the porch. Jorge was in the middle of the steps, holding his arms out wide, like the arms of a train crossing. When the blades finally stopped, he lowered his barricade and led the way down. The company's name, King Fisher, was emblazoned in gold script on the doors.

Upon exiting the aircraft, the pilots met the crowd halfway to the gravel. "Mr. O'Bannion?" said the older one, checking the clipboard in his hand. Jorge stepped forward. "Sir, good to meet you." They introduced themselves, Norm and Kevin, two Canadians, one middle-aged, one in his twenties, both looking ex-military with modified buzz cuts. The older one had a no-nonsense attitude about him. The younger, Kevin, threw a few sideways glances at Amy, who was not currently in a flirty mood.

"Why did you stop?" O'Bannion demanded. "Get back up in the air. I pay you to search."

"We didn't give up," said Norm. "On the contrary, I think we sighted your subject."

"My subject?" the estancia owner asked. "I don't understand."

"The subject you're looking for," said the younger one. "About three klicks north by northeast of here. There's a river, the Serrano. Big river. A human female body is in the water by the far bank. Facedown. Otherwise we would have initiated rescue procedures."

Amy avoided looking in her mother's direction. She was very familiar with Fanny's "I told you so" expression and didn't need to see it again.

"No, that's impossible." Jorge O'Bannion seemed genuinely shocked by the news. He held out a hand to steady himself. Edgar was at his side and supplied an arm to lean on. "It can't be. It's a mistake."

"No mistake, sir," said the older pilot. "That's why you hired us. That's what we did." Then he added, almost as an afterthought, "We're sorry for your loss."

"We didn't land or disturb the body," explained his copilot. "There's a clearing, a bend in the bank that looks solid enough to put down on. If you'd care to join us, sir?"

"I don't understand," said O'Bannion softly. Then, "Yes, of course." His hand, still steadying itself on Edgar's arm, began to shake.

"Are you going to be okay?" asked the older pilot. "Do you want someone to come with you?"

"I'll come," said Edgar. "If that's all right."

"My daughter and I are coming, too," said Fanny. "We're close friends."

"Mother, please," said Amy, although she didn't really object. She was just in the habit of saying "Mother, please" in a situation like this.

"We have plenty of room," the younger pilot said,

then quickly qualified his offer. "If that's what Mr. O'Bannion wants. It's his choice."

O'Bannion didn't seem capable of making a choice, so Fanny took him by his other arm and, along with Edgar, guided him toward the helicopter. "Come on, dear," she said in Amy's direction. "I trust you have your phone?"

Amy had flown in a few helicopters in her life, but this was by far the fanciest, perfect for any elite troop of millionaires who wanted to rough it. The seats were large and plush, complete with armrests and cup holders. The two main passenger doors were like picture windows with handles. Before restarting the engine, both pilots took a minute to reconfigure the interior. They wound up with four seats behind the cockpit area, two across and facing the other two. The two seats in the rear section had been folded down to provide cargo room, like the rear of an SUV. Amy didn't want to think about what the cargo section would be holding on the way back.

The interior noise level was surprisingly low, thanks in part to the noise-canceling headsets they were each given to wear. Before Amy realized the rotors were at full operational speed, the King Fisher was off the ground and heading north by northeast.

"How could she be north?" It was O'Bannion's voice over the headset, the question directed at no one in particular. "There are no real trails to the north. And she was riding south."

"We don't know, sir," came the disembodied voice of one of the Canadians.

"This is a mistake. You must have made a mistake."

"No, sir. We were focused on the southern terrain, per our instructions, when Norm made a wide swing up by the river. We flew along it, configuring our old maps, since not every spot in the world is GPS friendly all the time. Anyhow, I spotted her. It was almost a fluke." They were flying over a pathless swath of scrubby green. The gray-blue glint of a wide, meandering ribbon of water played among the low foothills.

Amy and Fanny were the first to see the condors. Two of them were gliding at about the same height as the chopper, with their long black wings and separated feathers at the tips, flying away from the noise of the rotors. Fanny let out a little yelp.

"Pardon me, ma'am?" asked one of the Canadians.

"Nothing," replied Fanny. "Just a little déjà vu." She nudged her daughter's arm and pointed to the phone in Amy's hand. Amy understood. She turned on her video feature and pointed the phone out the window toward the river. *Be judicious,* she reminded herself. *There might be a lot more that needs filming today.* With any luck, she wouldn't have to erase her glacier adventure, but she might. As they came in low, she could clearly see a small figure—red top and black pants—lying by the bank.

The Bell 407 circled once, then eased down onto a bend in the river, onto a large rocky patch in the midst of the solidified silt. The pilots cut the engine and reminded their passengers to stay on board until the doors were opened for them. When the young copilot opened Amy's picture window and helped her out, he saw her camera phone. It reminded him to take his own camera, probably last used to record the landing of a prize trout a hundred miles away. The older pilot saw the two cameras, and that reminded him to open up a small storage compartment on the outside of the hull and retrieve a large, thick black plastic bag. He tried to be nonchalant, but Amy had to wonder if they had packed it specifically for this job, or if all helicopters working in the wilderness came equipped with body bags.

"Get in front," said Fanny, elbowing Amy in the back. "I want good footage."

Amy toyed with the idea of obeying her mother, but there was something about Jorge O'Bannion that stopped her. She let him take the lead as they walked the twenty yards or so between the helicopter and the river. The man look so vulnerable, almost frightened. The younger pilot tried to point the way, but the body's location had been pretty obvious from their time circling the spot. Amy kept filming.

Lola Pisano's body was wedged in a little eddy, almost submerged as the river water swirled around it in a miniature whirlpool. It was a foot or two from the shoreline. Amy had never seen a human being dead in the water like this. There was more bloating than she'd expected, considering it had been in there for perhaps only thirty hours. The woman lay on her side, facing the shore, dressed in red and black, but the fabric was so muddied and tattered that little remained of the design. Her face had been pecked at by the scavengers, but not to a horrible degree. No, Amy rethought that assessment. Horrible, yes, but not to an unrecognizable degree. Although Amy had never spent much time with Lola, she thought back to the woman she'd seen on the horse—the hair, the sharp features, even the mole on the cheek, surprisingly unpecked, as if the condors had found it as distasteful as most humans had.

Jorge O'Bannion approached slowly, his eyes fixed on the face. And although the sight was exactly what

everybody had expected, his expression went from
vulnerability to wide-eyed wonder, then to a kind of
calm resignation. "It is Lola Pisano," he finally said.
"I didn't think . . . Until this minute, I didn't think it
could be. My dear Lola."

Amy caught what she could on tape—the face,
Jorge's reaction, the pilots and their catch of the day.
But at some point the whole thing became too personal, too intrusive. When she slid her finger off the
video button and lowered her phone, even Fanny
didn't object.

The rest of the recovery mission was simple but
mind-numbing. O'Bannion and the Abel women
stood by the banks of the Serrano, averting their
eyes, watching the muddy water flow down from the
distant Andes on its zigzag journey to the Pacific.
The two pilots, assisted by Edgar, lifted the body, settled it into the open body bag, zipped it tight, and
carried it—one at the head, one at the feet, Edgar
guiding them along—to the waiting helicopter.

After the pilots had finished their job and were escorting their living passengers into the chopper, Amy
couldn't avoid glancing into the cargo area. The
black bag was being held in place with built-in straps
meant to hold down equipment. Luckily for all concerned, the bag seemed to be airtight. On the short
ride back to the estancia, there were next to no
smells wafting up from the rear.

CHAPTER 20

Jorge remained with the aircraft, the pilots, and the body, while Amy, her mother, and Edgar walked from the meadow across the gravel drive, up to the Torre Vista porch and the small crowd that had gathered—all the other guests, plus Nicolas and a few of the staff. Fanny tried valiantly to preserve an aura of somber respect, but she nearly trotted the whole way.

"What happened?" Todd Drucker was at the front of the pack. "Was it her?"

"Was it the same as your vision?" asked Alicia Lindborn, who had apparently been able to put two and two together.

"What vision?" Todd's eyes went from Fanny to Alicia and back again.

"My vision four days ago, dear, the one you said I made up."

Gabriela stayed busy with her Furies and the Spanish-speaking staff, translating the drama step-by-step.

"I don't blame anyone for doubting me." Fanny was at her magnanimous best. "But as soon as I met Lola, I knew. I tried warning her, but she wouldn't listen. Not in English, anyway. I guess the lesson is we can't change the future, as hard as we may try. Amy, give me your phone."

For the next hour, Fanny held court on the porch. She began, with Alicia's support, by singing the praises of yerba maté as a vision-inducing drug.

"That's not what maté does," Todd protested, but no one cared.

From then on, the tale unfolded like a Greek tragedy. Fanny's vision in the wilderness, the cruel world doubting her, Alicia's brilliant suggestion, then the surprise arrival of Lola, and Fanny's futile attempt to stop the hand of fate. The finale was the video, raw and unedited. The audience watched it several times, passing it around and around again. Even her nemesis, the Toad, was awed into submission. In the sport of competitive traveling, Fanny had made a touchdown, a home run, and a hat trick combined.

Halfway through the saga, Amy melted away through the double doors and into the lounge. The younger of the two pilots was standing over the map, admiring their handiwork from yesterday's search. "You guys were organized," he said. "And I don't blame you for not looking up by the river. Not a logical spot."

His full name was Kevin Vanderhof, originally from Ottawa. As Amy had assumed, he was ex-military, having served with the Canadian Air Reserves, flying search and rescue in the frozen North until he opted for a change of scenery and came down to the frozen South. His love of fly-fishing had made this job a natural. He was almost exactly Amy's height, five-ten, but had a presence that made him seem taller.

"What are you going to do with Lola?" Amy couldn't bring herself to say "the body."

"My partner is arranging the flight plan now. After

lunch, we're taking her to the El Calafate airport in Argentina."

"We're that close to Argentina?"

"The geography here is deceptive," Kevin explained. "It can take you half a day to drive fifty miles as the crow flies. There's mountains and glaciers in the way. And the roads are crazy. Most of them were laid out a hundred years ago to connect sheep ranches. Nothing is direct."

"I think our train took that route."

"Then you know. The deceased's relatives are arranging the logistics. Someone will be meeting us in El Calafate and flying her back to Buenos Aires."

"Will Jorge be going with her?"

"I think he's got his hands full here." Kevin turned to face Amy. His eyes were hazel, she couldn't help noticing, just like Marcus's. He lowered his voice. "From what I overheard, I don't think the relatives were ever thrilled with Mr. O'Bannion. Even before she rode off and got killed."

When the noonday meal was announced, Amy asked Kevin and Norm to join their table. She knew her mother. Fanny would be preoccupied by her vision, trying out slightly different versions on her daughter as she endlessly retold the tale, barely able to eat. Having two strangers with them—two practical military types—might help to put a damper on her enthusiasm. But no. It just provided her with a new audience.

After lunch, a crowd gathered on the long porch and watched as the two pilots and their cargo took to the air, sprayed gravel along the drive and up the steps, then pivoted east and gained altitude over the meadows. Then their attention returned to the more serious matter of touring.

The monastery visit had been scheduled for a full
day, including a donkey ride up an Andean path that
hugged the mountain. The itinerary didn't say how
you were supposed to get down the mountain, but
Amy assumed it would be with the same donkeys.
The monastery's replacement, arranged by Nicolas
at the last minute, was an afternoon excursion. They
would off-road through a petrified forest to a small
working estancia, where the guests would witness a
sheepshearing demonstration. The travelers had put
on brave, concerned faces during the ordeal of the
last day and a half. But they'd all barely met the deceased, and hey, enough was enough.

Despite their eagerness for a good time, the afternoon did not turn out well. The off-roading part failed
to make allowances for the older bones and older
nerves of some of the travelers. And the sheepshearing
proved to be a little bloodier and less animal friendly
than any of them had imagined. The mood didn't im-
prove when they returned off-road through the same
petrified forest and found lamb chops and mutton
curry as two of the three selections on the evening
menu.

After dinner, Fanny took a long, hot bubble bath
in their claw-foot tub, easing out the aches of the day.
Amy sat on her bed within easy earshot and tried to
make sense of that morning's video. "Don't accidentally erase any of that," Fanny warned, her head half
under water. "It's great *TrippyGirl* stuff."

"I can't promise not to accidentally do something."

"Just be careful."

"How do you think she died?" Amy had frozen the
footage on a still of Lola's face. Something didn't

look quite right. Amy's insides began to knot up, a too-familiar sensation.

"She fell off a horse. Broke her neck."

Amy inched the footage ahead until the still was clearer. More knots. "There's a bruise on her left temple. Pretty nasty. I'm wondering if that was the cause of death."

"She fell and hit her head on a rock."

"Maybe." Amy pressed PLAY again and kept watching. "But it's a silty river, this part of it at least. I don't see any rocks."

"You're saying something other than a rock? Like a tree stump?"

"I never heard of anyone dying from a tree stump."

"What then?" It took Fanny several seconds to figure out the implication. Then her head jolted and went under the bubbles. She reemerged, sputtering and splashing.

"Mom, are you all right?"

"I was right. I was right," Fanny gasped between wet coughs. "It was murder. Murder and a vision. This is going to be a *TrippyGirl* gold mine."

Amy wagged her head, half yes, half no. "Only if I'm right and we solve it."

"Do you think her ghost came to me seeking revenge for her murder? No, that's right. She wasn't dead yet. Her pre-ghost."

"What's a pre-ghost?"

Fanny ignored the question. "So who do you think killed her? And why?"

"That's the hard part. Jorge O'Bannion's the only one who knew Lola, and he was at the estancia from the time she rode off until we got into the chopper."

"Do you want me to go into another trance?"

Fanny volunteered. "No problem, but I'll need more maté."

"Mother, it wasn't a vision."

"Then what was it?"

"I don't know. But I know we don't have enough information." She joined her mother in the bathroom, wiped the steam off the mirror and her glasses, checked her makeup, refreshed her lipstick, ran a brush through her hair and pulled it back into a loose chignon, the way most men seemed to like it.

"What's up? You got a hot date?"

"None of your business," said Amy. "I'll be back in half an hour, tops."

"Sounds like one of your dates."

When Amy walked into the lounge, she found several guests still up, sitting at the bar. She sat down on a far stool and caught the bartender's eye. "Campari y soda, por favor." It would help take the edge off what had been a long, edgy day.

"I apologize about the sheep," said Nicolas to someone else. He was at the other end of the bar, between Alicia and Gabriela. Amy waited for her Campari and listened in. "I thought it would be more pleasant. After all, they need to be sheared. For their health." He took a long draft from his bottle of beer. "Don't they?"

"You're the naturalist," said Alicia. She'd been the one most upset. The group had come to the demonstration at the end of the day's shearing, when the gauchos were tired and had had a few cervezas before picking up the shears again. There had been no real injuries to the sheep, just some cuts and scrapes and the kind of screaming lambs that a Jodie Foster character had once dreamed about.

"Naturalists don't need to know about sheep," Nicolas said, defending himself. "That's animal husbandry, I think you call it."

Gabriela nodded in sympathy. "You can't expect a boy from Buenos Aires to know. Nicolas has done a very good job, considering he was a replacement."

"I'm not from Buenos Aires." His tone had turned guarded.

"No?" Gabriela sipped her red wine and considered. "Your accent is *porteño*. And that beer you asked for, it's Quilmes. Most Chileans drink something local. Escudo."

"Escudo tastes like piss." Nicolas covered his mouth, coughed out a giggle. "Pardon my language. About my accent . . . I went to school with Argentineans. People say I sound like them."

"That must be it," Gabriela said. She didn't care to argue the point.

When Amy's Campari arrived, she took it with her to the corner of the lounge, by a sheepskin-covered love seat. Nestled behind the love seat was the Wi-Fi router. Within a minute, she had settled in and dialed her Skype call. It connected. "Is it two hours later there or earlier? I always forget."

"It's earlier," said Marcus, smiling up at her. "Dinnertime." He was in a familiar-looking kitchen, with a napkin tucked into the neck of his shirt. It was a habit she always found endearing.

"You prefer Mom's half of the house to mine?"

"She has plants that need watering, and her leftovers are better." He removed his napkin and made kissy lips. "Mwa, mwa. Good to see your beautiful face. What's up?"

"Why does something always have to be up? Maybe

I just called . . ." The screen froze for half a second, then unfroze. "The Wi-Fi's sketchy, so I won't waste time arguing."

"How sweet." He lowered his voice conspiratori- ally. "So, what's up? A murder?"

"Why do I always have to have a murder?" The screen froze another half second. "I think so, yes." She scooted over to the far end of the love seat and changed the phone's angle. Then she concisely, quietly reviewed the events of the past two days, in- cluding Gabriela's unexplained jaunt in the Land Cruiser. The screen froze twice more but recovered both times.

Marcus listened attentively. At the end, he was press- ing his temples together, as if massaging a headache. "So Fanny's a psychic? I don't get it."

"No one gets it," said Amy. "It's un-gettable. But if we solve the murder, then we'll probably also solve that."

"How will solving the murder explain away her vi- sion?"

"We won't know until we solve the murder. And for that, we need a suspect."

"What do the police say?"

Amy rolled her eyes. That was the great thing about video chats, the nonverbal thing. "Her body's been airlifted to Buenos Aires. It's going to be la- beled an accident, without anyone checking the scene or investigating."

"Humph. Next time I want to kill someone, re- mind me to do it in Chile."

"It's not their fault," said Amy. "She was found alone in a remote area. If her family wants to make waves, I'm sure the police will do more."

"Meanwhile, my two TrippyGirls are in the thick of it." The camera caught Marcus's impish grin. "Like old times."

Another roll of the eyes. "Don't even mention Trippy. I get apoplectic just thinking what Mom is going to do with this."

"Is she going to blog about the vision?"

"Of course she is. I don't think I can stop her."

"Well, you should try. At least until you know what's going on." There was something about his suddenly serious expression and his lack of eye contact.

"Why do you say that?" Amy asked.

"I'm just thinking about your fans. And the book deal. If your publisher sees Fanny making up some supernatural stuff, they may have second thoughts."

"Have you been talking to Sabrina?"

Marcus paused a beat too long. "No. I'm just saying that Fanny's exaggerations can go too far, especially now that you have real journalists hanging around. I wish I was there."

"I wish someone was here. In other countries I had the local police. In New York there was Lieutenant Rawlings. I never thought I'd say it, but he was actually better than nothing. And you, of course." She was suddenly feeling a little vulnerable. Taking a moment, she removed her glasses and cleaned them with one of the lens wipes she always carried in every pocket.

"How can I help?" Marcus asked. "There must be something."

Amy put her glasses back on, then took a sip of Campari. "I don't know what more I can do, to be honest. The tour moves on tomorrow. Plus I'm facing a language barrier. Plus the Wi-Fi is terrible. I

don't know how detectives found out anything before the Internet."

"You want me to check on some things." A statement, not a question. It was at times like this, Amy realized, that they were most in sync with each other.
"Gabriela Garcia? The woman who lied?"

"If you can find out about her . . . See what the
connection is between her and Lola. Also their late
husbands."

Marcus nodded.

"Thanks." Amy put her hand to her heart. "E-mail
me whatever you get. No attachments. That'll just
gum things up."

"Oops. I sent you an e-mail with six attachments."

"I got it, but I couldn't open it. Something about
the apartment search?"

"A few photos, nothing crucial. We'll talk about it
later."

"Good." Amy cracked a smile. It was good to think
about something else, even for a moment. "You've
been looking? In Manhattan, I hope. I can't wait to
see. I can't wait to get home and for us to move in together."

"I found some great possibilities," Marcus assured
her. "Meanwhile, I'll work on Gabriela and Lola . . .
try to find a motive."

"I'll check my e-mail when I can, but I don't want
to spend hundreds on roaming charges. There's a
limit to my civic nature."

"There's no limit at all to your nature," said Marcus, "whatever that means. Anyone else on your hit
list?"

"My hit list?" Amy glanced over at the lounge bar.

Nicolas was alone now, taking the last swig from his bottle of Quilmes. "Yes, a nature guide named Nicolas. I think he lied about being from Chile."

"Why would he do that? Where's he from? Is this important?"

"All good questions. Damn, I don't even know his last name. I'll call you back in five." The screen froze again, just as Amy was about to blurt out, "I love you," and she felt both cheated and a little relieved at having lost the moment to a glitch. Before she could reconsider, she instinctively pressed the red phone icon and ended the call. Then she crossed over to the bar.

"Ms. Abel, good evening." Nicolas abandoned his bottle to the bartender. He had turned over one of the cocktail menus and was now sketching on the blank reverse. Amy had seen him doing this fairly frequently in his off-hours, the ex-art student indulging in his old passion. He put down his pen. "Have you also come to complain about the sheep?"

"Tomorrow will be easier," she promised. "The Patagonian Express will be on its way, one more night. Then Puerto Natales and the end."

"The end," he echoed. "Except that everyone is complaining about missing the monastery at Monte Carmelo. I think they only want to go because now we can't."

Amy replied with a thin, sympathetic grin. "Dealing with us must be tough. We expect so much. Sometimes we treat you like servants instead of people just doing their jobs."

Nicolas thin-grinned her back. "Beware. You are talking like a socialist."

"No, just a fellow human being. For example . . ." She pretended to think. "Names. You obviously knew the name of everyone as soon as we met. And yet Todd Drucker forgets your name half the time. Even I don't know your last name. What is it?"

"It's not important."

"Weren't you the one who criticized the rich tourists who have no idea about your lives? How do you expect us to know your lives if you won't even share your name?"

"It could be anything. What difference? Why do you want to know my name?"

"I want to get to know you. As a person."

"As a person?" The guide seemed flattered but wary. He had already shared bits of his story on that magical night under the stars: of his schooling at the conservatory, his love of art. But now . . . "I must be honest with you, Ms. Abel. I have a girlfriend."

Amy kept her composure. She had actually seen this coming. "In Santiago? Where you live?"

"Yes, in Santiago. Not that I find you unbeautiful."

"Don't worry, Nicolas. I have a boyfriend of my own. I just think you're an interesting person." Her eyes fell on the reversed menu. "And an excellent artist. Someday I'll see your work in a gallery or a museum, and I won't even know it's you. May I look?"

Nicolas pushed the paper across the bar. It was a simple sketch, much different from his whimsical man in the moon. Done in ballpoint on white, it was the portrait, shoulders and up, of an older, heavyset man. The style was mostly angles, even the round-ness of the head, nearly bald, was done in sharp little angles. The man's features were thick, a bulbous nose and heavy lids above squinty, ratlike eyes. A scowling, angry face, almost cartoonish in its intensity. An average comic book villain. And yet somehow recognizable. Where had she seen this face before?

"Is this someone famous?" she had to ask.

"Famous? No. It's just imagination." Nicolas gently pulled the menu back across the bar. "If you want, I can draw you. May I?" He pointed to a second cocktail menu lying by his pen.

Amy took one last glimpse of the nightmarish face. "I'm not sure I want to see how you see me."

The corners of Nicolas's mouth turned up, just the corners. "This is not how I see you."

"Good. But I'm still going to pass."

"Are you sure? I'm a good artist."

"You're very good. But years from now, when I see your work in a museum, I won't know it's you, will I? Nicolas what?" She made the question sound casual.

"True." He studied her face closely as he considered the request. "Blanco," he replied.

"Nicolas Blanco." She would call Marcus. She knew that Blanco meant *white*, and that it was a common enough surname. It could be real. But she couldn't help thinking of the English word *blank*, that the name he'd given her was a blank and that Marcus would have no luck finding anything at all.

When she got back to the room, Fanny was already in bed and snoring. Amy knew there would be no point in waking her. Fanny would deny snoring, then would fall back asleep, and it would be even worse. On most nights, she tried to get to bed before her mother, hoping that she could nod off first. More often than not it worked. But tonight? The idea of lying there, trying to relax, trying not to listen as the noisy breaths grew promisingly softer or annoyingly louder, or halted for a blessed minute, only to start up again . . . She wasn't in the mood.

Amy used the bathroom, took a white bathrobe off the hook, then found her bottle of sleeping pills. These she reserved for intense jet lag or similar emergencies, and she washed one down with half a glass of water. The little balcony under the dormer on her side of the room would give her a pleasant place to sit while the medication took effect. She carried the smallest chair in the room, a tiny armchair, outside, wrapped herself in the pashmina shawl she'd bought in Buenos Aires, and settled in under the sliver of a new moon.

With the door open, she could still hear Fanny's performance. She tried to think of it as waves crashing on an unseen shore. The sound of waves had always been very soothing. Why should waves be soothing and her mother be annoying? She didn't know. Maybe another sleeping pill. She had just decided to get up and indulge in a second dose when a movement caught her eye below her on the gravel drive.

It was Nicolas. Nicolas Blanco? His light blue jacket was unmistakable, much too city-like in tone and prone to showing dirt. Amy watched from her perch, straining to get a better view, as the young guide treaded lightly over the gravel, heading past the white stables to the white garage. The sound of an engine momentarily drowned out Fanny's snoring. A good thirty seconds later, when no one had emerged from the estancia to question the sound, one of the Land Cruisers poked its hood out, no headlights, and began to make its way around the back side of the garage and onto the dirt road.

Amy continued to watch, even as the vehicle grew smaller in the distance. Following Nicolas would have been stupid, she told herself. He would be long gone, and she would have a sedative coursing through her system. Not that the pill was doing much good. Behind her, in the room, Fanny's decibel level was going into overdrive. Maybe she just needed another sleeping pill. Maybe that would do the trick.

CHAPTER 21

If she could have chosen a night in which to drug herself into oblivion, it probably wouldn't have been this one, despite her mother's provocation. When Amy woke the following day, she had missed both the early breakfast and the latest accident to befall the New Patagonian Express.

At some point during the night, the precarious chimney of the Torre Vista whistle-stop had collapsed. When the engineer and his crew had arrived at the station shortly after dawn to provision the train for its next journey, they found that a few tons of stone had fallen across the first carriage, Jorge O'Bannion's pride and joy, his personal sleeping car.

Amy was in the lounge, still swatting away the cobwebs with coffee and a Danish, as Todd Drucker breathlessly filled her in. "They're guessing it happened around three a.m., when the winds picked up. Luckily, it didn't hit the engine. Imagine having to get a new engine all the way out here. We'd be stuck for days." They were across from each other in the leather armchairs, facing the picture window framing the Torre del Paine peaks.

"Are they sure it was an accident?" Amy regretted the question almost before it left her lips.

"Interesting." Todd topped off her coffee with the last drops from the carafe. "A few days ago I would have ridiculed that. Over-the-top TrippyGirl creating chaos out of a coincidence. But I have to hand it to you, Trippy. We did find a body. I should keep an open mind."

"No, you shouldn't keep an open mind. Forget I said anything."

"You suspect someone of destroying O'Bannion's carriage? Who would want to do that?"

"No one," she emphasized. "It's a ridiculous idea."

The travel writer's mouth curled, and his eyebrows pulled together. "I get it. Protecting your secrets. Is that partly because I'm a suspect? Because I don't mind being a suspect." He leaned across. "As long as you get all your facts straight. When it comes to my reputation, please note, I can be litigious."

Amy spent a few seconds trying to come up with a snappy comeback. But it didn't matter. One of the vehicles had just pulled up and was letting off its passengers. Edgar and Fanny got out of the two back doors and hurried up the steps.

"We're going to the monastery," Fanny announced. "It's back on."

"I'll go tell the others," Edgar said and marched his way through the lounge.

"You mean today?" The first thing that came to Amy's mind was the donkey ride part and how it would aggravate her cobwebs.

"As soon as we can pull everyone together." Fanny

and Edgar had been at the whistle-stop, getting a firsthand look at the damage. Amy was sure there were pictures and probably video.

"What about the train?" Todd asked.

Fanny plopped herself down on the arm of Amy's chair. "Well, Jorge's beside himself, poor man. His car may take months to repair. But once they clear it from the track and get rid of the rocks, we'll be on our way. Tomorrow morning, if all goes well. He can rough it in another car."

"Does it look like an accident?" asked Todd.

Fanny looked at her daughter, then at Todd, then back again. "They're calling it an accident," she said carefully. "Is there something else I should know?"

"No," Amy told her with excess conviction. "We should all get ready for the trip."

Jorge O'Bannion returned a few minutes later, doing his best to put a positive spin on exactly the same news. The tour would be extended one more day, nine days of wonderful wonder instead of eight. All the connecting flights out of the tiny airport of Puerto Natales would be adjusted free of charge. He was dealing with them right now and would sit down with everyone individually and work out the details. Meanwhile, his honored guests would have the unique pleasure of seeing the mosaics of Monte Carmelo, the legendary Carmelite monastery.

Amy thought of her own connections. One day less in Valparaiso before their flight to New York. Yes, that would work out fine.

The estancia became the hub to a sudden flurry of activity. The staff prepared box lunches. The guests put on their most suitable clothes and filled their souvenir canteens. Jorge made an impassioned call to his cousin the abbot on the one landline connecting Monte Carmelo to the rest of civilization. The monastery's fleet of donkeys would be waiting for them halfway up the mountain.

Jorge O'Bannion talked as he drove one of the Land Cruisers up the winding hill, turning back to face his audience more than Amy would have liked. "There are monasteries of service who run hospitals and do good deeds. But Monte Carmelo is one of contemplation. For much of the day the brothers don't speak. They pray, sing hymns, study the scriptures, and tend the vegetables and other things they need to live."

"Got it," said Fanny. "And what's the point?" She was beside him, in the front passenger seat. Amy and Alicia shared the back, keeping their eyes on the road even when their driver wasn't.

"The point?" Jorge seemed confused. "Prayer and contemplation are good for the world. The church has always known this. Here in South America there are few such orders. But God still calls men to be hermits, to separate themselves and pray for all His children."

"And no one ever visits them?" asked Amy.

Fanny snorted. "Yes. Because they don't talk."

"Pay no attention to my mother. We're honored to be part of this."

"My mother's sister's son was very gracious." Jorge puffed his chest with pride. "The first time in fifty years that an outsider is allowed past the courtyard. And the first time ever for a woman."

All six of the women had worn skirts or dresses. Amy's choice was a black skirt and her all-purpose Liz Claiborne top with the high neckline. Her new pashmina shawl would cover her shoulders and also her head, if that was required.

As promised, the donkey ride began halfway up, at

the twenty-foot-tall gates and the stone wall that surrounded the monks' property, separating it from the rest of the mountain. Nicolas volunteered to help out Fanny, taking the steep path on foot and leading her stubborn donkey by the reins.

Amy's skirt was slightly too long and too tight for any comfortable donkey ride, but she hitched it up a little and made it work. It was actually a nice introduction, she felt, leaving behind all their twenty-first-century machines and approaching the stone fortress just as other pilgrims—all men—must have done for the past hundred years. Slow paced and silent, except for the hooves and the wind. Her only cheat was the camera phone, which Fanny had insisted she bring, hidden in one of her skirt pockets.

It came into view piecemeal above the trees, a stone turret here, a stone and slate cupola there. It reminded Amy of the Cloisters in Manhattan, a storybook monastery, but this one flanked by vegetable gardens and small wooden outbuildings. Jorge's cousin met them in front of the vaulted entryway.

The cousins were similar in age and appearance, although—and this might just have been Amy's imagination—the father abbot didn't look quite as stooped by the cares of the world. He didn't particularly seem to welcome the presence of women, but he didn't object. The Furies all had their heads covered, but not the North Americans. Amy decided she would remain uncovered until told differently.

"Bienvenidos, mis hermanos en Cristo." A welcome to brothers, not to sisters. The man's voice was soft, barely audible, befitting someone who didn't get a lot of vocal exercise. Jorge did the translation. The abbot was humbly proud of his island of devotion to Our Lady of Mount Carmel, the patron saint of Chile. His brothers currently included twenty-two monks, he said, men who came from all backgrounds, giving up their old identities to pray and study and work. By granting his guests a glimpse into their world, he hoped he might inspire them to lead more contemplative lives of their own. Then he motioned them through the carved oak doors.

In its basics, the tour was like a hundred other castle or monastery tours Amy had been on, except that this was no museum. The medieval-looking kitchen looked more deadly than most, with mallets and cleavers and foot-long knives, but it was a working kitchen. The sleeping cells were the brothers' real living spaces. The chapel and cloister were filled with real monks, performing their devotions and paying little heed to their visitors from the future. The father abbot saved the best for last, the crypt below the cloister, illuminated only by candlelight, where a century's worth of brotherly graves were covered over with bright mosaics, laid out in playful depictions of the birth of Jesus and his youth. A haloed baby. A child on his mother's knee. Playing with sheep. Learning carpentry from Joseph. It was the cheeriest crypt Amy had ever seen.

After the tour, the father abbot, in a generous gesture, gave them free rein. In twenty minutes, the bells would ring and the brothers would gather for their afternoon prayers in the chapel. Until then, the guests were free to roam the grounds and do their own meditations. His only request was that they didn't disturb the monks or talk to them.

The Furies, including Gabriela, headed for the vegetable garden. Edgar and Todd brought out their cameras, began with the mosaics, and worked their way up, discussing lighting and setups and possible captions. Nicolas said he was fascinated by the medieval kitchen.

Amy left her mother with Alicia, the two of them still marveling over the crypt mosaics, and wandered back up to the chapel. She expected it to be empty. The monks would return soon enough, and her fellow travelers, even the Furies, didn't seem the type given to acts of meditation. But Jorge O'Bannion was there in a side pew, on his knees. Amy stood in the back, not wanting to disturb him. He must have sensed her presence, because he turned almost as soon as she walked in. The Chilean gentleman leaned on the pew in front and pushed himself to his feet, a little shamefaced, as if he'd been caught doing something ridiculous.

"Prayer is good," he whispered, then made a space in his pew and motioned for her to join him.

They sat down, side by side, both of them staring at the white and gold of the altar. "It never hurts to pray. I think that's a proven fact."

"It can only help," he agreed. "The explosion, Lola's death, this disaster with the chimney . . . as if heaven itself is against me."

It was sad to see this naturally optimistic man looking so beaten down. "I hope you'll continue with the Patagonian Express," she said. "There's a real market for it."

"That's kind of you to say. And yes, I will continue. We have reservations for March and April, still a soft opening. When the bad weather comes, we'll shut down, like everyone, and make improvements. Then in the spring, with all the good publicity from my friends . . ." He shot her a sly smile. "We will go on, full steam ahead. That is the phrase, yes?"

"Full steam. It sounds right."

"We have the money until then, thanks to my dear old friend."

Amy meditated on the strangeness of the past week, her mind settling on last night, with the sight of Nicolas driving off in the direction of the train station. "Do you know anyone who would want to destroy your business?"

O'Bannion considered this, perhaps not for the first time. "I'm not the kind to have enemies, but . . . the Pisano family, her niece and nephew in Buenos Aires, they were against me from the start. To my face they called me a gigolo. It was the inheritance from their father that she was spending. But the money was already invested, so they would be stupid to want to hurt our chances."

"If they knew, yes." Amy's shoulders straightened. Perhaps the chapel was acting as an inspiration. She voiced her new theory, right or wrong, just as it came into her head. "The money was invested at the last minute, right before Lola died."

"Some of it was, yes. The day before. Your mother was our witness. I suppose the timing for me was lucky, if losing a beloved friend can ever be lucky."

"Forgive me for saying this." She stopped herself, then tried to phrase it as gently as possible. "If the Pisanos didn't know she had already signed the papers . . . if they thought she would continue to give you money time after time, good after bad, they would want to stop that. They would want to do things to discourage Lola, like cause accidents. If that didn't work, they might even want their aunt dead."

"Dead?" O'Bannion faced her, and his lower lip quivered. "Her death was an accident. Are you saying it wasn't?"

"I'm sorry, Jorge. I'm just thinking out loud. Did

you ever meet Lola's niece and nephew? Could her nephew be someone like Nicolas?"

"Nicolas? The useless guide?" O'Bannion's soft laugh echoed up to the rafters. "Yes, I have met the niece and nephew. Many times. And no, neither one of them is Nicolas."

Amy's face turned a bright red. But she went on, with a revised version of her theory. "I apologize if it sounds stupid. But his job became available as a result of the explosion. That's how Nicolas came to you. And he's from Buenos Aires, even though he says he's Chilean. And last night he borrowed a car and drove off right before the chimney collapsed."

"The chimney? Do you think that was an unnatural act? Like sabotage?"

"I'm just saying his behavior is suspicious."

O'Bannion considered this. "His accent does sound *porteño*," he agreed. "And it was lucky to find him so nearby and free. But the rest makes no sense. How, for example, could he kill Lola? And why would he destroy my poor carriage? It serves no purpose."

"You're right." Amy pushed herself up from the pew and exhaled. "Dumb idea."

O'Bannion joined her as they sidled out into the chapel's side aisle. He linked his arm through hers. "Not dumb. I like that you take my problems seriously. Just like TrippyGirl, yes? I've been reading how you do things. Fascinating. In India and Siberia when you ask questions and follow people."

"Not so much in Siberia."

"I am honored that you want to help."

As they approached a stone alcove, O'Bannion unlinked his arm. Reaching into the breast pocket of his wool blazer, he pulled out a plain gold band, then focused on the statue filling the alcove. To Amy's eye, it seemed a typical porcelain depiction of the Virgin Mary, on a cloud and holding the baby Jesus on display for all to see, although it varied in one important aspect. The entire statue was festooned with trinkets. *Trinkets* might not be the right word. *Offerings?* Among other things, there were gold coins, paper money, miniature framed photos, amulets, and rings. Hundreds of them. Jesus and Mary held as many as they could, clasping them in every crevice of their porcelain anatomy. The remaining offerings spilled over into the rest of the alcove.

Jorge O'Bannion moved a dusty pocket watch over a few inches to make room. Then he placed the ring in the empty space, took a deep breath, and made the sign of the cross. Amy didn't ask him to explain, but he did. "Our Lady of Monte Carmelo. My cousin told me, you put an offering here, something that represents the past, something you want to free yourself from. The Virgin will intercede with Jesus to help change your life."

"That was your wedding ring?"

"My late wife's ring. I had intended for Lola to wear it as my bride. That's why I came to the chapel now, to ask God to help me be at peace."

"Oh, I interrupted a private moment. I'm so sorry."

"Not at all. I was glad for the company."

Amy couldn't help thinking of her own past. What would she be willing to place in Our Lady's alcove? Would it be a tiny mirror like this one, representing vanity? A gold coin for greed? The photo of a loved one, symbolizing the rejection of physical love? "Before a brother takes his vows, it is a ritual for him to place a token here with the Virgin."

Every token had a story, Amy mused. She tried to

imagine what the stories might be. This huge gold ring in the Virgin's outstretched hand, for example. Obviously expensive, if somewhat tacky. It was the head of a roaring lion with red eyes. Garnets or tiny rubies. She couldn't tell in this light. As Amy leaned in for a closer look, her heart grew cold. There was something so familiar about the ring. Familiar and evil. Why was she thinking evil?

"Excuse me, Jorge." Amy stepped a few feet away to where the dappled sunlight was streaming through an arched stained-glass window. Taking her phone from her skirt pocket, she scrolled to her camera icon and tapped the screen a few times. On their first day in Buenos Aires, what did they do? In what order? Was it before the opera house? Was it after the Evita balcony? It was during their visit to La Boca; that much she remembered. Yes, here it was. The angry mural of the "disappeared ones."

She had taken six photos: of the menacing blue soldiers, the desperate citizens soon to be among the disappeared, the dungeons, the chaos, and in the far left of the mural, the orange general with his wet blob of a tongue and the gold, roaring lion on one of his fat fingers. It was the same ring. And the face? *Oh, my God!* It was the same face she'd seen last night on the back of the cocktail menu: the bulbous nose, the heavy lids, done in the same cartoonish style. The anonymous artist of La Boca wasn't anonymous anymore, not to Amy.

She turned from her phone back to O'Bannion, ignoring his disapproving stare. "How did you find Nicolas? He says he originally applied for the job, but you gave it to Pablo."

"That's true. Our engineer is Nicolas's uncle. But

Pablo was more qualified. Are you unhappy with Nicolas?"

"The engineer and Nicolas are related? The engineer who was injured?"

"Not so badly injured." O'Bannion looked distressed. "Pablo will be on our next tour, my dear friend. This was an emergency."

"Nicolas really wanted this job, didn't he?"

"He was very eager, yes. He called himself a nature expert. But that didn't seem to be the case."

The monastery bell began to ring, a soft, resonant dong that gained momentum and volume as the rope in the bell tower was pulled.

"The brothers will be here for afternoon prayers," said O'Bannion. "We should return to the gate. I promised my cousin."

"I . . ." Amy didn't know what to do. Her mind was still processing. "I will join you in a minute." And she rushed from the chapel out into the cloistered courtyard. O'Bannion came out seconds later, looking for her, but by then she was half hidden behind one of the chapel's open doors.

The bell continued to toll as O'Bannion walked away, across the grassy center of the cloister. Monks in their brown robes were emerging from every corner of the complex and making a slow processional toward the chapel. Their heads were bowed and their hoods were down, giving Amy a chance to see a few faces. Some she dismissed instantly. Too young or too old. Too tall or too thin. The abbot himself, who was certainly not the man she was looking for. Would she even be able to recognize him? Only after the fact did she think about counting the brothers. According to the abbot, there would be twenty-two.

But was that twenty-two including the abbot or not? If they were all present, that would be easy. The man would be one of them. And he would be safe. The last brother entered the chapel just as the bell stopped tolling.

From behind the door, Amy watched Fanny and Alicia come up the basement steps and follow O'Bannion across an edge of the cloister, toward the main courtyard. The three Furies met them halfway, crossing from another direction. When the cloister was once again empty, Amy eased out from behind her door. A chorus of male voices was starting to sing a dirgelike chant in unison and in Latin.

Amy assumed from the chapel's layout that the abbot and the monks would be facing the altar. That gave her the confidence she needed to poke her head around the edge and begin to count their heads. They were indeed all facing the altar, but she still counted fast. Then she counted again. Twenty-one, including the abbot, all of them unaware or unconcerned that one of their own was missing. She counted a third time with the same result.

Where the hell could he be? she wondered. He could be anywhere in the complex, a man who had long ago repented of his past, unaware that it had just caught up with him. Of course, Nicolas might not be here for revenge at all. He might just want to talk to the man. Or maybe the general wasn't here. Maybe there were a lot of golden lion rings with red eyes and this was just a coincidence. Or maybe . . . Oh, who was she kidding!

Where the hell could they be? Would they be in the crypt, among the mosaics, out of earshot of everyone? Or in the kitchen, with all its medieval-cooking utensils? There were dozens of hermit cells, some occupied, some not. A brotherhood of unsuspecting monks might not find him for hours or days. *Think, Amy. Think. You can't look everywhere. Pick some place. Do something. Don't just stand here, doing nothing.*

But she did nothing. What could she do? Even if she found him in time, even if she succeeded in warning him . . . was it her responsibility to put her life on the line? For a man who had probably done unconscionable things? Who was she to stand in the way of . . . whatever? Justice? She really didn't want to think about it. Better just to join the others and act surprised.

Then again, there was Fanny. How could she tell Fanny that she had known the truth as it was happening but had decided to ignore it? Whatever this man was, he was a human being, right? What was the line of poetry her father had always quoted? "Do not ask for whom the bell tolls." Something like that.

Do not ask for whom the bell tolls.

Amy gasped. *Do not ask. . . .* The answer had been right there. Why hadn't she thought of it? The twenty-second man. The one who would always come into the chapel last and hardly be noticed. The one who didn't come in today.

The bell ringer.

CHAPTER 22

The door to the bell tower was closed, the first closed door Amy had encountered. But the monastery prided itself on having no locks, and she was able to push open the heavy door to find a square empty space with a dirt floor. The four stone walls enclosed a hollow wooden scaffold that supported a staircase. The stairs circled the interior walls, climbing the height of the tower to a single huge bell suspended from a set of crossbeams at the top. She stood in the middle of the square and listened. There was something moving up there, a scuffling sound, something barely audible above her own gasps for breath and the beating of her heart.

Without thinking, on adrenaline alone, she crossed to the steps and began to climb, one foot in front of the other, circling the space as she went. The scuffling above grew louder. But the sight still caught her by surprise—a landing about halfway up the tower, made larger by an alcove in the wall and a pair of vertical arrow-slit windows. Amy stumbled up to the landing, and the two men froze, much more shocked to see her than she was to see them.

He was older than his cartoon self, sturdily built but thinner, in a brown robe instead of an army uniform. But he was still just as frightening, his face a sweating, straining, angry mass of flesh. There was a streak of blood on his cheek, and a red gash in the left sleeve of his robe. His strong hands were even more frightening than the rest of him, perhaps because they were encircling Nicolas's neck, pressing him down into the floorboards, in the process of squeezing the life out of the young guide.

Nicolas stared into Amy's eyes, his own eyes bulging with fear and desperation. "Help," he groaned between tightened lips. "Help me."

Amy took a second to survey the scene, scouring the landing for the weapon. It was there on the stone of the alcove, one of the medieval-looking knives from the kitchen, blood dripping from its blade.

"General," she said to the straining mass of flesh. "Stop. This isn't you. Not anymore." The second after she said it, she realized he probably didn't speak English. *"General, por favor. No."*

It didn't take much to make the ex-general stop. Just the sight of the intruder was enough to break the spell. He had been on his knees, straddling the smaller man. Now he rolled to one side with a loud pained grunt. His right hand went to the gash in his sleeve, trying to staunch the flow of blood.

"He attacked me." Nicolas coughed and rolled to the other side. "For no reason." He pointed to the knife. "The man is crazy."

Amy paused and nodded. She didn't mean to nod. She was still catching her breath. "Was it your father,

Nicolas? If that's your name. Was it your father or your mother that he killed?"

Nicolas nodded in return, his hands on his own throat now, trying to rub the air back in. "My father and my mother. They were professors. That was their crime." The fear in his eyes had changed to anger. "I was a baby, but I remember. Being ripped from my mother's arms."

"I killed no one," said the bleeding monk. His accent made him barely understandable. But the English was there, and his comprehension. "I did many things. I detained people. I followed the lists made by other generals. Many bad things I ignored."

"You were responsible," Nicolas growled.

"No. There was a court trial. Argentina said I was innocent. By the law," he added, as if he knew the difference and knew that the difference didn't matter.

The blood was seeping through his fingers. Amy considered using her pashmina shawl to help. The monk saw her about to take it from her shoulders and objected with a grunt. Was it because the shawl was too nice, she wondered, or because it would leave her shoulders uncovered? The monk looked at the hem of his own robe, then at the bloody knife on the stone.

"Nicolas," Amy said with an authority that surprised her. "Cut off part of his robe. We need to apply pressure."

The guide had a decision to make, and Amy knew that once he made it, she could trust him. A similar thought was probably going through the minds of the two men. And then Nicolas did it. He grabbed a section of the brown wool hem, pierced it with the knife's blade, and sawed until he had carved out a piece the size of a dish towel. He handed it to Amy and stepped back as she pressed it to the monk's upper arm.

"What was his name?" she asked Nicolas.

"*Is* his name. He remains General Juan Cortavos, butcher of La Boca."

"I deserve all your curses," mumbled the monk. He settled back against the stone, half sitting up, trying to regain his strength. Amy sat beside him and kept the pressure on. "For twenty years, every day I ask God to forgive me. To use me in His service. *Perdoname, te lo suplico.*"

The younger man ignored his plea for forgiveness. "How did you know?" he asked Amy. "Who told you?"

'You did," said Amy. "Your mural in Buenos Aires."

"You saw my mural?" Beneath his anger there was a glimmer of pride. "I worked for weeks. All alone in the middle of the night. I used the most expensive acrylics, so it would last forever."

"It's quite powerful," Amy admitted. "The size of it, the anger. I didn't connect it to your other drawings, not until you drew the general again. Then today, when I saw his gold ring in the chapel . . ."

"He still has the ring?" Nicolas asked. "I want it."

"The Virgin of Monte Carmelo has the ring." The general's wound gurgled red around Amy's hand. "An offering for my sins."

Amy tried to keep Nicolas focused and away from his victim. "All your life you wanted revenge. After his trial, the general must have disappeared. But you tracked him down—to the one place where you couldn't just go and kill him. It must have been maddening that he was so cut off from the world. But then you heard the gates of Monte Carmelo would open for one day. You and the train engineer. You were responsible for the accidents."

Nicolas shrugged. "The engineer was our neighbor in La Boca. He took me from the empty house and raised me by himself. A saint who called me his nephew. It was just luck, or maybe the hand of God, that he had worked as an engineer and could get hired if he made his money demands small. I was an art student, and I was not so lucky. Pablo was hired."

"The engineer caused the first delay in Buenos Aires?"

"That was an experiment, to see if the explosion would work. In Patagonia, it worked perfectly. We didn't want to hurt Pablo, just do enough to send him to the hospital in the middle of the wilds, where no one could take his place but me. "

"And the chimney? That was you?"

Nicolas made a face and shrugged again. "Senor O'Bannion was going to cancel the visit. After all we had gone through to get here. I had to make the train stay. A crowbar from the garage was all I needed. . . ." He broke off abruptly, his gaze going out to the hollow square in the middle of the staircase. Amy was about to say something when he raised his hand and stopped her.

There were people below, on the dirt floor, half the height of the tower down from them, speaking in hushed whispers. Two people at least, from the sound of it. "Amy? Nicolas?" None of the intruders wanted to raise their voices in the reverent hush of the monastery, not even Fanny. "Amy, sweetie. It's time to go."

The wounded monk, the guide, and the tourist waited in silence until the voices below them exited the bell tower and continued their search elsewhere.

"We have to go," Amy whispered. "This isn't easy for you, I know."

"He killed my mother and my father."

The old general sat himself a little straighter. "I am responsible, yes, God help me. So many were taken. This is horrible to say, but I do not remember your parents."

Nicolas took a step closer, almost reaching their feet. The knife that he'd used to cut the robe was still in his hand. *"No te acuerdas?"*

"Lo siento, pero no."

The conversation had switched into Spanish. Amy had no choice but to listen for a few recognizable words and watch their body language. What if the talk turned angry again? What would she do? Would she try to protect the general? Could she? And then what? Would Nicolas willingly turn himself in? Even though she wasn't a religious person, Amy couldn't help but say a muted prayer.

The monk who had been the general spoke softly. The orphaned boy didn't want to listen, but he did. Then it was his turn to say impassioned things while the man he had dreamed about all his life listened. For Amy, the exchange seemed to go on forever—while she sat by and continued to apply pressure. She had stopped the flow of blood, at least for the time being.

Fanny and Alicia returned to the main courtyard. Before anyone could blame her for anything, Fanny threw up her hands in frustration. It was one of her most effective tactics, to seem more annoyed than anyone else.

"We looked everywhere. This is not like my daughter to lose track of time." She glared at Jorge O'Bannion. "It must be your employee's fault."

The courtyard was filled with the seven tourists, showing various levels of concern; their leader, O'Bannion; his patient cousin, the abbot; and the ten impatient donkeys, braying and defecating and waiting to take their heavy loads back down the mountain. It had been no more than fifteen minutes since the group had realized that Amy and Nicolas were not showing up.

"What do we do now?" asked Alicia.

Fanny bristled. "Well, I'm certainly not leaving without my daughter."

"I would never ask you to," said O'Bannion. "But if they're not here, then they must have left on foot. The abbot is anxious to return his monastery to its normal life."

"So you are asking me to leave without my daughter."

"No, no. But if they are not here . . ."

"What if they fell down a well?" she asked. "What then? Or fell off a wall? Or if Nicolas decided to become a monk, and she's with him in one of those cells, trying to talk him out of it?" Fanny was just getting warmed up. "Or if the monks were so starved for female companionship that Nicolas sold my Amy into white slavery? No offense, but it's a possibility. Or if they both got sold into white slavery? Or if they . . . Oh, there you are, dear! It's about time."

Amy and Nicolas had just walked through the archway. They were smiling—fixed, artificial smiles—which only made the blood more obvious: the bloody streaks on Nicolas's neck and the dark, wet stain on Amy's skirt.

Todd Drucker was the first to speak up. "What the hell happened?"

Amy ignored his question and walked straight up

to O'Bannion and the abbot, then motioned the two men away from the crowd. Whatever Amy whispered seemed to have an immediate effect. O'Bannion's hands flew to his chest in shock, and seconds later, after the translation, his cousin had a similar reaction.

"Stay here," O'Bannion told his charges in both languages, foregoing any reassuring pleasantries. "Amy, make sure Nicolas doesn't move until we come back. Mr. Drucker. Mr. Wolowitz. Do as she tells you." And then the cousins hurried through the arch and vanished into the monastery proper. Nicolas didn't make any attempt to move.

"What the hell happened?" Todd repeated. "Is that blood yours? Is someone dead?"

"It's not mine," Amy said, holding up her hands. "It's not from Nicolas, either. We're okay."

Fanny collided into her daughter's arms. "Are you sure you're okay? I was so worried. What happened?"

"I'm fine."

Fanny stretched herself up toward her daughter's ear. Amy met her halfway. "Are you sure you're fine?" Fanny studied her face. "Was there white slavery involved? You can be honest."

"What? No. No white slavery." Amy straightened up and addressed the English speakers. "We had an accident, that's all." She tried to sound flippant, but her voice was shaky.

"An accident with blood marks around his neck?" Todd asked. "Is this a *TrippyGirl* murder? Is that it? I should have known."

"No murder," Nicolas said, the first words out of his mouth since they'd returned. "Thanks to Ms. Abel."

"Nicolas, be quiet," Amy said. "For your own sake, nothing happened."

Nicolas allowed himself a solemn half nod. He had calmed down and no longer looked like he was ready to flee.

"So you're not going to tell us?" Todd's sigh was extravagant. "Yes, Nicolas. We mustn't ruin the surprise. No one can know anything until it gets revealed on *TrippyGirl*. Never mind that we've all been worried sick."

"I thought you didn't believe in Trippy," Fanny reminded him. "According to you, Amy and I made it all up. Well, maybe that's what happened. She made it all up."

"Don't act so superior," Todd replied. "You don't know any more than I do."

"Oh, but I will," said Fanny. "I've had over thirty years of practice."

"No. I don't think I can tell anyone." Then Amy corrected herself. "I mean, it was a silly accident. Not worth talking about."

"Don't worry, Todd," said Fanny with a conspiratorial wink. "I'll get it out of her. Right, sweetie?" And she stretched up and kissed her daughter on the cheek.

CHAPTER 23

By 10:00 a.m. the next day they were back on the Patagonian Express. Jorge O'Bannion had managed to find lodgings somewhere among the eight remaining cars. The track had been cleared of debris. And the last leg of their trip was turning out to be scenic and uneventful. As always, the express moved at a snail's pace, meandering around the lakes and fjords and crossing broad rivers on Chile's ancient railway bridges.

On their last night, after repeated assurances from the engineer, the Abels decided to take their lives into their own hands and build a fire in their carriage's fireplace. Amy was glad they did. It was an amazing, almost surrealistic sensation—the earthy smell, the flames in the grate, the sparks popping in their Victorian living room, all combined with the passing late-evening scenery, the gentle rocking motion, and the long howl of the silver engine's steam whistle.

"The engineer was very accommodating," Fanny

said, then treated herself to another pinch of herbal
holly in her maté bowl.

"He should be," Amy replied. "I kept him and his
adopted son out of jail."

"A lot of that was Jorge's doing, don't you think?
He couldn't afford the bad publicity of the arrest.
Neither could the abbot. I mean, it's one thing to
preach God's forgiveness. It's another to be harbor-
ing a man who was so hated by so many."

"Mother, give me some credit. If it hadn't been
for me . . ."

"You're right, sweetie, you're right. If it hadn't
been for you, someone would be dead, instead of in
an infirmary for a day. The story would be all over
the media, and people's lives would be ruined. On
the plus side, I would have really juicy material for a
month's worth of *TrippyGirl* blogs, at least." She
mashed and stirred and took a sip. "Just kidding."

"You're only half kidding."

"I know. But there must be something we can use."

"You mean create a fake version of what happened?"

"You make *fake* sound so negative. You saved a life
and you deserve a story. The Toad will believe every
word. He was quite impressed."

"You have to stop calling him Toad."

"We'll come up with something involving blood
and a mountaintop monastery. There'll be no one to
deny it. A little disclaimer saying we changed the
names and certain details to protect the innocent.
Blah, blah, blah. It'll be our best Trippy ever, just in
time for the book release."

"Maybe," said Amy, a word she regularly utilized to
mean no. But in this case it was a qualified no. It all
depended on her mother's discretion and creativity,

which might just turn it into a yes. So, it was a real maybe, after all.

"Did you talk to Nicolas? Everyone's talking about the poor boy—in two languages that he understands. I'm surprised he got back on the train."

"I'm proud of him," Amy said. The fire was getting a little too warm, so she put aside her pashmina on the nearby ottoman. Would she ever be able to wear it without remembering that day? "I can't imagine nursing a hatred for so many years and then just letting it go. There must be such a void in his life."

"Or a peace," said Fanny. "Let's give him the benefit of the doubt."

They basked in the glow of the fire. A comfortable silence fell between them, broken only by the rattling of the tracks and the occasional slurping from the gourd.

"I guess there's no chance that Nicolas murdered Lola Pisano," Fanny suggested. "That would be too easy."

"Easy and impossible."

"How about the general? Maybe he got a day pass and went on a murder spree, for old time's sake."

Even after a lifetime together, Amy couldn't always tell when Fanny was joking. "Ha-ha."

"What do you mean, 'Ha-ha'? Why not? Someone had to kill her."

Amy gave it some thought, not her mother's suggestion, of course, which was ridiculous, but . . . "To be honest, Mom, I'm not even sure Lola was murdered. It's just the lack of a blunt object and my own nagging suspicion."

"Well, the trip's not over, sweetie. We may still get lucky."

* * *

Marcus was relieved to see that the Abel girls were still alive and blogging. It had been nearly two days without a call or a note—and right after Amy had asked him to run down information on possible suspects. But just as he was about to send off another e-mail, his computer pinged with an alert. A brand-new posting from TrippyGirl. A little after 8:00 p.m., 10:00 p.m. Patagonian time.

He read through it quickly and couldn't quite make sense of the logistics. He had expected the story to have something to do with the train explosion, the subject of the last blog, perhaps connecting it to Fanny's vision or Lola Pisano's death. But this was entirely different.

The resourceful TrippyGirl was still in Patagonia. She had somehow wound up on a runaway donkey and found herself banging on the door of a hilltop monastery during a thunderstorm. Faced with having a beautiful young traveler on their doorstep, one who was dying from exposure, the kindly abbot took her in. She spent the night on a cot in the bell tower, which acted just like a booming alarm clock one hour before dawn, when the monks got up for their morning vespers. The *TrippyGirl* blog was illustrated with several shots of Amy on a donkey in front of what could have been a real monastery. At the end, Marcus noticed for the first time a disclaimer printed in red: "Based loosely on true events."

While he was reading it through for the second time, a Skype window materialized in the corner of his screen, along with the familiar bongo beat. Before her face even popped up, he had to ask. "Did you really take shelter in a monastery? Are you still there? Did you take a vow of chastity? I hope not."

"Based loosely. I made Mom put that in." Amy straightened her glasses and smiled into the camera. "But there was a bell tower. We'll tell you the whole story later, over drinks."

"Tell me now."

"I promised Fanny we'd tell you together. Give her a chance to embellish. Where are you?"

Marcus turned the screen so that she could see the exposed brick walls and the dirty clothes on the sofa. "In my own apartment for once. Terry and Fiona drove up to Vermont for the weekend to ski. Was there another murder? Is Fanny all right?"

Amy pretended to pout. "You ask about Fanny before you ask about me?"

"I can see that you're all right. Better than all right."

"Yeah, yeah." Amy waved away the compliment. "And yes, Mom is fine. And no, there's no extra murder. We're in Puerto Natales." She moved her own screen to show a large but perfectly ordinary hotel room. It could have been a Holiday Inn.

"It looks like your Patagonian adventure is over," Marcus said.

"Pretty much. Last night was our last night on the train. The airport here is tiny, so everyone has to stay in town until morning. Sorry about the news blackout. I did get your e-mails. Thanks."

"There's not much info on your victim. I Googled the hell out of Lola Pisano. Her husband was Esteban Pisano. Like your friend O'Bannion, he came from an old ranching family. But he got into banking and real estate, where the big money apparently was. I'm telling you stuff from the e-mail."

"Go on. It's better to hear it from your face. I pay more attention."

"Glad to hear it. Were you able to open the obituary? It's from the Buenos Aires paper, the *Clarín*. Lola dressed to the nines at some society function. I know you said not to send attachments. . . ."

"It's fine. I was just looking at it," Amy said. "The picture's not very flattering. I think she liked to wear flashy jewelry to help distract the eye."

"There aren't many photos of her. At least not online. A society column or two. Pretty gossipy stuff. Her relationship with Jorge O'Bannion started about a year ago, although her family disapproved. Called him a wellborn gigolo. It actually said that in the paper. '*Un gigolo de buena cuna.*' And they hate that he's Chilean. To his credit, it seems like he brought the widow out of herself a little. There's a photo of them dancing in a tango parlor."

"That's where I met her," said Amy. "And she wasn't happy to see me talking to Jorge. Anything else in the obituaries? I couldn't read much of the text."

"I'll have to teach you Spanish someday. They say that the cause of death was a riding accident and that because of the 'animal damage,' it would be a closed casket."

"I think that's what she would have wanted."

"Ouch," said Marcus, even though he couldn't help laughing. "Bad joke."

"Sorry." From five thousand miles away, he could see her blushing. "Anything on Gabriela Garcia?" she asked.

Marcus nodded. "Gabriela is much more Google friendly. Her husband, Arturo, was quite the charmer. A full-page obituary for him, nothing but praise. A suicide, by the way. Did you know that?"

"That's what you said in the e-mail. Any details?"

According to Google and its minions, Arturo was a

Buenos Aires boy made good. He had begun as a young guide on the streets, arranging tours on the spot for North American visitors. By the age of twenty, he had married Gabriela and founded Hemispherio Travel. The two of them thrived and eventually expanded to vacation resorts and a cruise line.

"From all accounts, Arturo did a pretty amazing job of surviving the political and social upheavals." Marcus vanished from the screen and reappeared with a few pages of printouts to look at. "But he finally got hit by the recession. Big-time bank problems."

Amy scratched at her hairline. "Didn't you say Lola's husband had been a banker?"

"You're one step ahead of me. Banking and real estate."

"Gabriela mentioned something unpleasant about the Pisano legacy. That must be the connection. If Esteban Pisano had been personally responsible for her husband's financial problems . . . I can see why Lola would ride away and not want to confront her."

Marcus put aside his printouts and scowled. "You don't even need me, do you?"

"I need you plenty," Amy said. "So I'm right about the connection?"

"Arturo's obituaries were a little vague." Marcus returned to his printouts. "They mentioned loan defaults and business worries. But suicide is a complex thing."

"Not if you're a grieving widow. For a grieving widow, there's plenty of blame to go around." Amy's eyes shifted, and Marcus could tell she was checking out the clock in the corner of her camera. "I need to talk to Gabriela before she leaves in the morning, not that she'll tell me much."

"Oh, I almost forgot." Marcus reshuffled the pages. "I found out what I could on Nicolas Blanco. There was no such student at the art conservatory in Santiago, according to their online records, which go back ten years. I also checked the art schools in Buenos Aires."

"His name is Nicolas Bruno. Brown, not White. I got it all straightened out. He's not a suspect."

Marcus made a sound, a tight-lipped growl. "I spent hours on this, you know."

"I realize that, and I'm sorry. Things just started happening with Nicolas, and he came clean." Amy made her most girlish, helpless face, an expression Marcus knew well. "I still need you plenty."

"I'm not so sure about that." He set the printouts aside for the final time. "Did you ever open the photos I sent? Or did you find us an apartment all on your own?"

"I opened them, yes," said Amy. "One good thing about business hotels. They have decent Wi-Fi."

"And?" Marcus looked hopeful. "What do you think?"

Amy sighed. "I think New York rentals are crappy and overpriced. No offense. I'm sure you did your best."

"What about the place in the East Village?"

"Oh, my God. That was the worst. A fire escape for a balcony? And so much garbage. We'd have to fumigate."

"I told you it would be hard."

"Well, don't give up. As soon as I get back, we'll seriously look, both of us."

"Good," Marcus said. "I can't wait."

"Me too." She checked the time again. "Right now I have to grill Gabriela. She's the only lead we have. Love you," she added.

Marcus loved her back and wished her good luck. They hung up simultaneously.

Amy would have liked to obsess about her last two words to Marcus and what had made her say them. And what he'd meant by his reply. Had it been a simple "Ditto"? Or something more heartfelt? But obsessing seemed like a luxury right now. The twin mysteries of Fanny's vision and the corpse by the river were rushing away from her, any possible clues dispersing to the four winds. By tomorrow the suspects and everything else would be gone.

The last day on the train had been perfectly, maddeningly uneventful, a tourist's delight, with the Andes spilling scenically down toward the Pacific. The large town/small city of Puerto Natales marked the end of the rail line. It was where the first O'Bannion immigrant had sent his mutton and wool off on their journeys around the world. The sheep industry had almost abandoned the town now, replaced by ecotourism. It was a jumping-off point to the wild glories of Patagonia, a place to book tours and purchase gear. One of its busiest shops was the outlet for the popular U.S. brand that just happened to share the region's name.

The tour's closing ceremony had been much less extravagant than its opening one. The small old station was a wooden structure, its dilapidated state half hidden beneath festive coats of red and blue paint. The borrowed silver engine had done its job. The last plumes of steam drifted up from its boiler as an older-looking Jorge O'Bannion bravely feigned his satisfaction on the station platform, facing his eight guests and speaking of his company's bright future. After a few weeks spent making improvements and repairs, the service would begin in earnest. Reservations, he said, were already pouring in. And with the goodwill of these lovely, influential travel experts, the New Patagonian Express would quickly become one of the world's premier tours. He didn't mention the destruction of his beloved sleeping car.

Amy had observed the others out of the corners of her eyes. Alicia Lindborn was as pulled together and amiable as ever, the perfect guest. The Furies were their usual, inscrutable selves, Gabriela included. Edgar Wolowitz was nearly as congenial and polite as Alicia. And Todd Drucker was practicing his smirk, which could mean anything. Amy couldn't help feeling sorry for Jorge. The tour had not been a disaster, not compared to the other disasters she'd been part of. But it had not been the rousing success that he needed.

When Amy went from her room down to the hotel bar, she saw that everyone had shown up for a final drink. The two non-English-speaking Furies were in a corner by the entrance with more than half of the bar patrons, intently watching a televised soccer game. Amy edged her way around the crowded chairs and nearly stumbled into Edgar and Todd, standing at the bar—Todd with a martini, Edgar with a Guinness Stout.

"Sorry," she muttered.

"Amy," Todd said, a welcoming note in his voice. It was the first time the stubby little man had ever called her Amy. "Just read the new Trippy. Quite entertaining, although I don't remember the thunderstorm. Or anyone spending a night in the bell tower."

For once she wasn't unnerved by his snarky grin. "Did you notice the disclaimer, 'Based loosely . . .'?"

"A welcome addition, and one that just increases

the fascination. You know, I'm going to piece together what happened."

"That's all part of the fun, isn't it?"

"I've begun reading, as well," said Edgar. "I hope you don't mind, but the piece I just filed for the *Sunday Times* mentions your blog quite glowingly."

"I don't mind in the least." Amy kept her smile to a sophisticated minimum and looked past them to the bartender. *"Señor, buenas noches. Un Campari y soda, por favor, con un poco de hielo."* With a little ice. Let the Spanish lessons begin. Todd offered to pay for the drink, and Amy accepted.

They chatted amiably about nothing until the pale red liquor arrived. She thanked Todd again, wished them both a good evening, then crossed over to the woman with the henna dye job, seated at a small round table on the far side of the bar with Gabriela. Fanny had managed to separate the owner of Hemispherio Travel from her companions. Amy could see in her mother's body language that she was already engaged in an intimate, friendly, disarming interrogation. It was the same attitude Amy recalled from the very first time she'd come home from a date.

"Amy, come sit with us." Fanny scooted around, leaving a space at the table but no extra chair. Both women were drinking wine, Gabriela a red, Fanny a white. Amy was glad not to see a maté gourd anywhere on the table. "I was just telling Gabriela that you saw her driving one of the cars on the day Lola disappeared."

"What?" Amy was flabbergasted. "Mother!"

"Weren't you telling me that?" Fanny asked, all innocence. "I thought it strange, because that was the same day Gabriela was bedridden with that terrible headache." Fanny shrugged. "My little girl gets confused about dates. You wouldn't believe how many appointments she's missed in her life."

"Don't blame your daughter." Gabriela wasn't stupid. She could tell that this was all a ploy. "I did borrow an auto, as a matter of fact. To go look for Lola. No one was searching that side of the estancia."

"I remember," Fanny said.

"It seemed neglectful. So I took it upon myself to search. Amy was right. She did see me."

"And the pilots found her body not far away. Did you run into Lola? Oops." Fanny covered her mouth and giggled. "I don't mean run over her. Did you find her?"

"No, no. I didn't get so far. The ground there is rough. I got lost. Then the auto wheels got stuck in a hole. I had to rock back and forth many times." She lowered her voice to a confessional whisper. "I think maybe I scraped something underneath. That is why I lied about the headache. If the auto was damaged, I didn't want people to know. That was irresponsible. I feel bad. And after Jorge has been so nice to us."

"I didn't mean to be spying," said Amy defensively. "I just happened to be around when you came back."

"Understood. It's my fault, not yours."

True or not, this was a reasonable explanation. It explained why Gabriela had been so secretive, tiptoeing back out of the garage and then lying about her headache. But it didn't change the fact that she'd been the only searcher out on her own, in the very quadrant where Lola would later be found dead.

Amy stayed at the little table with Fanny and Gabriela until she'd transformed her Campari into pink ice, then excused herself. Tomorrow would be an early day, with their flight to the Santiago airport and an overnight stay in the nearby port city of Val-

paraiso. Then back home to New York. Back home
without any hope of finding an answer. *Oh, what the
hell! One more* Campari y soda. She returned to the
bar, held up her glass, and twirled her finger, the international sign for "one more round." The bartender nodded and got to work.

"Miss Abel?" She turned to see Nicolas Blanco/
Bruno. The soft-looking young man stood there
timidly in his jeans and wool jacket, looking out of
place in a tourist bar in a business hotel. She hadn't
expected to see him again. The moment felt quite
awkward.

"How are you doing?" she asked. "Can I buy you a
drink?"

"No," he said, then swallowed hard. "I'm at a back-
packing hostel not far off. I came to see you." And
with that, he held up a plastic supermarket bag with
JUMBO written in large yellow letters. "I couldn't find
any place to buy wrapping paper."

Amy accepted the bag without comment. Inside
was a rolled-up piece of good-quality art paper, held
in place with two rubber bands. She had no idea
what to expect, but she found a dry section of the
bar, undid the rubber bands, and unrolled. She examined the curled portrait, a classic head and shoulders, similar to the one he'd done of the general, but
in charcoal instead of ballpoint. In this one, the head
was at an angle and the eyes were focused straight at
the viewer.

"It's you," she said with some amusement. "Thank
you. It's beautiful. Looks just like you." That part wasn't
quite true. In the self-portrait, Nicolas's face seemed
calmer. Not necessary a younger face, but more at
peace. Or was she just reading this into it?

"It's an odd present, no?" Nicolas admitted. "A

likeness of me? I did have a photo of you I could have worked from, but then you would have just had a drawing of yourself. And you know already what you look like, so why do that? No. This way, you have a Nicolas Bruno original." He swallowed again. "A portrait of the man whose life you saved."

Amy pretended not to know what he meant. "The general wouldn't have killed you, even if I hadn't come."

"No. You still saved my life."

CHAPTER 24

The overnight stay in Valparaiso was on their own
dime, as Fanny liked to put it. During their one
New York meeting, when O'Bannion was trying to
entice the Abels with the charms of Chile, he had
mentioned the city. He had told them he kept an
apartment there, and he had praised the gritty
beauty of the old port, with its hills and its crescent
harbor, a site that sailors had once dubbed "Little
San Francisco." Amy loved the name, Valparaiso, so
evocative of Spanish explorers and trade routes. As
long as they'd traveled all this distance, she'd
thought it would be a good idea to spend two days
walking around, decompressing, visiting churches
and taking the old wooden funiculars, the hillside
cable cars, up and down the picturesque landscape.
Those two days had been reduced to one, thanks to
Nicolas and the chimney. But it was still enough, she
hoped, to get a feel for the town.

Amy had researched the hotels and settled on a
boutique establishment on one of the trendy hills,
Cerro Concepción, partly because Jorge had men-

tioned it as his own beloved neighborhood, with good restaurants and incredible views.

"So, what's happening with Trippy in the monastery?" Amy asked as she split the last of the bottle of chardonnay between them and signaled the waiter for a check. She'd been waiting for a moment like this, when they were alone and her mother had relaxed with a few glasses of wine. "Nothing too close to the truth, I hope."

"I thought you liked when I told the truth."

"Not when it hurts people. And you can't just change the names," she added, anticipating her mother's response. "That's the only monastery in Patagonia. And there can't be many Argentine generals who turned into monks. People are going to guess, especially journalists like Todd and Edgar, who happened to be there."

"So you're encouraging me to lie." Fanny laughed. "Don't worry. I've already come up with a better story. It involves an intruder, not unlike Nicolas but cuter, and TrippyGirl, of course—and a novice monk who hasn't yet taken his vow of chastity. I'm still working the details. Which is better? A jealous fight over you? Or a sexual threesome gone wrong? I think Todd will find the threesome more believable."

"I think we need to increase the size of the disclaimer and make it flashing red."

"I will not embarrass you."

Amy shook her head. "In what alternate universe do you not embarrass me?" It wasn't really something to laugh about, but they both laughed.

It had been spitting rain on and off all evening. They had walked down the hill from their hotel to have dinner. Amy hadn't expected Valparaiso to be such a working harbor, full of container ships and concrete piers. But they had managed to find a sea-food market/restaurant, one that was nearly empty. It wasn't a white tablecloth establishment, but the fish was fresh and the service friendly. Amy paid the check in cash, eager to use up the rest of her pesos, then asked the waiter to point them in the direction of the Concepción funicular to take them back up the hill.

In the train shed, they paid the one-way fee, stood by the open bay, and watched the two funicular cars—one coming down, the other going up—as they passed each other in the middle of the slope.

"What do you plan to do with the Lola story?" Amy asked. She lowered her voice, just in case there were other Americans in the small crowd that was gathering behind them.

"I was hoping we'd come up with the truth on that one."

"I'm not sure we ever will," Amy said with some resignation. "Our suspects are all gone."

"Then I suppose Trippy will get high in some fun, wild way and have a vision. She'll try to warn the poor woman, but to no avail. The victim will ride off, and they'll find her body with the condors." Fanny adjusted her rain bonnet, keeping it on even though their heads were protected by the shed. "It's close to the truth and fairly exciting in a ghost story way. But of course, it's not the whole story."

The wooden carriage, brightly painted with a sunrise on the front, had clacked its way into the shed. The passengers got out on one side, and Amy and Fanny were among the first to get in on the other, finding places to sit near the rear, which would become the front at the other end of the ascent. As the carriage filled up, Amy ran her fingers through her

hair, then used her pashmina to wipe the raindrops
from her glasses. The glasses nearly flew out of her
hand when her mother violently tapped her shoulder.

"Tell me that's not a vision," Fanny hissed. She was
pointing at a couple who had just entered the carriage, the last two on before the attendant slid the
door shut. "Do you see her, too?"

The man was clearly Jorge O'Bannion, which was
hardly worthy of a vision. They had sat behind him
on the plane here, and they both knew he lived in
the neighborhood near the top of the tracks. But the
woman at his side . . . He was treating her with the
same deference as before. She was the same height
and build and carried herself the same way. And although she was wearing a head scarf, the ash-blond
curls were also the same.

Amy leaned down to her mother's ear. "It can't be
her. She's dead."

"Hence my question about the vision."

"Well, it can't be. Does she have a mole?"

Jorge and the woman were at the other end, facing out through the rear window as the carriage
started climbing. By the time they'd arrived at the
top shed, they still hadn't turned. Amy was counting
on a view of them when they exited, but by then
everyone who'd been seated was standing. Mother
and daughter were standing now, too, pushing their
way to the exit door on the right.

"Do we say hello?" Fanny asked.

"I think that's a bad idea."

"Why?"

"I don't know exactly." There was something
about this whole situation that felt dangerous. To
her. Perhaps not dangerous, but definitely worthy of

a slower approach. "What if it is her?" Amy asked. "What do we say?"

"Well, I think that's their problem, not ours. Are you just being a baby about this? Amy Josephine Abel . . ."

"I am not being a baby. . . . Oh, shoot." In the few seconds it had taken them to argue, Jorge and the mystery woman had left the carriage and were walking out through the turnstile. "Come on."

Amy jostled through the crowd, which was still funneling through the door and the single turnstile beyond. Fanny rushed to stay in her wake. By the time Amy saw the couple again, they were heading uphill, scuttling between the raindrops, hurrying from one pool of streetlamp light to the next. The Abels broke from the pack of pedestrians and were just beginning to catch up. And that was when the downpour started.

The sudden onslaught caught everyone by surprise. People scurried for shelter under the nearest awning or in the nearest doorway. Children and tourists and well-dressed locals leaving the cafés all zigzagged in a frenzy. When Amy got her bearings again, she and Fanny were the only ones exposed to the elements. She spun in a slow circle, already totally soaked, and checked the few crowded dry spots. Jorge and the mystery woman were nowhere in sight.

"It's hopeless," Fanny shouted above the wet cacophony. "Let's just find someplace."

Fanny led the way down a shadowy alley. The rain here was a little less intense due to the narrowness of the street. Twice they nearly fell on the slippery cobblestones. Then miraculously, just before the next corner, they dove into an empty spot under a storefront canopy. Fanny removed her useless rain bonnet. Amy took the pashmina off her head and sighed. Why had she even brought it with her when there had been that threat of rain in the forecast?

The storm was beginning to let up, and soon the Abels were engaged in the age-old game. *Do I make a run for it, or do I wait? Will it stop completely or just get worse?* From around the corner they could hear the voices of another couple, male and female, probably under a similar canopy, probably considering the same options. Fanny was closest to the corner, and her ears pricked up. She leaned her head out, almost into the rain, then drew it back.

"It's them," she silently mouthed.

It took Amy a moment to realize. "Are you sure?" she mouthed back.

Before Amy could object, her mother stepped out into the rain, hugging the wall, then darted her face around the corner. She raced back to Amy and their canopy. "It's them," she confirmed.

"So?" Amy enunciated broadly, without sound, as if speaking to an unskilled lip-reader. "Is it really Lola?"

"She's wearing the pendant," Fanny enunciated back. "I didn't see the mole."

Mother and daughter traded places. The rain had devolved into sprinkles, allowing Amy to abandon the canopy and stand within inches of the building's corner. The man was speaking. It definitely sounded like Jorge O'Bannion, with his smooth, deep ring-master voice. Amy felt a light touch on her shoulder and turned to see her mother still under the edge of the canopy. "What are they saying?"

Amy shrugged helplessly, which meant "I don't speak Spanish."

Fanny clicked her tongue and rolled her eyes, which meant "That old excuse."

Amy tilted back toward the corner and considered her mother's argument. As was often the case, Fanny was being unreasonable but accurate. It was her go-to excuse, Amy knew, a ridiculous mental block. She was good at languages. There were certainly enough words that were similar to Italian. She should be able to glean some meaning from them, perhaps enough to positively identify the woman in the head scarf. Forcing herself to ignore the rain and the ruined pashmina, she focused all her attention on the voices. It was an intimate conversation but still loud enough. *Afortunado.* Jorge said it more than once. Was that the same as *fortunato*? *Lucky*? *El cuerpo*. Was that like *il corpo, the body*? *Tinte.* Was that *tinta*? The word *motocicleta* came up more than once. *Motorcycle*, she deduced, although she didn't know why Jorge would be bringing his motorcycle into the discussion.

Amy's intense focus blocked out everything else, even the rain. Or the sudden lack of it. Just as she was getting used to their vocal rhythms, growing adept at catching a few words and extrapolating the meaning of a sentence here and there, the voices started growing dimmer. Without thinking, she poked her head around and saw the couple walking away, down the lamp-lit cobblestones. Fanny must have known, too. She was right behind Amy as they once again picked up their trail, scurrying half a block behind their prey, mentally cursing all the other pedestrians who were also coming out from under their awnings and making life difficult.

The surveillance parade ended at the door to a small, well-maintained apartment building—ocher with red shutters and trim—that had probably been a private home in the old days. Jorge used a key on the outside door and chivalrously eased the woman inside.

Fanny waited a few moments, then walked up and checked the buzzers. "J. O'Bannion. Three-A."

Luckily for them—*afortunadamente?*—there was a café directly opposite the building, and it was open. The owner, a motherly middle-aged type, just a shade younger and thinner than Fanny, took pity on their bedraggled state and, without any translated request, brought out towels from the kitchen, two for each of them. Amy thanked her profusely and ordered an herbal tea, then talked Fanny into an herbal tea, instead of another maté jolt. They settled down at a table for two by the window, where they toweled off as they shared a view of Jorge's front door.

"So?" asked Fanny as she tried to rearrange her soggy head of henna. "What did they say?"

"I didn't understand everything," Amy admitted.

"But you understood enough."

"Enough to be confused." Amy wiped her tortoiseshell Tumi's with her napkin. "The word *lucky* came up. 'We were lucky.' Also the word *police*, more than once. And *motorcycle.*"

"Jorge's motorcycle? How did that come up?"

"I didn't ask," said Amy. "At some point Lola was angry with him. They were arguing about money. Jorge wanted more money, or she wanted more money. It wasn't clear. And they agreed not to see each other. Three months, that's what he said. *Tres meses.* She didn't seem happy with that."

Fanny waited for more. "And?"

"And . . . and it's hard enough eavesdropping in English." Amy gave it some more thought as she put her glasses back on. "He said she had to dye her hair. She told him that she liked it this way, but he insisted she had to dye it."

"Only logical if it's Lola and they faked her death."

"How could they fake her death? There was a real body."

Fanny waved this nit away. "As he said, they got lucky."

"Lucky there was another woman's body just lying around Patagonia?"

Fanny sipped her herbal tea and made a sour face. "How can you drink this tasteless stuff? Did Jorge ever call her by name?"

"Yes, he said the name Lola several times."

"So we know we have the right woman. I say we ring his doorbell right now and confront them. He's going to have a hard time explaining her."

"Really?" Amy had to laugh. "You actually think he'll let us in?"

Fanny made another sour face. "Then we'll just wait until she comes out. We'll do our own stakeout. I've never done a stakeout."

"We're not doing a stakeout."

"Why not? When this place closes, we'll set up on the street. Disguise ourselves as street beggars. It's a nice evening, if the rain has stopped for good. Do you think she's staying the night?" Fanny was warming up to her own idea. "Well, I'm glad we had a big dinner. But we should be sure to use the bathroom here before they close."

"I'm soaked to the bone. There has to be a better way."

"What way? Once we lose track of Lola, we're back to square one. We might as well go home."

"We are going home," Amy reminded her. "To-morrow."

"What? How can you think of going home? With a mystery so close to being solved? I'll bet you anything Trippy wouldn't go home."

"That's because Trippy's not wet and shivering and exhausted. Trippy is imaginary."

It was an irrelevant fact. "We're both Trippy," said Fanny. "And we're staying right here, staking them out until Lola . . . Oh, fudge!"

They had been barely aware of the street traffic outside the café. There wasn't much—a car barreling through a puddle, a few scooters buzzing by. Neither had expected anything to happen so quickly. But when Fanny happened to glance out just then, there was Lola out in front of Jorge's building, still under her head scarf, about to step into a waiting taxi. They continued to sit in front of their herbal teas, stunned, as the taxi sped off into the dimly lit city.

"This is not how I expected my first stakeout to go," Fanny said. "Truly."

CHAPTER 25

Amy stayed to pay the check, while her mother thanked the café owner and went outside. It always surprised Amy how quickly things could turn. In less than an hour they had gone from a dead end to the lucky sighting of a dead woman to another dead end. She tried to think of their next possible step. Nothing was coming to mind, and it didn't help that she was momentarily distracted by the exchange rate and whether ten thousand pesos would be too much to leave or too little. And then she remembered the towels and left twenty thousand.

When she stepped out into the street, the rain had stopped and the moon was just rising above the skyline. Fanny stood in front of Jorge's building, writing something on a piece of notepaper. She put the pen back in her purse, folded the paper in half, and handed it to Amy. "Put this in your pocket," she told her daughter. Amy did so. Then, without further explanation, Fanny pressed the buzzer: J. O'Bannion, 3A.

"What the hell are you doing?"

"I don't see what else we can do. Can you think of something?"

Before Amy could respond, a muffled voice erupted over the intercom. *"Bueno. Quién es?"*

"Jorge?" said Fanny chirpily into the speaker. "It's me, Fanny Abel. Amy and I happened to be in the neighborhood. Do you mind if we come up, dear? It's important."

There was a longish pause, followed by a buzz on the door.

"Follow my lead," Fanny whispered as she pushed open the door and began looking for the elevator. "And stay open to improvisation."

For the first time in their acquaintance, Jorge was not the perfect gentleman. When the elevator arrived on his floor, he was standing at his door in a black velvet dressing gown, his arms crossed, his hair still moist from the downpour. "How did you get my address?"

Fanny looked perplexed. "You gave it to us."

"I did not," he replied. "Not that my home address is a secret. But I don't make a habit of giving it to business clients."

"Well, you must have," said Fanny, leading the way from the elevator to the door. "Amy wrote it down. I suppose it must have been on an e-mail. Or maybe when you were telling us about Valparaiso. Lovely city, by the way. The hills. The adorable funiculars."

"I did not give out my address," he repeated.

"Of course you did," said Fanny. "Amy, show him where you wrote it down."

Amy took her cue, unfolding the paper from her pocket and holding it out for inspection. "I honestly can't say how we got your address," she said, which was true. She couldn't say.

"So . . . May we come in?" Fanny shook her whole body pitifully, like a wet dog. "We got caught in the rain. Looks like you did, too. Did you just get back from dinner? I hope you weren't eating alone. That can be depressing."

O'Bannion stood his ground in the doorway. "It's late, Mrs. Abel. What can I do for you?"

Amy could almost see the wheels turning in her mother's brain. "My little girl and I . . . I say little even though she's so much bigger than me. But that's a mother's prerogative, isn't it? We're staying just a few blocks away. Lovely hotel. If we'd only been thinking, we could all have had dinner together. Then you wouldn't have had to eat alone. Did you have to eat alone?"

O'Bannion ran a hand back through his hair, looking bemused and annoyed at the same time. "If you must know, I had a lovely dinner with a close friend."

"Oh, who was it?" asked Fanny. "I mean, was it someone we might know?"

"You think you may know my friends? In Valparaiso? Which friend do you know?"

"I don't know. Who did you have dinner with?"

The bemused part of his expression dissolved. "Mrs. Abel. It has been a long day. If there is not some urgent matter, I must please ask you to leave."

"Are you upset with me, dear?" Fanny pouted. At the same time, she insinuated herself a few inches over the threshold. "Did I do something to offend you? If so, I'm sorry."

"It's nothing."

"It's not nothing. I can tell."

It took O'Bannion a moment or two. He took a deep breath. "When I invited you on this tour, it was with the understanding that you would promote the New Patagonian Express. Today I read your latest episode of *TrippyGirl* and was so disappointed. The Express was barely mentioned. Instead, you have her, a woman, wandering into a monastery and spending the night. Is she going to have carnal relations with a monk, heaven forbid? Or worse, are you going to reveal what really happened in the bell tower? Do I need to warn my dear trusting cousin to prepare for a scandal?"

Fanny bristled, or at least pretended to. "I should remind you that my daughter single-handedly prevented something far worse than a scandal."

Amy shot her a look. "There'll be no scandal," she promised. "We agreed. And I apologize for not featuring the Express more prominently. It was a wonderful tour. Mother and I were just discussing how to best spread the word. Maybe a Trippy adventure lasting a month or two."

"Exactly," Fanny agreed. "It'll put our Siberian adventure to shame."

O'Bannion seemed interested. He almost smiled. "Something romantic perhaps?"

Amy nodded. "We were thinking that Trippy might fall in love with a handsome gaucho working at Torre Vista or at Glendaval. Maybe she goes camping with him."

"Camping?" O'Bannion sounded dubious.

"Glamping," Amy said, correcting herself. "It's all the rage. Glamorous camping, with champagne and hot outdoor showers. Then they get lost in the majestic mountains. I think our readers would love that."

"I would love it," Fanny said, pitching in. "And if

people love it enough, you can add it to your itinerary, except for the getting lost part."

"It sounds perfect," said O'Bannion. Unconsciously, he edged open the door a little more. "If that's indeed what you're planning to do."

"It is," said Fanny. "That's why we dropped by, to discuss the story before we leave tomorrow. But we can always discuss it by e-mail." She frowned. "Even though Amy is terrible with returning e-mails."

"No, we can discuss it now. Please." He stood aside, finally relenting. "I was behaving rudely."

"Thank you, dear." For Fanny, this had been the goal. She was not a long-term thinker, always focused on the very next step. *Get inside. Regain his trust.* After that, she had no idea. Something would come to her.

O'Bannion ushered them into an elegant but dimly lit living room. The furniture was old and huge, as if meant for a castle instead of a city apartment. The Abels made themselves uncomfortable in an oversize pair of stuffed chairs that squeezed down when you sat until you could feel the springs underneath. Their host settled on the front edge of a sofa that might have had the same problem.

"It's too bad you have to leave so soon." Once again he was the aristocratic gentleman.

"It is," said Fanny. "But if you have the time now, we'd love to pick your brain."

"Pick my brain how?"

"Oh . . ." Fanny scratched her temple. "Find out more about Lola Pisano, for example. We wouldn't use her name, but just knowing about her would help us create a believable character."

"Lola?" O'Bannion looked skeptical. "I thought

your story was about glamour camping with a gaucho."

"It is," Fanny repeated. "But maybe they find a
body when they're lost. That makes it exciting—and
closer to the truth."

O'Bannion balked. "I'm not certain you should
use Lola. She was a friend."

"We don't want to use her," said Fanny. "That's
why we need to know more, so we can make it different. We could invent a story—just off the top of my
head, um . . ." She thoughtfully stroked her chin. "A
rich woman wants the world to think she's dead
when she's not dead. That's a great twist. But we
can't make it even remotely like the truth."

"Why would she want you to think she's dead?"

"Aha!" Fanny clapped her hands. "That's the mystery. Why do *you* think this woman wanted to fake
her death? Off the top of your head."

"But she is dead. You saw her body."

"It's fiction, remember? Just a story."

"I don't like this," O'Bannion said emphatically.
"Romance with the young gaucho is better."

"Maybe," said Fanny. "Or maybe—and I'm just
spit-balling here—maybe the gaucho is really Lola's
nephew, and he wants to kill her. But Lola pretends
to be dead in order to foil this attempt on her life.
Later on, someone sees her alive, and this ruins her
plan."

O'Bannion eyed the door, obviously regretting
having let them in. "If you send me your ideas, I may
be able to help. But please don't include Lola. It
would be disrespectful." He pushed himself up from
the sofa, a little unsteady on his feet. "I'm grateful
with your intent to include the New Patagonian Express. Every ounce of publicity helps. And now I

must say good night." He held out his hands in a farewell gesture. "It was an honor to know you. You are two remarkable women. Have a safe journey back to New York."

"Are you sure you don't want to talk about Lola? You must have been very good friends." Fanny stayed seated and eyed Amy, instructing her to do the same.

"We were, Fanny. But that's a private part of my life. What time did you say you leave tomorrow?"

"It's a late flight. So if you want to have lunch or even an early dinner . . ."

"I'm afraid not."

Amy was surprised, almost stunned, to see her mother fail so completely. It filled her with a kind of panic, as if the axis of the globe had shifted and she could no longer count on Fanny's gravitational pull. Panic was probably the only explanation for what she did next. "Where are you going to from here, Jorge?" Amy said. "Are you staying in Valparaiso?"

"Tomorrow I go to my estancia at Glendaval. There are improvements I need to oversee."

"Can we go with you?" asked Amy.

It took O'Bannion a moment to comprehend the request. "You wish to return to the estancia? Why?"

Amy didn't quite know why. She knew only that she had to stay close to Jorge O'Bannion if she ever hoped to figure this one out. "We want to see your improvements."

"So we can write about them," added Fanny.

"What about your flight home?" O'Bannion asked. "What about your work?"

Amy and her mother exchanged glances. Fanny raised an eyebrow, combining it with a half smile. "My dear, this is much more important. We believe in the New Patagonian Express."

"You are willing to do this?" Jorge O'Bannion seemed deeply touched. "Both of you?"

"Absolutely," Fanny said. "It shouldn't take us more than a day or two of nosing around."

"Nosing around?"

"A North American expression," Amy explained. "It means, uh . . . um . . . ." She was drawing a blank.

Fanny jumped in. "It means smelling out all the fabulous possibilities that Trippy can put in her stories. Do we have a deal?"

"Did you get a chance to look at the studio on Orchard?" Marcus was on Amy's laptop, sitting in the sunroom office at the rear of the Barrow Street brownstone, just behind her bedroom. She could see him glancing at several printed-out pages, then back at the computer's camera. "It's small, but it's got a nicer layout than the one-bedroom on Chambers Street. We can see them both on Saturday, if you're not jet-lagged."

"Yeah." Amy bit her lip. "Marcus, about my flight . . ."

Fanny was in the bathroom doorway, in a bathrobe, using the hair dryer but still managing to eavesdrop.

"Don't be put off by the photos. The air shaft doesn't allow much natural light. On a sunny day it's actually not bad."

"Saturday might be a problem," Amy mumbled into her phone.

"If you want, we can postpone until Sunday. But I was hoping to see the two listings out in Queens on Sunday. One actually claims to be a two-bedroom."

"Mom and I canceled our flight." She said it fast and clean, like ripping off a Band-Aid. "Now, don't get upset. We're not in danger. We just need to stay a few days, do some amateur sleuthing."

Marcus made a face. "Sleuthing? Did Fanny talk you into this?"

"What do you mean? I've sleuthed plenty."

"Not without Fanny and me forcing you to."

The drone of the hair dryer clicked off. "Hello, Marcus," Fanny shouted from the doorway.

"Hey, Fanny." Marcus waved. "Are you forcing Amy? Is it dangerous? Should I fly down and join you? I will. On the next flight." They could tell he felt left out.

"Not necessary," Fanny assured him. "It's just an intriguing puzzle." She brought out her hairbrush and joined Amy in front of the cell phone. Together, they informed him of the Lola sighting, the visit to Jorge's apartment, and their plan to keep spying on him.

Marcus listened and nodded. "So, you suspect Jorge. Of doing what? Helping Lola fake her death? Why would they do that? And here's a better question. How would they do that? The body was shipped back to her family in Buenos Aires, right?"

"That's what the obituaries said."

"So the Pisano family would recognize the real Lola."

"There was some disfiguring from the condors," Amy suggested.

"Still, her own family being fooled? The mole alone is pretty distinctive." He waited for her reply. "Did the screen freeze again? Amy?"

Amy's face came to life. "It didn't freeze. I'm just thinking. Obviously, we don't have all the facts. "

"That's why we need to investigate," said Fanny.

"And how are you going to investigate?" Marcus asked. "Follow Jorge around until he confesses?"

"I don't know," said Amy, sounding exasperated. "But we have to do something."

Amy's boyfriend allowed himself a crooked grin. "Are you sure this isn't just some sort of mother-daughter bonding experience? Is that why you don't want me to come?"

"Good God, no," Fanny said.

Amy agreed with an exaggerated roll of her eyes.

"Are you sure?" Marcus asked. "Nothing brings people closer than a murder. Amy and I can vouch for that."

"This is not a bonding experience," Amy said emphatically. "And we don't need you showing up."

"I suppose." Marcus sounded resigned. "Even if I caught the next plane, I probably wouldn't be much help."

"Don't take the next plane," said Amy. "Promise me. You showing up will just make Jorge more suspicious."

Marcus promised. In return, Amy promised they would spend a maximum of two days at the estancia. That was what they'd arranged with Jorge. Any longer and their welcome would be worn out.

"We'll be home in three days," she told Marcus. "Then we'll look at all those apartments. Maybe the one in Queens? Now I really have to go. I'm exhausted."

All three said their good-byes, and Fanny smirked as the other two made kissy faces over their devices.

Fanny returned her hairbrush to the bathroom. "You know he's playing you, right? About the apartments?"

"If you mean that he's showing me the absolute worst ones? Yes, I know."

"So?" Fanny reached for her toothbrush. "Do you find that annoying or endearing? I'd go with endearing."

"It's annoying. But I can fight only one battle at a time. Let's get some sleep."

CHAPTER 26

By mid-afternoon the next day they had arrived at the estancia. What had seemed like a weeklong pioneering journey by rail across treacherous terrain had been reduced, in the opposite direction, to a single flight and a five-hour drive. Jorge O'Bannion played chauffeur, while Amy and Fanny sat in the back, mostly silent, gazing out at a landscape that appeared surprisingly untreacherous.

"It is not so far on a map," Jorge told them at one point as the road looped gently around one more ravine-like tear in the earth, "but like the joke says, you cannot get there from here."

Glendaval, the family's Montana-like lodge, looked as inviting to Amy as an old friend, its front doors flung open to embrace the lightest of breezes. Oscar the gaucho was there to meet them, festooned in his usual poncho, beret, and enviable thigh-high boots. From the moment Jorge opened the car door, the two men became immersed in whatever business a resort owner and a gaucho could be immersed in. They strode off together, and the Abels settled into their old room toward the rear of the second floor. Fanny immediately went to the chest of drawers and found the plastic bag of yerba maté that she'd accidentally left when they'd vacated the room. She placed it next to the thermos and gourd on her bedside table.

One of their windows faced the apple orchard on the rise behind the lodge. The summer foliage obscured Fanny's view of O'Bannion's office, the little log cabin nestled among the trees a hundred yards away. "I can't tell if he's there or not," she complained.

Amy had positioned herself by the side window. "I think Jorge and Oscar drove off somewhere. Do you want to risk it?"

Fanny grunted in the affirmative. "It's probably the best chance we'll get."

"What about the middle of the night? That might be safer."

"But then we'd need the lights on, which could be dangerous. Plus, who wants to wait? Plus, we'll probably be tired after a big meal. Plus, you'll have had a few glasses of wine by then, knowing you. Plus, Jorge might decide to work late or might have insomnia. . . ."

"Fine," Amy sighed. "Let's go break and enter."

Their pretext, if anyone bothered to ask, would be an afternoon stroll. Fanny was in the lead, whistling nonchalantly as they disappeared behind the lodge, walking up the rise and through the first barrier of apple trees. The cabin's front door was unlocked, which was both convenient and disappointing.

"I certainly hope he has something worth locking up," Fanny said, closing the door behind her.

Amy took the outer office. Her smattering of Spanish might be able to help her with the file cabinet or the contents of the desk drawers or the computer. Meanwhile, Fanny went through to the rustic living room. Neither one knew what they were looking for. Anything mentioning Lola Pisano would be a good start.

Moving a chair cushion to the floor gave Amy a place to sit cross-legged by the file cabinet in quasi-comfort. It was a short, single wooden cabinet, and her head wound up at the same height as a framed photo sitting on top: Jorge and Lola elegantly dressed for a night on the town. Jorge was beaming. As usual, Lola's face was turned at an angle to hide the mole. Amy took this as her inspiration. "What are you up to, Lola?" she muttered, opening the cabinet and starting in the front.

Jorge's filing system seemed almost as disorganized as Amy's own. First of all, the folders weren't alphabetized. The front one was labeled *IMPUESTOS*. She had no idea. But upon opening it, she saw the forms from the Gobierno Federal de Chile and deduced that *impuestos* must mean "taxes," not close at all to the Italian word. Amy scanned the rest of the tabs, hoping, ridiculously, to see something labeled *L. PISANO* or, better yet, *MUERTE DE L. PISANO*. No such luck.

"You don't make it easy," Amy said, continuing her one-sided conversation. Lola stared back, glistening in her rings and earrings and a blue-stoned necklace, all intended to be distractions from the quarter-sized dot on her cheek. Behind the tax files were various business folders, some from architects and contractors, some holding financial spreadsheets. Amy didn't even bother with the spreadsheets. Toward the back were files of promotional material, much of which Amy had already seen. Her pulse quickened when she saw the folder labeled *MOTOCICLETA*, "motorcycle."

Jorge and Lola had both said the word, but the folder contained nothing but a ten-year-old sales receipt and maintenance records.

"Tell me something, Lola," she begged the photo. But all Lola did was stare, half hidden in the protective luster of her jewelry. The blue stone seemed almost to wink. Was it a necklace, Amy wondered, or a pendant on a silver chain? And what was in the center of the blue stone? A little starburst? Amy stood up from her cushion, grabbed the frame, and took a closer look. Then she leaned toward the doorway to the next room. "Mother?" she whispered.

Fanny emerged, wearing a pair of winter woolen gloves she'd brought to safeguard against leaving fingerprints. "Tell me you found something, dear, because all I have are fingernail clippings and an old yachting magazine."

Amy bit her lip. "Remember that turquoise pendant Lola Pisano wore? On the silver chain, with the starburst in the middle?"

Fanny took the photo and looked. "Of course. She was wearing it at the second ranch. I remember when I signed some contract for her, as a witness. She was also wearing it in the rainstorm, after her death."

"Right. But the first time I saw it was in this room." Amy pointed. "It was right there, by Jorge's computer. He saw me looking at it. He said it was an O'Bannion family heirloom and that he was going to give it to Lola the next time they met."

"That was very sweet of him."

"Then, when we arrived at Torre Vista, I saw him at the station, giving it to her."

"You're just full of jewelry facts, aren't you?"

"And yet Lola is wearing the same pendant in that old photo, which had to be taken some time ago."

Fanny had another wisecrack all prepared. But this stopped her. "So it wasn't an O'Bannion heirloom. If anything, it's a Pisano heirloom. Hold on!" And she scratched her head with a gloved finger. "No. Sorry. I don't have any possible explanation for this."

"Do you think Lola was actually here?" Amy asked. "At the same time we were?"

"You mean in secret?" Fanny glanced out the window at the tree-obstructed view of the estancia. "It's possible. There's a back road leading up here. But why?"

Amy thought out loud. "Maybe Jorge and Lola were plotting something and didn't want to be seen together. But she accidentally left her pendant. When I noticed it, Jorge made up his heirloom story to explain away a piece of woman's jewelry in his office. Then, when I saw them at the Torre Vista station, he wasn't giving it to her. He was returning it."

"That fits with the facts," Fanny conceded. "It creates more questions than answers, but it fits."

"Oscar's daughter, Juanita, says she saw a car driving toward the estancia. But when we checked with the staff, they hadn't seen anyone arriving. This would explain it, a secret meeting."

"Well, it looks like we found a clue."

"I know." Amy felt a surge of pride. "And it was right here in front of me."

"Congratulations," said Fanny with less enthusiasm. "Not that I want to look a gift clue in the mouth, but aren't clues supposed to clear things up? This one does just the opposite."

A long, thoughtful pause fell between the two Abels, and it was in this silence that they first heard the faraway, throaty whirl of the helicopter.

* * *

When Amy and Fanny walked out onto the front meadow, the sheep had scattered, replaced by the familiar form of the Bell 407, its blades slowed to the leisurely speed of a ceiling fan. Jorge and Oscar were at the pilot's door as it swung open, and Kevin Vanderhof, the younger, hazel-eyed Canadian, stepped out to greet them. Amy and Fanny stopped at a respectful distance, not wanting to seem to eavesdrop, then did their best to eavesdrop. From what they could see, Kevin had arrived alone.

The King Fisher pilot saw them and, with a wave, invited them over. "Amy," he shouted into the breeze. "I didn't expect to see you here."

"Flirt with him," Fanny barked in her ear as they crossed the meadow. "You can never tell."

"I didn't expect to see you, either," Amy said, sweeping back her hair with one hand, straightening her glasses with the other, and feeling a bit foolish. "I hope there's no emergency this time."

"Quite the contrary." Jorge O'Bannion welcomed them with an ingratiating grin. "When I hired the helicopter in Torre Vista, it gave me an idea. Not all guests will want to ride horses, especially older guests." He had almost looked at Fanny as he said this. "The King Fisher people and I are working out an arrangement to share their machines, perhaps to lease my own at some point."

"They sent me here to scope out the sights," Kevin said.

"Marvelous idea," Fanny agreed. "For those older travelers."

"I'm taking Mr. O'Bannion and his man up to look around. If you'd care to join us . . ." It took Amy a second to realize he was talking to her and not to her mother. "If that's okay with Mr. O'Bannion."

"If you would be so kind." O'Bannion made a courtly bow. "You've already done our land excursion. I think your input would be invaluable."

And just like that it was settled. Amy would accompany the pilot, Jorge, and Oscar on their joyride, while Fanny would stay at the estancia and rest up after her day of travel.

"Perhaps you can do some more nosing around," Jorge suggested. "Smell out the possibilities."

Fanny promised him that she would indeed do some nosing around.

On Kevin's insistence, Amy took the copilot's seat. All four would be connected through their headsets.

"Torre Vista may be the more scenic," Jorge announced as the rotors reached full speed and the King Fisher became airborne. "But we will see."

"Absolutely," said Kevin. He took his eyes off the instruments just long enough to wink her way, leaving Amy to deduce that there must not be that many young, eligible, English-speaking women in this neck of the woods.

Once past the sheep meadow, the helicopter rose above the sea of small-leafed bushes, rooted stubbornly in the dust, and an optical illusion took over, giving them the impression of a green and fertile plain below. Jorge and his gaucho chatted back and forth, pointing at landmarks and discussing options. Every minute or so, Jorge would have new instructions or questions for Kevin. "Go north through the canyon." "How far are we from the estancia now?" "How low can you fly above the ravine?"

It was scenic enough, thought Amy, feeling a little guilty about feeling so jaded. She had seen much of this landscape at ground level. Flying over it at seventy miles an hour almost trivialized the vastness. Oscar and Jorge talked some more. Jorge translated it into English. "Oscar wants to know how far we are from the river."

Kevin pushed a few buttons on his navigation screen. "Pretty close. Do you want me to swing by?" The pilot made a show of tilting into a ninety-degree turn and zooming out toward a sandy plateau. Amy braced herself on the window and tried to ignore another wink from Kevin.

After a few minutes in the air, all the landscape had started to look familiar. Some parts were more familiar than others. *Like now*, Amy thought. Right below their flight path was a meandering animal path, carved through the scrub by generations of guanacos and wild horses. Had they actually ridden along that path? she wondered. It seemed like ages ago, all of them following Oscar as they tried to locate the spot where Fanny had seen her disappearing corpse. In front of them was a sandy cliff and the spot just below it. . . .

Amy glanced behind her. "Oscar?" she said, catching the gaucho's attention. *"Perdona."* Of all the times she'd wished she spoke Spanish, this had to be in the top five. *"Este es el lugar. . . ."*

"Sí," he answered, then trained his eye back on the animal path, actually a small, concentrated collection of paths, well trodden by the horses and the police in their fruitless search. It might have been Amy's imagination, but Oscar seemed more focused now, focused and perhaps a little puzzled.

"Do you see something?" Kevin asked Amy. Before she could answer, Kevin was slowing down to circle the spot. He circled the general area twice.

"Why are you stopping here?" It was O'Bannion, almost shouting.

Kevin eyed Amy, who gave him no response, just a blank stare. "Sorry, sir," he replied, then gained altitude and straightened his course. Within seconds the Rio Grey came into view, a fast-flowing, deep-looking black ribbon of water flowing east, away from the lengthening shadows.

"You want me to land by the river?" Kevin asked. "Should I circle? Sir?"

No one answered. Through the headsets, Amy could hear a hushed, rushed conversation in Spanish from the seats behind her. The words were impossible to decipher, but the tone . . . Jorge O'Bannion's voice sounded defensive, perhaps a little belligerent, while Oscar's tone . . . Amy couldn't quite figure it out.

Kevin was already circling. "Should I land, sir?" he asked. "Do you want me to follow the river? Whatever you want. We have plenty of fuel." Again no one answered.

Amy tapped Kevin on the shoulder and caught his eye long enough to mouth silently, "What are they saying?"

Kevin mouthed back, "I have no idea."

CHAPTER 27

"When we landed, they were still talking. They totally ignored Kevin and me and went straight up to Jorge's cabin. Poor Kevin didn't know what to do."

Amy and her mother were on the porch, in side-by-side rockers, primitive but well-polished creations with curving branches cut and pieced together to form the arms and the backs. The women leaned inward, keeping their rocking synchronized and their voices low.

"Jorge and Oscar must have had something to talk about," Fanny said.

"Something to do with the site of your vision."

"Did you mentally just put the word *vision* in quotes?"

"We both know it wasn't," Amy said. "We just don't know what it was."

Fanny had stopped rocking. "Who is that girl with Oscar?" She pointed with her head toward the small corral just to the left of the meadow where the King Fisher was still parked. A compact but attractive teenager stood holding the reins of a brown- and white-spotted horse, a little larger than a pony. Oscar was in the cab of a weathered pickup, talking to her through the driver-side window.

"That's his daughter, Juanita," said Amy. "I told you."

"Ah, yes. The girl practicing her English. She looks happy."

She did indeed look happy, Amy thought. They both did, with closed-mouth smiles they didn't try to hide. The weathered gaucho leaned his head out of the window and kissed her on the cheek. Then the truck chugged reluctantly to life, was thrown into gear, and traveled around the meadow and toward the road.

"Yoo-hoo," Fanny called out, waving at young Juanita. "How are you, dear?"

Juanita turned and looked perplexed, until she noticed Amy in the other rocker. Her smile returned. She tied her spotted horse to the railing and came up to the porch to greet her one-time tutor. "Hello, Miss Amy Abel. To see you is a lovely shock. How are you feeling?"

Amy stated that she was just fine and got up to find Juanita a chair. "This is my mother. Mom, this is Juanita Jones."

"Oh, please," said Juanita, hands raised in gentle protest. "I cannot stay. I was practicing with the waiter, my friend Alejandro. He tells me of that unlucky woman who died by the river at the other estancia."

Amy was surprised. "News travels fast."

"I think it does," Juanita agreed. "People say she was the owner of the company, with Senor O'Bannion."

"That's right," said Amy. "She was his friend."

"So sad." Juanita gave it a moment, a young person's innocent mourning for the world. Then her smile returned. "My father says I must ride home now. Very important."

"It looks like your father had good news," said Fanny. "He was smiling."

"It is good." Her natural modesty seemed at battle with her desire to divulge. "I will be going to school in Puerto Montt," she said in a breathless whisper. "A thing I always wanted. My family never had the money to send me to the Sisters of Grace and to pay for my stay."

"But your father has found the money," Amy said, guessing. "That's wonderful."

"He says God will provide. And I must thank you, Miss Abel, for helping."

"I'm not sure . . . How did I help?"

Juanita lowered her gaze and stared at her own folded hands. "When you and the ladies came to our house. He saw how you took time and talked to me like an equal person."

Amy felt guilty. Her interrogation, disguised as an English lesson, had obviously touched the gaucho family in an unexpected way. "I liked talking to you."

"My father likes you."

"Really?" This was news. She didn't think Oscar even noticed. The two of them had barely spoken.

"My father is a quiet man who does not like many. After that day, he understood. He will pay for my uniform and my clothing and books. And soon, in the autumn . . . Is that the right word? Is it *autumn* or the other word? *Fall?*"

"Both words are right," Fanny said.

"Actually . . ." Amy wagged a hand back and forth. "*Fall* is an American word—*fall* or *autumn*. In England they don't say fall, just autumn."

"Is that true?" Fanny asked her daughter, then shrugged. "Well, what do the English know?"

"Then I will say autumn," Juanita decided. "That way I can speak to everyone."

Fanny wanted to ask more about Oscar Jones's sudden good fortune. But she could see that Juanita was eager to hop on her spotted steed, gallop home, and plan out her future. They wished her the best of luck, then watched and waved as the gaucho's daughter leaped into her saddle and pulled her horse's head toward the empty road. The sound of hoof beats died off in the breeze.

Fanny started to rock. "That's probably the best use of blackmail money I've ever heard."

"What?" Amy mulled over the possibility, then joined her mother, rocking once again in the same cadence. "It does sound like blackmail, doesn't it?"

"It must be what they were discussing in the helicopter. If you spoke Spanish, this mystery would be solved."

"If I spoke Spanish, they wouldn't have been discussing it over the headsets."

Fanny begrudgingly allowed this. "If we do our part and Jorge gets arrested for . . . whatever . . . does Oscar have to give back the money? I hope not."

"I hope not, too. But I don't think that can be our priority."

"Agreed." Fanny grunted as she pushed herself up from the rocker. "I'm thinking Oscar's blackmail has to be something he saw from the helicopter."

"That makes the most sense."

"Do we have a map? I think I saw a framed map in the hallway."

There were in fact two framed maps in the hallway off the great room, facing each other on opposite walls. One was similar to the topographical map they'd disfigured in Torre Vista in their attempt to find Lola, only this one had the Glendaval estancia at the epicenter instead of Torre Vista. The other was a larger, less detailed map of this entire section of Patagonia. Together, Amy and Fanny lifted it from the wall, carried it into the great room, and laid it out on the huge coffee table in front of the two-story walk-in fireplace.

"Okay," said Fanny, slapping the dust from her hands. "Where are we?"

Amy leaned over the coffee table and looked for anything familiar. There were names, mostly of lakes and rivers, mountain peaks and glaciers. A green dotted line showed the boundaries of the national park. A red dotted line showed the border with Argentina. Smaller symbols denoted campsites and the rare hotel in the park interior. "There's Lago Grey." She pointed to an armlike length of blue. "I think the river we saw today was the Rio Grey."

"You having a geography lesson?" It was Kevin Vanderhof, just walking in, nursing a fresh cup of coffee, looking young and adorable in his standard-issue bomber jacket with the fleece collar.

"Kevin." Amy couldn't hide her pleasure at seeing him, then immediately hoped he wouldn't take it the wrong way. "Hi." She straightened her smile. "You're just the man we need. Where exactly are we?"

Kevin crossed to the far side of the coffee table and peered down. They were almost head-to-head, and he took his time. "Right here," he said, his right index finger showing off the tiny print. "Glendaval," about two inches below the blue of Lago Grey.

"And where is Rio Grey?" Amy asked. "The river we saw today?"

Kevin's finger moved an inch or two to the right. "The Grey Glacier melts into Lago Grey, and the lake drains into the river." His finger went south on the map. "Rio Grey bends around here. It joins up with Rio Serrano and keeps going until it empties into Ultima Esperanza Sound. Last Hope Sound. Great name, huh? Some explorer thought it would be his last hope to find a passage into the Strait of Magellan. It didn't work out for him."

"The Rio Serrano?" Amy moved her own finger away from Kevin's. "That's where you found Lola Pisano's body."

"Right." Kevin moved to the other side of the table, giving Amy's finger a little breathing room. "Here's Torre Vista," he said. The print was the same size as that of "Glendaval," nearly invisible to the eye. "And here's the spot where we found her, give or take a kilometer."

"Really?" Amy's eyes went from one microscopic piece of typeface to the other. "I didn't realize how close the two estancias are."

"They're not really close," Kevin said. "As the crow flies, maybe fifty miles. But the ranches were built in the old days."

"It took us a full overnight trip on the train," said Fanny. "Not that I'm complaining. It was lovely."

Amy continued to stare, her focus traveling from the source of the Rio Grey to its merger with the Rio Serrano and beyond. Impossible terrain, but connected by rivers.

My God, could it be that simple? she wondered. All the wild complexities answered by the flow of a river? Simple and lucky. And clever, requiring a killer who could stay cool and solve problems on the fly—solve one little problem after another, until there were no problems left and he was in the clear.

"Amy, dear, what's wrong?" Fanny waved a hand in front of her daughter's eyes, still focused on the map. "Blink if you can hear my voice."

"Is she all right?" asked Kevin.

When Amy came back to life, she didn't speak. Instead, she took out her phone, pressed the camera button, and began to take close-up shots of the map—of Glendaval, of Torre Vista, of the rambling rivers nearly connecting the two.

"Mr. Vanderhof?" It was Jorge O'Bannion, striding down the curved staircase, his voice echoing off the rafters.

Amy blinked, feeling as if she'd been punched back into reality. "I'm okay," she reassured Kevin and Fanny, even though she didn't mean it. "Really."

O'Bannion was still talking as he approached. "Don't you need to fly before sunset? For safety, yes?"

"I should get back," agreed the young pilot. "Bright and early tomorrow we have a full flight to Dickson Lake area. Two days of trout." He straightened up, and O'Bannion could finally see what they'd been leaning over.

"Another map taken from the wall?" There was a disapproving note in his query. "Is the light not good enough in the hallway?"

Fanny tittered girlishly. "Oh, poor Jorge. We promise not to draw on this one. We just wanted to see where we are."

"That's why we have maps on the walls," said the resort owner. "So that everyone can see."

"I'm the one who took it down," said Kevin. "My fault." His wink to Amy could best be described as chivalrous. "I wanted to show them. The geography can be confusing."

"The other map is a closer view. Also the brochure."

"We wanted to see the big picture," said Amy, her mouth suddenly dry. "The helicopter ride piqued my curiosity."

"I was telling them about Last Hope Sound," said Kevin. "That would make a great title for a book, wouldn't it? Last Hope Sound. The Sound of Last Hope. Kind of a double meaning."

"Last hope," echoed O'Bannion. Then he stepped between Amy and Kevin and grabbed both sides of the picture frame. Kevin tried to help, but the older man refused. He stumbled away with the large, awkward rectangle between his outstretched arms, grunting with each step.

Kevin followed him toward the hall, apologizing again. Fanny was going to follow, but Amy touched her arm, and the Abels stayed behind.

"He's upset with us," Fanny said softly. "The poor man has a right to be."

"He's suspicious," Amy whispered back. "He suspects we know the truth."

Fanny drew her chin back. "And do we, dear? Know the truth?"

Amy nodded.

"From the map? Is that what your disturbing little trance was about?" Amy nodded again, and Fanny gasped. "Well, no wonder the man's upset. Tell me, tell me."

"Not now. Not here."

Fanny could barely stand it. "Is Jorge a killer? Tell me that much."

"Yes," Amy confirmed.

"Was it some lost backpacker they made up to look like Lola?"

Amy wanted to say more. But saying more would have meant saying everything. As simple as it was, there wasn't one answer that didn't lead to another question, and she couldn't risk explaining any of it in public. "We have to behave like nothing's wrong."

Fanny said she understood. Fighting every instinct, she managed to take her time. She visited the kitchen, heated up water for her thermos, opened a fresh packet of maté herbs, and washed out her gourd. When no one else was left in sight, she raced up the back stairs to the privacy of their room.

Meanwhile, Amy returned to the front porch. She leaned back against a post, arms folded, and watched as the engine roared, the rotors spun, and the helicopter wobbled into the air, carrying away the one friendly face, their one possible ally—the man who had, just before leaving, written down his e-mail address and shyly handed it to her—to another sector of the Patagonian wilderness.

CHAPTER 28

For Fanny, it was second nature now—mashing and stirring with her shiny *bombilla*. She curled herself up in the window seat overlooking the orchard and the cabin beyond, while Amy paced their room and tried to explain.

"I don't have all the pieces," Amy said haltingly. "But what I have makes sense. It's the only possibility that makes sense, even though it's wild."

"You apologize too much," said Fanny between long sips. "Just speak."

"Okay." Amy took a deep breath. "We start with the fact that Lola visited this estancia. I don't know if this was a surprise or if Jorge had been expecting her. But she was a private person and could easily have arrived at his cabin without anyone at the ranch seeing her."

"And you know this because of the pendant?"

"Right. Lola left behind her pendant. Also, Juanita saw a strange car on the road that day." Amy turned the corner and paced back. "My guess is she wasn't happy with the way business was going. The delays, the explosion, the expenses. I don't know how it happened, but Jorge killed her."

Fanny raised a hand. "You mean at the second estancia, not this one."

"No, I mean this one. Just hear me out."

"Oh, excuse me!" said Fanny and returned to her gourd.

Amy ignored the sarcasm. "Perhaps Jorge and Lola argued, and he lost his temper. Whatever happened, she was dead and he needed to hide the body. My guess is he used his motorcycle with the sidecar to drive it to some inaccessible spot."

"Out where the animals would eat it?"

Amy shrugged in the affirmative. "I don't know what he did with the car or her clothes. He didn't go on any of our excursions, so I assume he used that time to get rid of them. When Lola's family finally missed her and made inquiries, he could plead ignorance. She never arrived. He never saw her."

"But then I found the body. Yes!" Fanny pumped a fist in the air. "I'm so good."

"You found the body," Amy confirmed. "Nicolas and Oscar called Jorge on the two-way radio. They thought he was back here. Wherever Jorge really was, he returned to the scene and disposed of her body."

Fanny stopped slurping, quickly enough to make her choke. "How could he dispose of it? The police searched the whole area."

"Patagonia's best transportation system. He took the body fifty yards or so to the Rio Grey, slipped it in, and watched it float downstream."

"Okay . . ." Fanny drew out the word, then paused and cleared her throat. "I have about fifty questions."

"Just let me go on." Amy stopped pacing and settled onto the other half of the window seat, knee to knee with her mother, staring into her eyes. "Jorge had gotten away with murder. But he had a problem. He needed more of Lola's money. So he called someone. An actress friend from Valparaiso. Or just some woman who bore a resemblance. The fact that Lola was a bit of a recluse probably gave him the idea. With a fake mole and dyed hair, she could pass, especially since no one here knew the real Lola. When she arrived at Torre Vista, Jorge gave her Lola's pendant, just to make it more authentic."

"You're saying the Lola I met—"

"She was the fake, yes. The plan was for fake Lola to sign some documents, write a few checks, and disappear, never to be seen again."

Fanny thought it over, warming to the idea. "You know, when I ran into her and I started ranting on about death, she seemed definitely rattled."

"Everyone rattled her. That's why she stayed out of sight. Gabriela Garcia in particular was a threat, even though the two women had never met. When fake Lola rode off on her horse, it was partly to avoid Gabriela."

"And where did fake Lola go?"

"I don't know," Amy admitted. "But I remember in the Torre Vista garage . . . Jorge's sidecar was there, but not his motorcycle. If the motorcycle was waiting somewhere with a full tank of gas, fake Lola could have escaped to any little town and caught a bus."

"And so the Lola we saw in Valparaiso? That was the friend?"

"It had to be. She had removed the fake mole. But she hadn't changed the hair color or the curls. And the words I overheard—*hair dye, motorcycle, police, lucky*—they all fit in with my theory."

"Lucky," Fanny repeated. "I'll say the bastard was lucky."

"Remember how shocked he was when the pilots told him they'd found a body? He was a wreck. Kept saying it was impossible—until he saw for himself. Lola had floated into the Rio Serrano. If the helicopter hadn't accidentally flown over and spotted her, she would have just disappeared into the wilderness, eaten by condors and washed away."

"But he didn't count on the body getting found. How could he count on that?"

"He couldn't. He would have been happy just to have her disappear."

Fanny placed her gourd on the windowsill and got up to stretch. She hated saying anything negative to her daughter, about solving mysteries at least. "It's a little far-fetched, don't you think?"

"All in all, yes. But if you take it a step at a time, why not?"

"Wouldn't it be easier just to say that I'm psychic?"

"You're not psychic."

"No. According to you, I just saw the same corpse twice."

"It's the truth. The first time, she'd been dead only a short time. The condors must have just gotten there. Be honest, Mother. You exaggerated about all the condor pecking."

"It makes for a better Trippy."

"So you agree? That's how it must have happened?"

Fanny reluctantly agreed. Amy's theory did answer all the impossible questions. "So what was his mistake?" she asked, her natural optimism bubbling up. "Every killer makes a mistake. How do we nail Jorge O'Bannion?"

Amy didn't share her optimism. "I can't think of a single mistake. We have no way of finding his mysterious friend. And everything else is buttoned up."

"What about Oscar?" Fanny asked. "If he's getting money from Jorge, he must know something."

Amy thought about this. "From their behavior in the chopper, maybe Oscar noticed the tire tracks from Jorge's motorcycle going off to the river. I don't know if he pieced together the same thing I did, but he knows something's wrong. Our Jorge doesn't have much of a poker face."

Fanny was pleased. "So we should talk to Oscar. Juanita can translate."

"You want her to translate about how her father is blackmailing Jorge? Mother!"

"Come on!" Over the decades, Fanny had perfected this, the art of looking offended. "I can be subtle. Give me some credit."

It was a testament to their abject desperation that Amy didn't argue harder and longer than she did.

That night, after a simple dinner of trout, a present from Kevin's visit, Amy and Fanny complimented the chef and warmly thanked Jorge for his continued hospitality. Then they walked out of the empty dining room and went for a stroll. After circling back up toward the orchard, the Abels sneaked down to the service area and found a set of keys just where they expected to, in the ignition of the Land Rover parked farthest from the estancia.

Amy had a good memory for directions. She drove, lights off for the first minute, then lights on. Fanny took care of opening and closing the three sets of barbed-wire gates. The gaucho home was easier to find in the darkness, a constellation of incandescent lights nestled in the prairie.

All three of the Joneses came out to greet the guests. Juanita was still as excited as she'd been a few hours earlier. "Miss Abel, it is an honor to have you visit our home again. Mrs. Abel, welcome."

Oscar stepped off the porch and shook their hands. He also seemed to welcome them—although that was soon to change. They apologized for the late hour and their unexpected arrival. Oscar's wife, Maria, remained on the porch, near the door, observing.

"Can you tell your father we need to speak to him?" asked Amy. "And maybe you could translate for us."

"Translate? I will do my best." Juanita seemed to understand that it was a big responsibility.

Her mother understood enough to retreat back inside, while Oscar and his daughter sat themselves on the porch steps. Amy and Fanny said that they would prefer to stand. Oscar offered them some tea or maté. He would be happy to heat up the water and share a gourd. Fanny refused—"Please don't go to the trouble"—which signaled to everyone that this was not to be a friendly, neighborly visit.

"Please tell your father . . ." Amy had agonized over how best to say this. "We know what he and Senor O'Bannion were talking about this afternoon."

When Oscar heard the translation, he stiffened. "Do you understand Spanish?" Juanita asked on his behalf.

"No. But we saw what you saw from the helicopter." The Spanish word was close enough so that Juanita understood. *Helicóptero.*

"Jorge O'Bannion is a bad man." Fanny said this

directly to Oscar. "You need to tell the police what you know."

Juanita did her part. Then she asked her father a question of her own. He answered. She asked another and received a sterner, more forceful reply. "My father says he doesn't know what you are talking about. But I think he is lying to you."

"I think he is lying, too," Fanny said. "No, don't translate that, dear."

She didn't. But the three-part conversation deteriorated from that moment. Rather quickly. Oscar was angry with them for presuming to lecture him on right and wrong, for coming to his home only to insult him and, most of all, for involving his daughter. Juanita, as Amy had feared, was caught in the middle, trying to please her new American friends and trying not to antagonize her father.

"Did my father do something bad? Is he going to be arrested?"

"No," said Amy. "Your father's a good man."

"Is his job in danger?" she asked next. When Amy wasn't quick to reassure her, the teenager grew anxious and upset. "This is Mr. O'Bannion's land. Are we going to have to move? Where will we get work after this? What about my school?"

Amy and Fanny didn't have any answers. They tried their best to be vague with her and direct with her father, but they didn't stand a chance of succeeding at either. Juanita was sent inside the house, and Oscar Jones began shouting obscenities, what they assumed were obscenities, as he ushered them back, nearly pushed them back, to the Land Rover and pointed to the barbed-wire gate. This last portion of his tirade did not require any translation.

Inside the truck, a guilt-infused silence prevailed.

It was only after Fanny had returned from dealing with the third gate that anyone spoke.

"What were we thinking?" Amy asked softly.

"We're trying to catch a killer," Fanny said, settling back in and fastening her seat belt.

Amy bit her lip. "What is wrong with us? Why didn't I think this through? How could we be so arrogant?"

Fanny shrugged. "From Oscar's behavior just now, I'd say your theory is right on the money. For what it's worth."

"It's not worth much." Even on high, the headlights barely illuminated the dark, dusty trail. "People out here live on the edge. If Oscar tells the truth and Jorge isn't convicted, Juanita loses her education. Oscar loses his job, and the lives of three good people are ruined. If he is convicted, the New Patagonian Express will be over. Who would own the estates? Would they throw Oscar and his family out? And all this upheaval and damage for what? To get justice for a woman we never knew? For a woman who was probably mean and selfish to begin with?" Amy stepped heavy on the gas.

"The law doesn't care if a victim was bad or good. Even in Chile."

"Well, we did our part," Amy said. "More than our part. We have our answers, and it's over. We'll be home, safe in New York. With any luck, we won't have ruined Juanita's life. And you can invent some Trippy story that makes sense, even if it involves a maté vision."

"I think you're going a little overboard."

"I don't know where I'm going. It's been a long day."

"You don't know where you're going?" Fanny looked concerned.

"I know where I'm going." Amy made a sharp left turn with the last of the road. "The parking lot's right up here. The lodge is around the ridge."

The Land Rover pulled into the same spot it had evacuated less than an hour before. Amy cut the lights, throwing the lot into darkness. "We should have brought a flashlight," she grumbled. And just like that, it happened. A flashlight snapped on, its beam shining into the Land Rover's windshield.

Before they even saw his face, they knew it was O'Bannion. He turned the beam away from their eyes, and they could see in the spill of light the two-way radio in his other hand. His voice was even deeper than usual. "I am going to have to ask you to leave tomorrow."

"Really?" Fanny feigned the innocence of a newborn puppy. "I thought we had one more day."

"After what you did? After what I know you've been doing all along?"

"What have we been doing?" Fanny asked. "You mean taking the truck for a little joyride? I'm sorry. But we brought it back. No scratches. You can check."

"Oscar called me."

"Oscar called?" Amy asked. Of course he'd called. He was protecting his family.

"That's where we went for our little ride." Fanny laughed. "You should have been there. We don't communicate well, Oscar and I. He got upset about something. . . . Some misunderstanding."

"Enough." They could see Jorge struggling with his anger, wanting to say more, to accuse them of betrayal, of spying on him, but not daring even to bring up the subject. "In the morning I will have a man drive you into Puerto Natales. You can arrange your transportation from there."

And with that, Jorge turned and marched away, through the parking area and around the bend toward the lodge. In a matter of half a minute, the beam of his light flickered and disappeared.

"Hello?" Fanny shouted into the darkness. "Hello! You could have left the flashlight!"

CHAPTER 29

The next morning Amy woke up slowly. Through the cobwebs, she could sense that her mother was already up—not up and trying to be politely quiet, but up and trying with every movement to lure her out of bed. This went on for some time. The rustling of pages, the dropping of a shoe, the closing of a door, all designed to make her show some sign of human life. But Fanny's efforts had the opposite effect, like on those mornings at home, when Amy would be lying half awake and the alarm clock would go off. Whatever energy she might have had right before the alarm sounded would be sapped away by the sound of the alarm.

"What time is it?" She mumbled the words reproachfully, head still under the covers.

"Around five forty-five," answered Fanny. "Good morning, sunshine."

"Five forty-five a.m.? How long have you been up?"

"An hour maybe. I couldn't sleep."

"I can tell."

"I kept thinking about all the footage I took, all of it lost. So I decided to read the instruction manual, just for fun."

"Instruction manual?" She oozed her head out of her cocoon to see her mother, fully dressed, sitting at their imitation Chippendale desk, studying a black credit card–sized device and the contents of two open pamphlets. "Are you talking about the camera?" Amy asked, then produced her first big yawn of the day.

"It's the VITA Pro Action Camera," Fanny announced without looking up. "You know your Uncle Joe, always pushing me to buy the latest crap. Like this little doohickey that came with it." She fingered the thick black credit card. "It's a remote. They say you can turn on the VITA Pro from a distance of six hundred feet."

"Interesting."

"I guess it makes sense if you're a nature photographer or you're sending up the camera in a hot air balloon, or whatever else people do with them."

"Very interesting."

Fanny grinned. "That's what I thought. And then I was checking the camera's battery life. You know, to see if it might still be working out there in the middle of nowhere."

Amy was listening now, the cobwebs magically dispersing. "Very, very interesting."

"After half an hour the VITA Pro Action has an automatic shutoff, unless you change the settings, which I didn't." Fanny flipped to the next page. "When you turn it back on with this doohickey, the camera lights up and beeps. Oh, and the best part. Once it's on, it sends a signal, unless again you change the settings, which again I didn't. You can track it on a little map on your phone. I just spent half an hour downloading the app."

"And the camera's battery life?"

"A maximum of four hours." Fanny finally looked over at the newly hatched creature. "And to spare you the great exertion of asking, yes, I charged the battery right before I lost it. My estimate is that we have at least an hour—between the time we remotely turn on the camera and the time its battery dies and it stops sending the signal."

"Are you suggesting we wander around where you were on your horse, pressing the remote?"

"Uh-huh. Apparently, people lose and re-find these cameras all the time."

Amy was impressed. "I'd completely forgotten about that."

"Pretty smart of your old mother."

"So, all we have to do is get within six hundred feet." Amy was already out of bed, sniffing through the bedside drawer for a clean pair of underwear. "It's a long shot."

"What's six hundred feet? A couple football fields? Not a bad long shot." Fanny had gone to the closet, looking for a pair of comfortable shoes. "Think of what's on that video. Lola's body, time-stamped, days before she died. How is Jorge going to explain that?"

"Are you sure you caught her face?"

"Ten seconds, at least. I made myself do it for Trippy."

Amy was at the same closet now, grabbing a pair of jeans and thinking through the logistics. "Should we contact Kevin and his helicopter? He'd be glad to help, although it would be expensive."

Fanny gave her that look. "What do you mean,

contact him? Did you ask that cute boy for his number? What would Marcus say?"

"I didn't ask for his number. He gave me his e-mail, and I haven't thrown it out."

"Well, Kevin's busy. Two days of trout fishing, remember? It's just you and me, sweetie. Well?"

Normally, it took Amy five minutes to pick out a top. Now she grabbed the first thing she saw on a hanger, Marcus's oversize plaid shirt. "Okay. Let's do it." For Amy, the mental jolt was better than five alarm clocks and ten cups of coffee. They had gone to bed defeated and had gotten up within reach of success. She didn't even need a hot shower. The earlier they got out, the less chance they would have of being seen.

Within ten minutes they were in the same Land Rover, this time with Fanny behind the wheel, her Peruvian Batman hat pulled snugly over her hair, the pompom flapping in the breeze of an open window.

In the passenger seat, Amy checked her phone. Kevin had been nice enough to point out the spot on the map where Jorge had gotten so nervous, and she'd been smart enough to take photos of the map. Mother and daughter had each grabbed an apple from the bowl in the great room and hoped it would last until they either succeeded or gave up.

According to this section of the map, now expanded on the phone until the lines and swirls went blurry, the route out of the Glendaval valley was fairly clear. "We're basically heading for the Rio Grey." Even with her seat belt on, Amy's head bounced up against the dome light, and she regretted leaving her mother in charge of the driving. "Can you slow down and maybe not aim for the ruts?"

"No. The ruts are aiming for me." But she did slow down enough to keep Amy's head dome-free.

"We need to head more toward that butte," Amy advised, pointing to a small, sandy mesa in the distance. "Take a right." There wasn't much of a right to take, just a path with fewer scrubby bushes than the non-paths. Fanny did as she was told, and Amy was satisfied that they were drawing closer to the site of Fanny's vision and the river just beyond.

The terrain was changing into familiar foothills, but now there were even more ruts aiming themselves under the Land Rover. After one particularly nasty bump, the rear tires got stuck in a waterless gully, bringing the vehicle to an abrupt, shuddering stop. The seat belts saved them both from the dashboard.

When the dust cleared, Amy got out to push. And when the tires and undercarriage were finally free, she took over behind the wheel. Fewer ruts wound up attacking them after that, but not a lot fewer.

They were driving parallel to the sandy butte now. "I remember riding along here," Fanny said.

"Before or after your vision?"

"After, I think. Do you want to try the remote?"

"Sure," said Amy. "We'll give it a shot." She had no idea if being in a vehicle in motion would affect the remote's ability to function. Deciding to err on the side of being outside and stationary, she stepped off the pedal and waited until they rolled to a stop.

On getting out of the Land Rover, they wordlessly agreed to make a production of it. Fanny opened the app, while Amy aimed the thick black credit card everywhere and nowhere in particular. Pressing the button resulted in a tiny beep. But there was no answering beep from anywhere, not within earshot.

They hovered over the phone together and watched the little dotted circle on the app revolve until the appearance of the words *no signal* signaled their failure.

Amy hadn't really expected it to work on their first try. She would have been amazed. But still there was a feeling of disappointment, and the nagging suspicion that it wouldn't work at all, even if they accidentally parked themselves right on top of the camera.

Neither Abel spoke. They got back into their four-wheel drive and continued down the path along the bottom of the butte.

"I definitely remember coming by here," Fanny said. Amy appreciated the deception, if it was a deception, which she had no way of knowing. But she appreciated it.

When they were half a kilometer farther along, around the next bend, Amy eased off the gas and they tried again. She was prepared this time for failure. Maybe in an hour, a signal might miraculously hit the phone. Maybe after a few more turns, she hoped, after they'd made their way around and down to the Rio Grey. Maybe on their way back it would happen, she hoped, when all seemed lost. It would be a process. They wouldn't give up. And either it would work or it wouldn't.

Again, they got out. Again, they went through the procedure, with the remote aimed into the heavens and the dotted circle on the phone spinning and spinning. Again, the words *no signal* replaced the dotted circle. Fanny sighed and was in the process of fingering the *OFF* button when the dotted circle reappeared. This was enough encouragement to make her hold the phone aloft and wave it slowly back and forth, like a lighter at an eighties rock concert.

"What?" Amy shouted, her voice echoing off the cliff walls. "What is it?"

When Fanny lowered the phone to eye level, there was a new map on the screen, barely a map, since there were no details except a tiny compass and quadrants of vertical and horizontal lines. A little red dot pulsed not far from a little black *X*. "I can't believe it." There was awe in her voice.

Amy peered over her shoulder. "Are we the *X*?"

"I didn't get around to all the instructions. But the dot must be the camera." Fanny pressed the plus sign in the bottom right. The view zoomed in, and the symbols grew farther apart. "I think if we walk this direction . . ." They left the vehicle and headed farther along the bottom edge of the cliff, almost tripping over the rocks and roots, their eyes still glued to the screen.

"We're getting closer," Amy said.

It certainly seemed to be true. The *X* was moving with each correction of the screen, coming closer and closer to the pulsing dot. They were almost on top of it now. Amy started scouring their surroundings, alert for the little black box of a camera. When Fanny checked the phone again, maybe fifty feet farther along the path, her face grew confused. She blinked, then pressed the plus sign again and squinted. The screen corrected. "Um, I think we just passed it."

"How could we pass it?" Amy asked. She grabbed the phone and checked for herself. "How could we pass it?" she repeated, then pressed the plus sign again until it hit the maximum close-up setting. She crossed back and forth over the same few dozen yards. "Mom, take the phone and stand here. I'll look around."

"Why do *you* get to look around?"

"Because I'm younger and my eyes are better."

"You wear glasses."

"And you wear contacts. Just do it, okay?"

Reluctantly, Fanny did as she was told, acting as a pivot point while her daughter walked in larger and larger semicircles from the cliff face outward, her eyes alert to any smooth man-made object, pressing her boots into thick, prickly bushes and focusing on little holes in the dirt.

"Do they have groundhogs here?" Amy wondered out loud. "Maybe a groundhog came and buried it." She retraced her steps and started again. When she returned to her maternal pivot point, Amy's hands were empty.

"Are you done now, Miss Eagle Eye?" asked Fanny, looking up from the display. There was a familiar smugness in her tone. "'Cause if you are, you should check this out."

While Amy had been searching, Fanny had changed screens. The red dot and the *X* were still there, practically on top of each other. But the on-screen compass was larger, and there were numbers across the bottom, followed by *ft.* "We're thirty-five feet away," Amy deduced. "Does it say which direction? Because I've looked farther than thirty-five feet."

"It doesn't say the direction." Fanny was still smug. "We're right on top of it, and yet it's thirty-five feet away." And with that, she turned dramatically toward the butte and pointed straight up. "There."

The cliff above them was craggy and worn. Thousands of years of wind and rain had created crevices in the stratified stone wall, some mere indentations, some of them large enough to resemble caves.

"Up there?" Amy asked. "How did it get up there?"

"I don't know. I certainly wasn't riding up there."

Amy stood, hands on her hips, and tried to make sense of it. "How tall is that cliff?" she asked.

Fanny snorted. "What am I? Some sort of nature expert?"

"How tall of a building?"

"Oh, when you put it that way . . ." Fanny craned her neck and adjusted her thinking. "Five stories at least."

"Fifty-something feet. And yet our app says the camera's thirty-five feet away."

"So the app is malfunctioning?"

"Or the camera's in one of those openings."

Fanny bit her lower lip. "Do you think a hermit found it and brought it back to his cave?"

"I'm not sure they have hermits here—or any-where these days." Amy situated herself under one of the cave-like crevices and saw that the GPS distance was the shortest here. Straight up, thirty feet. "Come on," she said. "There's a little ledge in front of it. I think we can get up there."

"Up to the cave? How?"

"Give me a minute, would you?"

There didn't seem to be any direct path up to the ledge or the crevice. But Amy remembered walking past a break in the wall, a natural fault line where millions of years ago the sandy sedimentary rock had been pushed up at an angle to form part of the cliff, jutting up at a not-impossible angle and worn almost into a path by the millennia of rainy runoff. If a climber were to hug the wall and go sideways . . . if the climber was lucky and sure-footed enough . . . Amy kept one eye on the crevice as she walked back, seeing if and how it would line up with the fault.

They were almost back to the Land Rover when she saw that the ledges did line up, both part of the same stratum of prehistoric soil turned into rock. It was like a long, narrow, distressed ramp. And it wouldn't be all that far.

"I think I can do it," she called back to her mother, who was lagging behind, as always.

"We can both do it," Fanny said, waddling to catch up.

Amy didn't waste her time arguing. "Go in front, where I can keep my eye on you."

Fanny stopped and took a glance at the precarious ledge. "Really? You're going to let me risk my life?"

"Mom. We don't have time for games. Yes or no?"

The answer was yes, of course. Amy bent over and linked her fingers. Fanny grunted as she lifted a leg and stepped into her daughter's hand. She straightened her knee into a precarious stand. And then somehow Amy managed to straighten her own knees. The ledge was just low enough to allow Fanny to step onto it and hug the rock face.

Amy watched her mother take a few side steps up the angled ledge. When she was satisfied with Fanny's footing, she followed, using her greater height and agility to clamber up without any assistance.

"All right," she mumbled, her mouth pressed into the rock. "Step by step. And don't look down."

CHAPTER 30

The climb took longer than Amy had expected but wasn't nearly as terrifying. Several yards from their starting point, the natural ledge actually widened under their feet and the feeling of imminent disaster faded into an excruciatingly slow but careful crab walk as the two women felt for a foothold with every step. Fanny was doing well, Amy marveled to herself. Her mother wasn't being impatient or reckless, two of her more distinctive traits. She was taking her time. And while a fall from this height probably wouldn't kill either of them, it would definitely be unpleasant.

They were only a few steps away from the crevice, the black hole they'd pinpointed from the ground, thirty or so feet up, the spot where, according to the app on Fanny's phone, the VITA Pro Action was waiting for them, as improbable as that seemed.

Two more steps and Fanny grabbed the lip of the crevice.

"Good job," Amy muttered into the rock face. She took a second to smile in her mother's direction but had to look away. "Augh." The mirrorlike Batman insignia on the Peruvian wool cap was catching the sunlight and causing her to see spots.

The hole in the rock face was maybe six feet in diameter, wide enough and deep enough to accommodate them both. Fanny was just about to pull herself off the ledge and into the blackness when something in the cave erupted.

Fanny screamed but held on. Her grip was loosening, and she had no choice but to pull herself into the now empty hole. Amy screamed, too, and teetered on a loose spot of gravel on the ledge, her fingers trying to grasp the stone.

The eruption had been a huge gray swirl of movement and air, like a ghost, flying out of the darkness of the crevice and spreading its wings. Amy steadied herself first, then turned her head and watched as the Andean condor sailed down, flapping its long, jagged wings and catching just enough wind to lift it into the cloudless blue.

"Mom? Are you okay? Mom?" Amy took a half dozen quick baby steps, grabbed the lip, and followed her mother into the mouth of the cave. It took her eyes a moment to adjust.

"I think we disturbed its nest," Fanny's voice announced calmly from the shadows. "See?" She was pointing.

Amy had never seen a condor's nest before. It was larger than she'd imagined, not that she'd ever imagined a condor's nest. It sat less than two feet back into the chamber; was about the same size and shape as a truck tire; and was constructed of twigs, bits of brownish moss, and a few little strings of bright red fabric. Fanny was staring down into it. Reaching down into it.

"Don't touch the eggs," Amy shouted.

"There are no eggs," Fanny shouted back. Then she straightened up and displayed the stringy remains of a frayed red strap, with a small black camera hanging from the end. "But there is this."

Amy laughed. "A condor stole your camera?" She felt almost giddy. They were no longer balancing on a ledge, no longer facing a wild, meat-eating bird, and suddenly, amazingly, in possession of their goal. "It must have liked the strap."

"I can't believe this actually worked," Fanny said. Then she took the camera to the lip of the cave, where a patch of sun gave her enough light to see the buttons. Neither one said a word as the little machine whirred to life. There seemed to be enough juice left to power up the rectangular display on the rear. Fanny pressed a few buttons, reversing and fast-forwarding. Reversing and fast-forwarding, with a few grunts along the way. "Ooh, remember our tour of La Boca? That was fun."

"It was after that."

"Of course it was. Give me a minute." A few more fast-forwards and reverses. And then . . . "I got her," Fanny said. She pressed *PAUSE* and held out the display.

Amy tried to look at the frozen image but was once again blinded by the Batman mirror on Fanny's forehead. "Jeez, Mom, can you please take that off?"

"Take what off? Oh! I think we have more important things to do than discuss fashion."

Amy moved the camera out of the direct sunlight to check for herself. "It's her," she confirmed, taking off her glasses and squinting. "I think so."

She had met the real, living Lola Pisano only once, in a dim tango hall in Buenos Aires. But the face—

bloody, perhaps from a fall or a wound, damaged by a few condor pecks—matched the face in her memory, mole and all. And it perfectly matched that of the much more damaged, bloated corpse they'd found in the Rio Serrano.

"Yes, definitely her."

"Then we got him," Fanny crowed as she took back the camera and kissed it on the lens. "Our charmingly smug cold-blooded killer. All we have to do is find our way back to the ranch, behave like nothing happened, take the next whatever to Santiago or wherever the real police are, and show them." Fanny's celebration was interrupted by a flapping shadow, the sound of beating wings, and a guttural hiss echoing off the rock. "But first we should get out of here." Just for good measure, she walked back into the sunlight and started waving her arms. "Shoo!"

Amy joined her mother at the mouth of the shallow cave. Off in the distance, but not far enough off for their comfort, were two condors now, circling on the thermals in a tight little pattern. They had retreated from their approach but were starting to circle closer. "I think they want their cave back."

"That's reasonable," Fanny agreed. "Want me to go first? It should be easier going down." She wound what was left of the red strap tightly around her wrist, letting the camera dangle and keeping her hands free, and took a first tentative step out to the ledge.

"Mom, wait." Amy put a hand on her mother's shoulder and pulled her back. Out on the Patagonian plain, below and beyond the condors, they could see a moving column of dust. It was approaching on the same dirt trail that they themselves had just used. "You think it's Jorge?"

Reverberating up from the stubbled plain came

the soft but distinctive sound of a truck engine. Fanny shrugged. "Well, he was bound to notice we were gone. Should we hurry down and drive off?"

Amy shook her head. "He's going to see our dust, like we're seeing his. It'll look like we're running away."

"We don't even know he's coming this way."

"My guess is he followed our tracks."

"Maybe it's not him."

"Really? Who else?"

The Abels went back and forth like this, arguing the pros and cons of going down or staying or meeting Jorge halfway, waiting for him on the ledge or waiting for him by the truck, until it just didn't matter anymore. The dust column was coming straight for them, growing into a Land Rover like their own. Amy pulled her mother back into the crevice, and they watched as it slowed and stopped, parking maybe a dozen yards away from their abandoned vehicle.

Jorge emerged from the passenger side, and a few seconds later, Oscar, the gaucho, emerged from the driver's. The men approached the other Land Rover, one on each side, and looked through the tinted windows, talking back and forth.

"We should let them know we're here," Amy whispered.

"Why?" Fanny whispered back.

"Because . . ." Amy sighed. "Because I left the keys in the ignition."

"You did what? Well, that was irresponsible. What if they take it?"

"You know, that possibility didn't really occur to me."

"Mrs. Abel?" a voice echoed up. Jorge O'Bannion was turning in a circle, hands cupped to his mouth. "Fanny? Amy? Where are you?" He turned toward the cliff, his eyes drawn to the top directly above him and not fifty yards farther along and halfway up the rock face. "Fanny? Amy?" They stood perfectly still, becoming just another pair of irregularly shaped shadows in one of the multiple weatherworn openings. "Where are you?"

"We should answer," Amy hissed into her mother's ear.

"What do we say?"

"Well, we don't tell him about the camera in the condor's nest."

"But what do we tell him?" Fanny asked. "That we took up rock climbing?"

"It's better than saying nothing and getting abandoned."

"I suppose." Fanny stepped six inches forward into the sunlight, staring at Jorge and mulling over their options. The choice didn't remain theirs for long. The aristocratic man in his jeans and sheepskin jacket noticed something on the ground under his feet, a moving bright spot shaped roughly like a rectangle. He bent at the waist for a closer look, then reached down, as if to touch it. When he straightened, he was already facing in their direction, a hand shielding his eyes. Jorge O'Bannion was staring directly at them.

Amy was the first to realize. "Mom, it's your hat!"

"Don't start in about my hat."

"No, the reflection."

It took Fanny a moment to see that the mirrored Batman logo on her Peruvian wool cap had acted as an unintended bat signal. She snatched it off her head and threw it into the condor's nest.

"Fanny?" Jorge O'Bannion was walking toward them now, squinting up at the cliff face. "What in the world are you doing there?"

Amy's gut reaction was to retreat as far as the shallow cave would let her, but it was too late. "We came up here for the view," she said, improvising.

"The view of what?" Jorge asked, glancing back at the flat expanse of scrub. The man had a point.

"We got lost," Amy said. "We were hoping we could get a view of the estancia."

"The estancia? It's too far. And you could hurt yourself climbing like this." There was concern in his words but not in his tone. His tone was full of suspicion. "Well, now you are found. Lucky for you, Oscar is a professional tracker."

"Yes, very lucky," said Amy. "We can get down by ourselves. Don't worry."

"Good. Oscar will drive you to Puerto Natales. But you have to come now. Enough is enough."

"We need to talk to you first," Fanny said.

"Talk?" Jorge threw his hands in the air. "No. No, I am very busy. And this foolhardy excursion has made my schedule worse. Oscar will help you down and drive you. Meanwhile, I'm leaving. I have been more than patient."

"All the same, we need to talk," Fanny insisted.

"We do not need to talk." O'Bannion was near enough to speak in an almost normal voice, but he was shouting. "We are through with talking, Senora Abel. You crazy women stole my property and worried me and wasted hours of my morning. I never want to talk to either of you again. Is that clear? Good-bye." He was about to retreat to the spot where Oscar stood now, arms crossed, between the two trucks.

"We know you killed Lola Pisano," Fanny shouted back.

"Mother?" The word came out as an elongated moan. "What the hell?"

O'Bannion stiffened. Then he returned to the foot of the cliff, three stories below. "What do you know, Senora Abel?"

Fanny smiled a thin, nasty smile and squared her shoulders. "We know you dumped her in the river and she floated downstream. We know you hired some woman to impersonate her."

"Interesting." Jorge choked out a laugh. "And how do you know this?"

"We figured it out," Fanny answered, "after that night in Valparaiso. We saw you and the woman together. Did you hire her for your masquerade? Or is she your lady friend? Your coconspirator? Not that it matters."

"Is that it?" O'Bannion looked relieved. "Seeing her? So you are just guessing."

"It's more than guessing," Fanny said. "When we tell the police what we know, they'll talk to your Valparaiso friends and they'll track her down. I think she'll confess."

O'Bannion laughed. "I doubt that very much."

"What do you doubt? That they can track her down or that she'll confess?"

Amy had been struck dumb by her mother's reckless antagonism. Her one consolation was that Fanny wasn't stupid. Impetuous and willful, but not stupid. Annoying and unfocused, but not stupid. Amy kept her mouth shut and tried to think it through. What was the point of all this? What could possibly be the point? And why was her mother standing stiffly like that and off centered, with her weight on her left side?

Quickly enough, Amy saw it—the VITA Pro Action, balanced in the crook of Fanny's left arm, its lens pointed out and downward. A flash of red pulsated against her jacket. Impetuous and willful, but not stupid at all.

"You can tell us," Fanny continued. "It might be cathartic. And we don't have to worry about Oscar hearing."

O'Bannion glanced in Oscar's direction, curled his lip, then turned back up to face the Abels. "It was an accident."

"You killed her accidentally?" Amy had joined in.

"Yes, accidentally. I'm not a murderer, despite your opinion of me."

"What?" Fanny adjusted her arm. "My hearing isn't what it used to be. Can you speak up?"

Surprisingly enough, O'Bannion complied. "When Lola paid her visit, she was upset." His voice was loud and clear. "The money. The problems. But I could talk her into things. Given time, she would see how important it was. With a little more faith, the business would be a success. My father's dream. My legacy. All I needed was time. But she was stubborn. When she tried to walk out . . ." He cricked his neck uncomfortably. "I had no choice but to stop her."

It took all of Amy's self-control not to glance at the camera. "I understand."

Fanny also seemed to understand. "It must feel good to get that off your chest," she said.

"To be honest, no," said O'Bannion. "But it makes no difference, does it? Since no one will ever hear me say that again." And with that, he began walking back toward the vehicles. "Oscar?" he shouted, then followed up with a sharp sentence or two in Spanish.

Fanny stepped out of his line of vision and switched off the camera. Amy joined her. "Pretty smart of your old mother, huh? Even if the video is a little jerky, the audio alone . . ."

"Very smart," Amy agreed, although she didn't quite feel like celebrating. There had been something about Jorge O'Bannion's tone just now. "We should get off this cliff."

"Agreed," said Fanny. This time she secured the camera inside her nylon Windbreaker, where it would be camouflaged by her natural contours, and zipped up tight.

When they next looked down to ground level, one of the Land Rovers, the one driven by Oscar, was on the move. It made a tight little circle and began to pick up speed, retracing its path back toward civilization. Jorge O'Bannion stood there, watching it go. When the vehicle was kicking up dust a good kilometer away, he pivoted back to the cliff, gave a soldier's salute to the two women, got into the second Land Rover, and made a similar tight little circle.

Then he drove off.

CHAPTER 31

It had seemed a very doable hike, at least at first, when the day was young and they weren't yet so hungry and dehydrated, to follow the trail of tire tracks back to Glendaval. At the estancia there would be a few sympathetic employees, they thought, including their English-speaking waiter Alejandro. They would find Alejandro and explain their situation, and they would be safe. If Jorge O'Bannion was counting on them to just give up and die in the middle of nowhere, then the man was a bad judge of character.

The last food they'd eaten had been the apples in the truck. The last water had been from the water bottles in the truck. Amy led the way for the first hour, keeping a steady pace in the bright sunlight, walking into a light breeze, which kept them both from overheating. She had promised herself she wouldn't look back until the hour mark. It might have been a few minutes before the hour when she finally did and saw just how close the cliff face still seemed. An optical illusion, of course. But a disheartening one. Amy said nothing to her mother but kept up the pace. After that she kept looking back every few minutes, just to check.

The landscape was not as easy to navigate as they'd thought. On closer inspection, taken step by laborious step, the topography was not a straight plain, but was littered with dry arroyos and small foothills. The cliffs, such a prominent starting point, would disappear every now and then, only to reappear in what seemed like a slightly different location. Amy tried to use the sun as a reconnoitering point, but of course the sun kept moving. Their only sure guide, their lifeline, was the line of tracks, and she maintained her focus on that.

Through all of this, Fanny kept up, trudging without complaint, her head protected by that damned Peruvian cap. Amy's own head was uncovered, and she could feel the beginning of a sunburn on the top of her head and the back of her neck. Luckily, she was dark complected, but that didn't help her lips. More than once she rummaged through her pockets, hoping to find a small, forgotten tube of lip balm. How many times had she roamed around New York, carrying forgotten tubes of lip balm that she never used? In place of the balm, she started licking her lips to keep them from chapping, but she succeeded only in making her mouth feel even drier.

Twice so far Fanny had stopped to get pebbles out of her walking shoes, balancing herself on Amy's arm as she untied the shoe, slipped it off, shook it out, and replaced it. After the second adjustment, Amy felt her mother's pace slow down. Amy slowed her own pace, and they fell in side by side. And because it felt so unnatural, so depressing, to continue without saying anything . . .

"How are you holding up?"

"Fine," Fanny said. "And you?"

"Fine," Amy said. This lively exchange was followed by another unnatural, depressing pause.

"What are you thinking?"

"Oh." Amy decided to be honest. "I was thinking that Jorge knows these parts better than we do. He was raised around here."

Fanny raised a plucked eyebrow. "Your point?"

"My point is Jorge thinks we won't make it. I'm not trying to be pessimistic."

"Well, he doesn't know us, does he? We'll make it."

"And if we don't?"

"You're a cheery one."

"What do you think he'll tell the authorities? I mean, he has to acknowledge that we were at the estancia. Marcus knows. People there know. He'll probably say we went out for a hike. And he'll probably wait as long as possible before telling anyone. Just to make sure we're dead."

"What about Oscar?" asked Fanny. "When Jorge drives back without us, what will Oscar say? He's not a killer."

Amy had had plenty of time to think. She'd thought about Oscar, the one outsider who knew at least part of the truth. "Oscar showed his colors when he ratted us out. Maybe he'll feel bad. I hope he does. But he's not going to ruin his life to save a pair of crazy gringos. He's also not going to ruin his daughter's chance at a future. Juanita is his whole life."

Fanny mulled this over. A few seconds later she broke into a chuckle. More of a snigger than a chuckle. "The joke will be on them, won't it? Because someone's going to find our bodies. And when they do . . ." She patted the bulging pocket of her jacket. "They're also going to find Jorge's confession."

"You're right. That's a great joke."

"I'd like to see him talk his way out of that."

"Unless he's the one who finds our bodies—which is perfectly plausible since he's the one who knows approximately where to look."

Fanny sighed but didn't break stride. "You are a walking, talking depressant."

"Me? I'm not the one who brought up the idea of dying here."

"Forgive me for trying to look on the bright side."

"You made me feel so much better."

Amy actually did feel better. The fact that she and her mother could still banter, even when trekking through the Patagonian prairie, abandoned by a killer, with no water or map or supplies, that had to be a good sign, didn't it? Honestly, how bad could things be?

It was around that point that Amy looked down at the trail of tire tracks and saw that there was no longer a trail. At some point—two minutes ago, ten?—it had disappeared in the breeze or they had wandered off it.

After the sun dipped below the mountains in the west, the temperature dropped. And dusk, the afterglow of sunset, came and went dangerously fast, leaving them in near-total darkness. Only the stars and a sliver of the moon supplied any light at all. They had tried out several gullies, but the first two were aligned with the prevailing breeze, acting as wind tunnels instead of buffers. The third gully was deeper and flowed perpendicular to the others.

It was here that they set up for the night, not that

there was much to set up. Amy cleared away a few rocks and settled her mother in first. The two of them curled up in back-to-back fetal positions, drawing every piece of clothing tightly around their bodies. They had both worn jeans; that was good. Fanny had her Windbreaker. And the heavy shirt, Marcus's flannel, had been a lucky choice for Amy that morning.

"I'm so thirsty," Fanny groaned, almost inaudibly. "Not to mention hungry. What are we going to do?"

Amy had the same question. The hunger was painful and constant. But the thirst was worse. It affected everything: her joints, her ability to think and move. Even her eyesight. She could feel her mother's back against hers as they both struggled to find a good position. "They say if you suck on a button, it helps. It can help retain the moisture in your mouth."

Fanny didn't answer, even though the suggestion of sucking on a button would have provoked five minutes of banter under a different set of circumstances. Amy tore the two buttons from the breast pockets of her shirt, popped one into her own mouth, and handed the other around to her mother.

"It's relatively clean. Don't swallow."

Half a minute later, Fanny answered. "Thank you. I think it helps." The moon had just disappeared behind the clouds. The stars were disappearing, too.

"Good," replied Amy. The button did help. Her own mouth was no longer quite so dry. "Just take it out before you fall asleep. The last thing I need is you choking to death." Again, a perfect opening for Fanny Abel's legendary banter. Again, nothing.

"Amy?" She only rarely called her daughter by her first name.

"Yes, Mom."

"I'm sorry," Fanny mumbled.

"Don't swallow your button."

"It's all my fault. The one time I tag along and what happens? I get you stuck in the wilderness, sucking buttons, and . . . I won't say dying. I won't say that. Trying to survive."

"We'll survive."

"You warned me. Before we even started. But would I listen to you? No."

"Mom, it's not your fault."

"Really? Do you think Jorge would have abandoned us if I hadn't been so clever? We had all the evidence we needed. But I had to push it. You're right. I'm impulsive and reckless. You never should have brought me along."

"I'm glad you're here," Amy said. "I can't imagine being out here on my own."

Fanny had been hoping for Amy to give her more of an argument. But, to be honest, it was her fault, and she felt horrible and helpless about everything. When the warm body behind her began to convulse in little shakes, Fanny knew that her daughter was crying, her soft sobs half lost in the wind. Slowly, the shakes subsided.

"If you cry, you'll get more dehydrated." Fanny advised.

"I don't think any water came out." Amy sniffled and cleared her throat. "I was just thinking about Marcus."

"He loves you."

"I love him. That's what makes it sad. I didn't think anyone could replace Eddie."

"No one can replace Eddie."

"But I kept comparing them, and that wasn't fair. Whatever I have with Marcus is different. He's infuriating and unpredictable, and he lies whenever it suits him. But that doesn't make it any less valid. All my talk about finding an apartment, what was that about? We have the perfect place already. Marcus knew it. You knew it. It was just a dumb excuse."

"So you're going to let him move in?"

"It's all theoretical now, isn't it?"

Fanny didn't have an answer. Her usual phrases of comfort and reassurance felt suddenly hollow and couldn't force themselves past her lips. Perhaps she was just too exhausted and hungry and dehydrated. Perhaps she had already said them so often that they felt false, and now was not the time or place for false hope. In the silence, she could feel her daughter's body start to shake again. The sobs were barely audible—until the last few erupted into something that resembled a cough.

"Are you all right?" asked Fanny.

"I swallowed my button."

"Oh, well. That's the least of our problems." But just to be on the safe side, Fanny spat out her own and slipped it into her pocket for later. She burrowed down farther into the arroyo, trying to get a smidgen less uncomfortable. When she felt the first fat drops of water on her hand, she assumed that Amy was crying again and that the tears had somehow been carried on the breeze. It took her a second to realize. "Rain," she muttered grumpily. "Just what we need."

"What?" Amy had stopped crying.

"I said, 'Rain. Just what we . . .' Wait a minute. It *is* what we need." The drops were coming heavier now, falling closer together.

Fanny and Amy stumbled to their feet, colliding as they did. Their impulse was to tilt their heads back and just drink it in. That worked for half a minute, until the rain escalated into a downpour and they both began to choke.

"Your Windbreaker," Amy shouted. "We can use it like a tarp."

Fanny understood. She unzipped the waterproof jacket, took it off, and together they held it open, leaving it slack in the center to funnel the rain into a little plastic pool. They were getting drenched, Amy in her flannel and Fanny in her thin wool pullover. In the near total darkness, she could visualize the pool growing from a few drops to maybe a few ounces.

Fanny turned her head back up to the sky. She hooted victoriously, long and loud, feeling like a wild animal. Amy didn't join her, since she wasn't much of a hooter. After the howl, Fanny kept her mouth open, relishing the cool wetness in her throat, being sure to swallow occasionally and not choke. Until it stopped. It took her a moment to realize the rain had ended. A few stars were starting to reappear above her open mouth, shimmering through a scudding band of low clouds. Fanny licked her lips. "So that's it?"

"A passing shower," said Amy, eyeing the Windbreaker's glistening center. "Oh, well. It's better than before."

"Better than before?" Fanny had always been the optimistic one. *Never say die.* But this was just too much. "I'm cold and wet. My bed is cold and wet. My jacket is cold and wet. How is this better than before?"

*   *   *

Amy had read about survivors. She'd seen the movies, although they'd never been her favorites, in which ordinary people survived for weeks in deserts or on mountaintops or on rafts in the middle of the sea. Before, if anyone had asked her about her own chances on a sunny, temperate prairie, without any food or water or survival gear, she probably would have given herself a week. Not a fun week, granted, but a week of staying alive and relatively coherent.

It was the middle of the afternoon, and they had been on the move since the light of dawn had given them something, anything, to look at. The previous night, before settling into the gully, she had reconnoitered their position, picking out a landmark on the horizon, a space between two ridges, that was her best guess for the Glendaval estancia. When the sun rose in the east, Amy had reconfirmed the landmark and had been reasonably confident that their direction was correct—southeast, according to the photo of the map on her phone.

With the exception of the short, stingy shower, their night had been uneventful. They had heard a few unsettling howls echoing in the distance. Was the cougar the one big predator in this region? Or was it the puma? Or were they the same thing? Nicholas had told them, but who really paid attention to the nature guide? She'd never seen any snakes in Patagonia. But she knew there were scorpions. As for the condors, she assumed they didn't fly at night and wouldn't bother them, anyway, not until it no longer mattered. The night had been uneventful but long, and whatever sleep she got had come and gone without her being aware of it.

Amy spent much of the long, silent trudge today second-guessing her decisions. Walking back to Glendaval had seemed the logical choice. But it had exposed them to the elements and the reality of getting lost. In those survival movies, didn't the characters tell each other to stay in one place? Conserve your energy? Drink your own urine? Wait for help to arrive? But that option, staying in the protection of one of the caves, would have been wrong, Amy knew, since no one would be out looking for them for a day or more. They had done the right thing, she told herself. There was some perverse consolation in having done the right thing, even if you wound up sunburned and dehydrated and dead.

"I need to stop for a while." Fanny was limping badly. It wasn't quite as noticeable now, because she was limping on both legs, turning her gait into a kind of John Wayne shuffle. They had been walking since yesterday morning and didn't seem any closer to the space between the two ridges. "Just a little while."

"I'll find some shade," Amy said. The shadows were starting to lengthen across the plains. Looking around, she spotted a deep arroyo ahead and to their left, where they could lie down with at least half of their bodies out of the direct sun. "We'll rest for a few minutes. I know we're close. I think we can get back by sunset, I do."

"Are we totally lost?" Fanny asked as she hobbled to catch up.

"No, no. We're getting close, Mom. You'll see." She skidded down the sloped side of the arroyo and cleared a few rocks away from the most shaded section before helping her mother down.

They settled in quickly, without any of the fuss they'd made the night before. Fanny pulled off her Batman cap. She considered using it as a pillow, but there was something about the smell that made her change her mind. She placed it on the gully rim above her head, then faced the mirror away, where it wouldn't shine in anyone's eyes.

Amy laid herself down a few feet away, feeling as weary as her mother looked. But she was kept alert by the unsettling sensation that this arroyo was just too familiar. Of course, they all looked familiar, she told herself. And this couldn't possibly be the same place where they'd spent last night. Could it? After a full day of walking, without water, without food, that would be just too cruel. She had heard the stories of people being lost and accidentally walking in circles. It had something to do with having an uneven pace or being right handed or having one leg longer than the other. She couldn't quite recall the logic.

Despite her anxiety, the fatigue of the day caught up with her. Amy closed her eyes and felt suddenly, inexplicably comfy. It would be all right, she thought, to fall asleep now. They could sleep until sunset, then walk at night. No, they couldn't walk at night. *That's right. No light.* Maybe it would be better for them just to sleep until morning. Then they would get up, take a shower, drink a gallon of water, and have a nice big breakfast. Eggs and hash browns. Orange juice. Bacon, maybe. She never allowed herself to eat enough bacon. One of her big regrets in life.

Maybe the people in the car were bringing the bacon. That would be nice. Amy could hear the car now, coming closer, barreling over the plains. Was it Marcus? she wondered. She had told him not to come. But wouldn't it be just like this incorrigible man to come, anyway? He had probably flown all night. He was driving up right now, ready to apologize for ignoring her wishes and then to save her and propose. She would accept, of course. It was about time. Although she would make him repeat the proposal at a more appropriate moment, when she wasn't dying from dehydration and hallucinations.

Or maybe it was Kevin, her adorable pilot. And maybe it wasn't a car, after all, but Kevin's helicopter. Or both. Car and helicopter. *Uh-oh.* That would be awkward, wouldn't it, if both Marcus and Kevin came to rescue her at the same time? She would have a lot of explaining to do, even though she had never meant to lead Kevin on.

Or maybe it was Oscar, she mused. The gaucho had gone home and told everything to his daughter, Juanita. Juanita was a good girl. She would make him come out to find them. Oscar and Juanita would follow their trail from the condor's nest. And then . . . But how would they find them here, sleeping in the arroyo? Oh, that was easy enough. Child's play. Fanny's bat signal. It had led Jorge to them before. Now the flashing light would lead Oscar and Juanita to their little nesting place, and she and Fanny would be saved.

The car engine stopped. Five seconds later, Amy forced her eyes open and did her best to focus. She was well aware that she might be hallucinating, like a lost soul in the desert, seeing a cool, lifesaving oasis that would turn out to be a mirage.

But then again, maybe not.

EPILOGUE

Amy had been staring at the red light, willing it to go on. Why was it taking so long?

Fanny was at her side, blithely checking her e-mail. She chuckled. "Todd Drucker has reduced himself to begging. Trippy's biggest fan. He's dying to know."

"It was on the news," said Amy. "Jorge's arrest. His plea of accidental death."

"Please." Fanny chortled. "Todd knows there's more involved. But O'Bannion is one of Chile's great old names, and the police are being very close-mouthed. Of course, that will change once they find Jorge's girlfriend and she testifies."

"If they find her." Amy kept staring at the light. "Are you going to tell the truth? In the blog?"

"You mean, will Trippy tell? Honesty, I don't know. According to our disclaimer, it's based loosely on true events, so I don't want to make it too real. It'll ruin the fun."

"Almost dying wasn't enough fun?"

"It wasn't fun at all," admitted Fanny. "But it also

wasn't very dramatic. I mean, one minute you're passing out from exhaustion, and the next minute you're
being revived in a bumpy Jeep. Where's the drama?"

"Sorry to disappoint."

"I'm just saying that we might want to add gun-
shots. Or a fistfight."

"Have you ever been in a fistfight?"

"You could have fallen off a cliff and broken some
bones. Then we could post the photos."

"So you want to disfigure me? Just to make a better
blog?"

"You can't take it personally."

"Maybe next time." Amy checked. The damned
light was still unlit.

Fanny's e-mail dinged. "Todd again, I'll bet. Ooh.
No. It's Juanita."

"Juanita!" Amy momentarily forgot the red light.
"How is she? Is she excited about school?"

Fanny read. "Very. Her English gets better every
day, although I wish she didn't use so many smiley
emojis. It's a lazy habit."

"Did the Pisanos take her shopping today?"

"Three smiley emojis worth of shopping. I think
Carmen's falling in love with our Juanita."

"She *should* fall in love with Juanita. I'm in love
with Juanita."

Amy's last hallucination from that Patagonian afternoon four days ago had been amazingly accurate.
When Jorge O'Bannion arrived back at the estancia
without the Abels, Oscar suspected the truth. But it
took him a day of wrestling with his conscience to tell
his daughter the real reason why Amy hadn't dropped
in to say good-bye. Without hesitation, without a moment's thought to her own future, Juanita had in-

sisted that she and her father go out and find them.
And it was the reflected light from Fanny's bat signal
that had guided them the last hundred yards or so.

After a full day between the hospital and the police, Amy had taken it upon herself to sit down with
the Pisanos. On learning of O'Bannion's arrest,
Lola's niece flew in from Buenos Aires. Carmen and
her brother would soon be principal owners of the
New Patagonian Express, including the Chilean estancias. Amy did everything she could to credit the
Jones family, Juanita in particular. If Oscar and
Juanita hadn't been willing to sacrifice their own
interests, then O'Bannion would have succeeded
and the Pisanos would have lost out.

Despite what Jorge had indicated, Amy had found
the Pisanos to be good people. Carmen Pisano took
an immediate and understandable liking to the Joneses. Oscar, she agreed, should maintain his position
at Glendaval, working as a tenant rancher and over-
seeing the property. And Juanita would still be able
to attend school with the Sisters of Grace in Puerto
Montt.

The red light finally flashed, the alarm went off,
and the baggage claim conveyor belt began moving
clockwise on its path. Clockwise was good. Amy had
guessed correctly and positioned herself right by the
rubber flaps. Now she stared intently at the flaps.

"A little anxious to see Marcus, are we?" Fanny was
smirking, but it was a pleasant smirk.

She ignored her mother and focused. *First bag, no.
Second bag, no. Third bag, a set of golf clubs. Who the hell
brings golf clubs back from Patagonia?* Fourth bag looked
like hers—except for the red ribbon tied around the
handle. She already had her carry-on bag and her cus-

toms form, so she would be ready to go. As soon as her black, oversize . . . Ah, there it was.

Amy leaned in, grabbed it with both hands, set it on the floor, and started wheeling it toward the NOTHING TO DECLARE line at the customs exit.

"Hey," Fanny shouted from somewhere far behind. "What about me?"

Amy walked through the open doors and saw him before he saw her.

She stopped, half hidden in the exiting crowd. Beyond the dozens of car-service drivers holding up their name boards, in a side space on the left, which gave him a little more privacy, stood Marcus Alvarez, dressed in his best and favorite suit. He, too, was holding a sign, straining his neck to see who might be coming through the open double doors of International Arrivals.

Amy watched as complete strangers read Marcus's sign and smiled. Marcus smiled back. The strangers, Amy could see, would read his sign, smile, then loiter at a respectful distance, a few of them pulling out their cell phones to record what might come next.

Amy's heart was pounding now. She took a deep breath, then another deep breath. She straightened her glasses and ran both hands through her hair. She did her best to keep calm as she took her big suitcase and her carry-on and her purse and joined the throng.

But her calm didn't last. As soon as she caught Marcus's eye, as soon as she saw him light up with his devilish grin, as soon as she could make out the words on his sign—AMY ABEL. WILL YOU MARRY ME?—she broke into a run, heading straight for him, dragging her luggage behind her, heedless of the chaos of the other emerging passengers and their own bags and their excited waiting families and the black-clad drivers with their signs.

She didn't see the huge, pink, old fashioned make-up case plopped carelessly in the middle of the floor, not until it was too late, not until a dozen cell phone cameras were already recording her horrific, bone-crunching fall.

Marcus was at her side almost instantly. On his knees. "Oh, my God. Are you all right?"

Amy answered with a groan. "Absolutely yes," she added. But she was answering his sign and not his question.

The airport emergency responders would arrive within five minutes. The total damages would amount to a broken leg, two cracked ribs, a black eye, various cuts and bruises, and an almost irreparable pair of black Lafont frames, her absolute favorites.

Amy would always remember it as one of the happiest moments of her life.

Fanny and Amy Abel, the dynamic mother-and-daughter owners of a NYC travel agency, have just booked their biggest trip yet. But the itinerary may include murder in . . .

DEARLY DEPARTED

Enjoy the following excerpt from *Dearly Departed* . . .

PROLOGUE

Peter Borg was pissed.

Under normal circumstances, he enjoyed visiting clients. It got him out of the office and into some phenomenal homes. It also, in the case of new clients, gave him some sense of their taste and history. For example, if he walked into a living room filled with dark, intricately carved teak, he would know (a) these people had an affinity for Southeast Asia and (b) they'd already done the Cambodia/Thailand/Vietnam circuit. Much better to push the more exotic Micronesian islands, preferably on a leased private jet.

Peter's assistant had set up this particular visit. Eleven a.m. at 142 Sutton Place. Penthouse 2. It wasn't until he was on the street, approaching the polished chrome entrance and the Burberry-clad doorman, that he even checked the name. Miss Paisley MacGregor. Otherwise known as MacGregor. Otherwise known as his ex-maid.

Peter Borg was very pissed.

MacGregor had been glowingly recommended by

Maury and Laila Steinberg. The couple had just sold their business and were moving to Maui. They seemed devastated by the upcoming separation from their full-time maid, much more than by the separation from the two grown children from Laila's first marriage. As he listened and pretended to sympathize, Peter grew intrigued by the notion of employing a maid. It was an extravagance he felt he deserved.

At first, he'd been thrilled with his decision. Mac-Gregor was large and warm and capable, with hair the color of lemon Jell-O and the texture of Brillo. He'd estimated her age at around forty-five, but she had probably looked the same since twenty and would remain basically the same until sixty.

Every morning MacGregor had been there, a human alarm clock who pulled back the curtains at exactly seven, to the smell of coffee and sizzling bacon drifting in from the kitchen. Granted, it had been a bit odd that she was actually in his bedroom, pulling back the curtains. Perhaps that should have been a warning.

For a moment, Peter had thought about canceling—texting his assistant with a few abbreviated profanities and having her phone in some excuse. But he was already here. And MacGregor had obviously transferred her affections onto someone else, someone with a posher address.

The thick white door opened into a startlingly white oval foyer with bunches of ghost lilies posing on a tabletop. Peter girded himself with a fake smile, ready to kiss MacGregor on both cheeks and say how happy he was to see her and how he'd been meaning to get in touch, but wasn't that just how it went?

Instead, he found himself staring at a middle-aged, patrician face that stared back with mild curiosity. His irritation grew. "So sorry. I don't mean to intrude. I'm here to see . . . This is awkward. I came to visit your maid. Why she asked me to come to your home . . ."

"Quite all right," the aristocratic woman replied with a Boston Brahmin accent and the hint of a smile. "Please come in." Peter was relieved by how accommodating she was, considering the situation. *Just another example*, he thought, *of how MacGregor could insinuate herself into your life*. "Can I take your coat?" she asked.

Peter refused the offer, then followed her through the all-white leather and plush living room.

"Miss MacGregor." She knocked on a bedroom door and called softly, "There's someone to see you."

It was at this point that Peter pushed aside all speculation, his mind growing numb.

MacGregor was sitting up in bed, framed in a spectacular view of the Fifty-Ninth Street Bridge. Like everything else, the bed was white and large and luxurious. The linens were smooth and crisp and served to accentuate the wrinkled head in the middle, propped up on a goose-down pillow, with wispy lemon hair framing it flatly. She had shrunken considerably since the last time he'd seen her—not aged so much as grown unmistakably ill. *Perhaps this explains it*, he thought, his mind unfreezing. Her employer had taken pity on a sick maid and was taking care . . .

"You can go, Archer," MacGregor said with a wave. The woman left the room, and Peter's mind froze again.

Paisley MacGregor's laugh was soft and affectionate. "Yes, Petey, dear. She's the maid."

"Did you win the lottery?" It was the only possibility he could think of.

"Inheritance." And, of course, that made sense. MacGregor must have had half a dozen employers during her years of service. All of them except one or two, maybe just one, must have considered her a treasured part of the family. Someone was bound to leave her something. "It came around six years ago."

"Six years?" Another brain freeze, but this one he powered his way through. "So . . . when you were working for me . . ."

"I was already rich. This place is more than I need, but I'm renting it from some friends."

"Did you have a maid when you worked as a maid?"

"Yes. And I pay her more than you paid me." She seemed to be enjoying his befuddlement. "I loved my work, Petey. I got to be part of all your fascinating lives, all your dreams, your worries."

Peter flashed back to the time he came home and found that she had taken it upon herself to re-arrange the personal files in his study. Her system was actually much better than his, but that wasn't the point, as he tried to explain. Peter had never stopped to analyze exactly what was so unsettling about Mac-Gregor. She was totally supportive of her clients, even loving. But she could also be quietly judgmental, like a nanny you were deathly afraid of disappointing.

"Why would I give up my life?" she said, following the statement with a slight shiver.

"Are you very sick?" He reached out to touch a spidery hand. He had never been completely immune to her homey charms.

"I'm dying, Petey."

"No, no," he said instinctively. "You'll get better. You should be in a hospital."

"I was in a hospital."

"I didn't know."

"All my families expect me to live forever. But I didn't ask you here to talk about my health." Her bluntness served to smooth over the awkward moment. "I need your professional services."

"You want to take one last trip?" he guessed. Peter had done deathbed trips before. They were difficult, yes, but given the right planning and the right money . . .

"No," she said with a wag of the head. "I'm much too ill. But I used to dust so many photographs on mantels and piano tops. Families posing by the pyramids or on the Great Wall. I would look at them for hours, imagining myself there, instead of staying home alone, feeding their goldfish and walking their dogs." Her eyes strayed to another part of the room, and Peter's eyes followed.

"A Steinway grand?" he blurted out. "In your bedroom?" Yes, there it was, by the flowing white gauze of the balcony curtains. A concert grand, barely taking up a corner of the room. Every inch of the lacquered white top was covered in framed photographs—wealthy, happy travelers, all shiny and neat and smiling directly into the lens.

"I had to special order it," MacGregor explained. "I don't play. But I like the way they look on a white piano."

Peter's mind went from one improbability to the next. "And people gave you their travel photos?" he deduced. "Why would they give—"

"I asked them. They were all tickled by the idea, made special prints, threw in expensive frames. Except you, Petey. Yours I had to borrow and make a copy. Actually, Archer made a copy. Isn't it lovely to be able to indulge in a little staff?"

Peter crossed to the Steinway and quickly found it, a small print in a silver frame, near the back. He had the original sitting on his own secondhand spinet. It had been taken in Belize, on a jungle-side beach, with Amy Abel nestled in the crook of his arm, her face framed by her signature eyeglasses. His eyes were half shut and his face was peeling red, but Amy looked great.

His face remained expressionless as he returned to Paisley MacGregor's bedside. He had been tempted to react to this new invasion of privacy but didn't want to give her the satisfaction. Besides, she was dying. "How can I help?"

"It's all written out," said the ex-maid, her voice a little cottony.

Peter handed her the glass of water from the nightstand. *Baccarat crystal.*

"Thank you." She handed back the glass. "I want to be cremated. And I want the ashes to be strewn around the world."

"Literally?" Peter was already envisioning some kind of NASA mission or perhaps a high-altitude jet releasing several pounds of MacGregor powder into the stratosphere of an unsuspecting earth.

"Yes, literally," MacGregor answered. "I want all my families to fly around the world and to hold these little wakes along the way. I want them to dance and drink and tell stories and spread little bits of me around. Take loads of pictures. Then fly off to the next. All first class and all on me. All the spots I've dreamed of but will never go to—until then, of course. Then I'll be there forever. Isn't that nice?"

"Oh," said Peter, relieved, and then it hit him.

"Oh!" Maybe it wasn't as bad as a NASA trip, but it still had the makings of a logistical nightmare. "Will they all want to do this? It'll take a week or two."

"There aren't that many. And yes, they'll want to." A practiced, slightly hurt expression wrinkled her eyes and mouth. "You want to, don't you, dear? A last tribute to your old MacGregor?"

"Of course." Hey, it was a job, probably with an un-limited budget. "But let's hope that's years away."

Ten minutes later, Peter was walking back out through the white marble foyer, with the contact infor-mation for the lawyers and bankers and ex-employers. *Would they really do this?* he wondered. *Circle the globe with the ashes of their maid?* And then there was the matter of transporting human remains through half a dozen countries—some with tight security and drug-sniffing dogs, some with unstable governments.

"What did you think of him?" Paisley MacGregor asked her own maid after the thick white door had closed and they were alone. The interview had taken a lot out of her. She was just a few nods away from a nap, but she wanted Archer's opinion.

"He's pretty much how you described him." Over the years, Archer had found that this was always a safe response.

"Yes." MacGregor chuckled, and her eyes wan-dered over toward the grand piano. She'd had the building's handyman and his brother move it in here from the living room just so she could lie in bed and look at the photos. Even from a distance, with her fad-ing eyesight, she recognized every face and pose and familiar monument. Why, there was young Nicole, straining every muscle as she propped up the Leaning Tower of Pisa. There were Evan and Barbara Corns, grinning on either side of a Buddhist monk, solemn

faced in his saffron robes. There was one of her favorite families, posing in front of . . .

MacGregor's face wrinkled itself more than usual
as she tried to recall. She remembered their names,
of course. That was easy. But there was some drama
involved with this one family, wasn't there? Some secret. Some responsibility that someone had given to
her, MacGregor, the trusted maid. That was the trouble with pain and medication and the cancer eating
through her insides. Facts and memories came and
went.

"Is there something wrong, ma'am?" Archer asked.

Damn. It had been on the tip of her mind. "No,
dear," she whispered. It was important, whatever it
was. It was something that she had fretted about during the past few years, as she routinely checked her
mail and her e-mail and the newspapers and Facebook and the obituaries. Something with life and
death importance. Something that would never get
taken care of now . . .

If only she could remember.

Connect with Us

Visit us online at
KensingtonBooks.com
to read more from your favorite authors, see books
by series, view reading group guides, and more.

for sneak peeks, chances to win books and prize packs,
and to share your thoughts with other readers.

facebook.com/kensingtonpublishing
twitter.com/kensingtonbooks

Tell us what you think!

To share your thoughts, submit a review,
or sign up for our eNewsletters, please visit:
KensingtonBooks.com/TellUs.